A killer among us . . .

The door opened, cutting me off. I was ready to scowl—but then I saw who stood in the doorway. It was our headmaster. Silence smothered the room, sudden and complete.

Headmaster Claude Fournier rarely made an appearance in the classroom. This was unprecedented. Unheard of.

He didn't bother with niceties; he just dug right in. "A girl has been discovered," he said, only a hint of his French accent detectable. "Just beyond the cove. A dead girl." His tone was flat, but his quiet delivery told me just how furious he was. "Somebody killed her, anonymously and without permission. Someone on this island bled her dry."

I'd thought it was already silent—until we all held our breath. This was shocking news. Nobody on this island acted—or killed—without it being somehow sanctioned by the vampires in charge.

Sure, deaths happened all the time. But random, anonymous slaughter? There was no such thing. Nobody crossed the Directorate.

For Headmaster to stoop to a classroom visit meant this death had upset them. It meant this was a mystery.

And then an even more frightening question popped into my head: Why had he come to *this* class? Was he visiting all the classes? Why not just hold a general assembly?

The hairs on the back of my neck prickled. Headmaster Fournier scanned the room with his shuttered gaze. "The question is, who among us would want to see Guidon Trinity dead?" He pinned that icy stare on me.

My nerves became nausea.

ALSO BY VERONICA WOLFF

Isle of Night

Vampire's Kiss

BLOOD FEVER

the watchers

VERONICA WOLFF

 NEW AMERICAN LIBRARY

NEW AMERICAN LIBRARY
Published by New American Library,
a division of Penguin Group (USA) Inc.,
375 Hudson Street, New York, New York 10014, USA
Penguin Group (Canada), 90 Eglinton Avenue East, Suite 700, Toronto,
Ontario M4P 2Y3, Canada (a division of Pearson Penguin Canada Inc.)
Penguin Books Ltd., 80 Strand, London WC2R 0RL, England
Penguin Ireland, 25 St. Stephen's Green, Dublin 2,
Ireland (a division of Penguin Books Ltd.)
Penguin Group (Australia), 250 Camberwell Road, Camberwell,
Victoria 3124, Australia (a division of Pearson Australia Group Pty. Ltd.)
Penguin Books India Pvt. Ltd., 11 Community Centre,
Panchsheel Park, New Delhi - 110 017, India
Penguin Group (NZ), 67 Apollo Drive, Rosedale, Auckland 0632,
New Zealand (a division of Pearson New Zealand Ltd.)
Penguin Books (South Africa) (Pty.) Ltd., 24 Sturdee Avenue,
Rosebank, Johannesburg 2196, South Africa

Penguin Books Ltd., Registered Offices:
80 Strand, London WC2R 0RL, England

First published by New American Library,
a division of Penguin Group (USA) Inc.

First Printing, August 2012
1   3   5   7   9   10   8   6   4   2

REGISTERED TRADEMARK—MARCA REGISTRADA

LIBRARY OF CONGRESS CATALOGING-IN-PUBLICATION DATA:

Wolff, Veronica.
Blood fever: the watchers/Veronica Wolff.
p. cm.
ISBN 978-0-451-23703-3 (pbk.)
1. Women college students—Fiction. 2. Vampires—Fiction. I. Title.
PS3623.O575B58 2012
813'.6—dc23   2012008366

Set in Bembo
Designed by Ginger Legato

Printed in the United States of America

PUBLISHER'S NOTE

This is a work of fiction. Names, characters, places, and incidents either are the product of the author's imagination or are used fictitiously, and any resemblance to actual persons, living or dead, business establishments, events, or locales is entirely coincidental.

The publisher does not have any control over and does not assume any responsibility for author or third-party Web sites or their content.

For Ivan Wolff,
who treats me like his own kid,
and also for Susan Goldstein—
I might write books about women who fight,
but she's a lesson in real guts and grace.

ACKNOWLEDGMENTS

I owe so much to so many:

Thanks, as always, go to my amazing editor, Cindy Hwang, who gets it, then helps me get it on paper.

Publicist extraordinaire Rosanne Romanello, whose hard work and enthusiasm blow me away.

Leis Pederson and all the impressive talent working on Drew's behalf at Penguin.

Robin Rue for the unflagging support, and Beth Miller, who's a dream to work with.

I owe so much to Kate Perry—she's been my critique partner from almost the beginning, and her wisdom and sparkle make my writing that much better.

It's great to have a Viking in the family—thanks, Gudmundur Audunsson, for the continued Icelandic expertise.

Thanks to Iris Krause for help with German translation.

Big, grateful hugs to my friends: Tracy Grant for always being ready to brainstorm over palak paneer. Martha Flynn, Connie O'Donovan, Joey Wolff, Jami Alden, Monica McCarty, and Anne Mallory for being such encouraging early readers. And Carol Grace Culver, Barbara Freethy, and Bella Andre, who also always have my back.

Last but not least, this book wouldn't be in your hands if not for the support of my dearest husband and partner, Adam.

BLOOD
FEVER

CHAPTER ONE

——⟨∞⟩——

H is mouth.

Not quite full, not quite thin. Just the right shape for an easy smile. It hitched up at the corner when he got that look—the one that said he was thinking of doing something reckless.

I'd move closer, and he'd part his lips. His eyes would drift to my—

"Acari Drew."

The stern voice brought me back to myself. *Crap.* I was doing it again. Thinking about *him*. The vampire. *My* vampire. Carden McCloud.

"Are you paying attention?" my teacher asked. Thankfully, it was just Tracer Judge and not one of the vamps. Daydreaming in class when a vampire was your teacher was high on the list of Stupid and Possibly Deadly Things to Do.

Just after bonding with a vampire.

Like I'd bonded with Carden McCloud.

⟨∞ 1 ∞⟩

His mouth. A glimpse of fang, shimmering. I'd felt that fang, an accidental slip, a hot kiss. . . .

"Acari Drew?"

"Yes, Tracer Judge," I said automatically. I gave a quick shake to my head to clear it.

Focus. I was in class. Combat Medicine. It was actually kind of cool. I wanted to focus.

I wouldn't call myself a teacher's pet, but I was the smartest thing they had going around here. My brains were what made me stand out. But it'd been my abusive, deadbeat dad who'd hardened me, landed me here on the Isle of Night.

Generally, every girl here had been an outcast in her former life. There were girls who'd called juvie home. Druggies and gang girls. Bad seeds. We were the sorts of girls who'd never be missed.

Only the most elite eventually became Watchers, and so vampires recruited only the strongest, the most ruthless. The best among society's bad girls. But training was lethal, and survival demanded *more.* Something extra. Something special.

In the normal world, my genius IQ had made me a loser. A social reject. But here? Here it made me an object of fascination. Someone with possibilities. In a place that valued secrecy and cunning, smarts meant potential.

We all had talents, but all too often these were things like a proclivity for knife play or an inability to feel pain. (My pyromaniac, maybe-dead/maybe-not former roomie-slash-nemesis, Lilac, came to mind.)

Roommate. Now, there was a topic to consider.

As in where was mine? Fall classes had begun and there was still no sign of Lilac's replacement.

Rather than seeing the empty bed in my room as a good sign,

it freaked me out. There was no way the vampires were letting me have a double room all to myself, and it didn't bode well that something was holding up whomever this new roomie was.

Had she already been selected? What would *her* gifts be? And would she view me as a freak, as Lilac had?

But, most important, would I be able to hide my relationship with Carden from her? Because this blood bond was proving to be . . . immersive.

I couldn't get him out of my mind. And believe me, I tried. But I was drawn to him—his touch, his eyes. *That mouth.*

Kissing that mouth, I'd tasted the vampire blood I'd been drinking since my arrival on the island. The difference was, from Carden, it hadn't been some refrigerated dose in a shot glass. It was hot and pulsing from the source, ringing with his life essence.

A tug of desire pulsed through my core, as though he were summoning me.

I scrubbed my hands through my hair. *Must focus.* I would *not* think about Carden's blood. His blood had done something to me, altered me in a way I didn't understand.

Things I didn't understand made me *intensely* uncomfortable. And this was one thing I couldn't ask anyone about. Carden's warning echoed loudly in my head. Nobody could know about our bond.

"Answer my question," Tracer Judge said with a peculiar note in his voice. He sounded annoyed, testy. "Preferably sometime today."

I gritted my teeth and brightened my smile. A *whoops-sorry-I-zoned-out* sort of smile. "It's a compelling question, Tracer Judge. Perhaps you'll rephrase it for me."

Judge didn't smirk, though. Normally he would've smirked.

Tracers were hard-core enough, ruthless enough, to do what it took to find and bring girls like me to this bleak rock. Some of them were decent, though, deep down. And Tracer Judge fell into that category.

He often let me stay after class to do independent studies. He taught topics in science such as infiltration, forensics, combat medicine—the cool stuff that I loved. He was okay, for a Tracer.

Except these days there was something fundamentally *not* okay about him. Not since his secret love, my Proctor, Amanda, had been killed.

Though *killed* was a pretty tame word for what'd happened to her. Ronan had given me details I was certain I wasn't supposed to know. She'd been tortured. Dismembered. Flung from a cliff.

I suspected Master Alcántara had been responsible for Amanda's death. On our mission, I'd gotten a peek into the Spanish vampire's interrogation techniques. They weren't pretty.

Amanda had been going to meet Judge so they could escape. *Together.* And I was sure I wasn't supposed to know *that* bit.

I had no idea what Judge would do if he found out I knew. Kill me? Who could guess? I'd learned not to trust anyone on this island. People—and I use that term loosely—played for keeps around here.

I still didn't understand why Ronan had confided in me. For a Tracer who'd sneakily relied on his hypnotic, persuasive power of touch in order to get me here in the first place, he sure could act like a friend sometimes.

But as I was constantly reminded, friends were a bad idea. Friends could die.

Enemies, though—I had those crawling out of my ears. There were any number of girls—Acari, as well as the older Initiates and Guidons—who wanted to see my ass in a sling. Especially Masha and her pal Trinity—they were Annelise Drew Enemies #1 and #2.

Just the thought sent a chill creeping along my flesh. *I'd* wanted to escape. That could've been me . . . tortured, mangled, discarded.

When I'd taken the assignment to go off the island for a mission with Alcántara, I'd thought it would be my chance to make a break for it. To run as far away from *Eyja næturinnar*, this Isle of Night, as I could get.

Should I have tried to escape when I'd gotten the chance? There had been a moment on our mission when I could've fled. Would Carden have killed me if I'd tried?

Somehow I knew he wouldn't have. In the same way I knew I couldn't go far from his side if I tried.

All I'd wanted was to free myself, and yet I now found myself more entangled than ever. What I felt for Carden, this sensation in my body, was beyond thirst. It was a yearning. An emptiness that only Carden could fill. And I didn't want that—*at all*.

Except, part of me really did. Want it.

Want him.

"Earth to Drew." It was my pal Yasuo, sitting next to me. A tall, cute vampire Trainee, he had the bluster that came with growing up in LA and the sensitivity that came from watching his Japanese gangster dad murder his mother. He singsonged under his breath, "Drew and McCloud, sitting in a tree—"

Yas could be such a *guy* sometimes. At the moment, his real damage was probably that he'd overheard Emma—his girlfriend and my best friend—mention how cute Carden was.

I stared ahead, hissing into my fist, "Shut up." But I forgave him instantly. I knew Yasuo had my back, and in a place like this, that was all that mattered.

Tracer Judge silenced both of us. "Is there a problem?" He said it with uncharacteristic sternness.

"No," I told Judge quietly. "There's no problem."

Ever since bonding with Carden, I'd been scattered. Fragmented. Unable to pay attention. Aware only of this itch I needed to scratch. It was like experiencing the surliness of PMS, a parched thirst, a fever chill, and a deep-down wiggly boy-wanting feeling all at the same time.

I was off, and whenever I tuned in to the feeling, asking, *What is my deal?*, I'd remember: Carden.

Master Carden McCloud, ancient Scottish vampire, was my *deal*. I blamed him.

But I could never admit to that, so instead I lied. "It's my fault, Tracer Judge. I let my focus wander for a moment. I apologize."

My formality seemed to mollify him, and the glare in his tired eyes eased a bit. "I repeat: What is the basic difference between combat medicine and emergency medical technique?"

Inhaling deeply, I used my breath to sweep my mind clear of Carden. Any once or future roommates, all conceivable friends or enemies, Amanda and Judge, Ronan . . . I relegated the lot of them into a tiny corner of my brain.

I sat straight in my chair, attentive Acari Drew once more. "The primary difference is that the EMT is the first responder, whereas, on a mission, if someone gets injured, the Watcher is the only respon—"

The door opened, cutting me off. I was ready to scowl—I'd assembled quite the pretty little answer in my head. But then I saw who stood in the doorway.

It was our headmaster. Silence smothered the room, sudden and complete.

Headmaster Claude Fournier rarely made an appearance in the classroom. This was unprecedented. Unheard of.

He didn't bother with niceties; he just dug right in. "A girl has been discovered," he said, only a hint of his French accent detectable. "Just beyond the cove. A dead girl." His tone was flat, but his quiet delivery told me just how furious he was. "Somebody killed her, anonymously and without permission. Someone on this island bled her dry."

I'd thought it was already silent—until we all held our breath. This was shocking news. Nobody on this island acted—or killed—without it being somehow sanctioned by the vampires in charge.

Killing without permission. Did that mean someone had actually granted permission for Amanda's death? I shuddered.

Sure, deaths happened all the time. In a combat ring. During hazing. At the hand of a bored vampire merely wanting to teach a lesson. But random, anonymous slaughter? There was no such thing.

Most of all, there were no abandoned bodies. Every corpse was repurposed for some other grisly means. Nobody killed and left the body to rot.

Nobody crossed the Directorate.

For Headmaster to stoop to a classroom visit meant this death had upset them. It meant this was a mystery.

And then an even more frightening question popped into my head: Why had he come to *this* class? Was he visiting all the classes? Why not just hold a general assembly?

The hairs on the back of my neck prickled. I didn't want to

be in their sights, not even in their line of vision, considering my bond with Carden.

Headmaster Fournier scanned the room with his shuttered gaze. "The question is, who among us would want to see Guidon Trinity dead?" He pinned that icy stare on me.

My nerves became nausea.

CHAPTER TWO

There was a burst of sound as people turned in their seats. All eyes landed on me.

I slid down in my chair, trying to hide. Because I knew who'd want Trinity dead. So did everyone else.

The list was easy:

1. Emma, who'd suffered much at the hands of the redheaded Guidon.
2. By extension, Yasuo, her boyfriend. *Duh*.

And Three?

Number Three was the ringer.

Number Three was the only one who would've been capable of seeing such a thing through.

Number Three was the only person who'd want Trinity dead and who also happened to come equipped with a new vampire buddy who operated just enough outside the official

Eyja næturinnar ecosystem to do something like feed on an Initiate.

Number Three was me.

Headmaster Fournier asked who wanted Guidon Trinity dead, and the answer was: I did. I'd fantasized about the many ways in which I'd obliterate both her and Masha pretty much every day since day one.

Headmaster glided to the doorway. When he spoke again, it seemed his gaze was trained on everyone *but* me. "Keep your eyes open, Acari, Trainees. The student who discovers and reports the identity of the culprit will know great honor."

The moment he left, Acari Loren turned to me. She was one of the many girls who'd dance a jig if I were to come to a gruesome ending. "You knew Trinity, didn't you, Drew? Didn't you hate Trinity?" Her tone was saccharine sweet.

When I'd left on my mission, I'd been public enemy number one in everyone's sights. But that I returned with a new—and let's be honest—super-stud vampire? I was now under a microscope.

If anyone discovered that Carden and I shared a bond and turned us in, it would garner them major brownie points. My sure and subsequent death would just be icing on the cake.

Yas whispered under his breath, "Bitch." His bemused, marveling tone was like armor for me.

I consciously slowed my heartbeat enough to speak. "I seem to recall Trinity kicking your ass a time or two, Acari Loren. Easy enough with such a wide target." The girl was built like a rock.

Yasuo chuckled. "Snap."

I hated stooping to such ridiculously adolescent taunts, but sometimes you needed to speak the native tongue. I'd seen Loren in the locker room, noticed how she always stole a quick glance to make sure nobody was looking before she changed. I don't know why she was self-conscious—she could probably bench-press the lot of us with a solid strength that I envied—but who was I to understand? Girls and their stupid hang-ups were beyond me.

"But it was you and your little friend who Trinity hated the most," an Acari said from the back of the room. "How lucky for you that she's out of the picture."

Nobody tried to hide their open stares, aimed at me.

Another girl chimed in, "How convenient she shows up dead just after you showed up with your new vampire pal."

Pal. So people had noticed me spending time with Carden. What else had they seen? Could they sense my obsession with him? Had they caught me casting longing stares whenever he was nearby?

I had to stop. *This* had to stop.

I had to figure out what this bond was so I could break it. In the meantime, I had to deal with the disrespect. I couldn't let my fellow classmates sniff my vulnerability.

I steeled myself. Looking over my shoulder, I said, "I didn't realize you were in a position to accuse any of the vampires. Impressive. You should definitely bring your concerns to Master McCloud's attention."

That shut people up. For now.

But it wasn't good enough. I'd thought my focus was shot before, but now I really couldn't pay attention to anything having to do with my class. Because who *had* killed Trinity?

Girls died all the time, but not like that. There was ceremony around it. God forbid the vampires missed an excuse for a tournament or a feast.

Guidon Trinity had been a bully bent on tormenting and sabotaging me. She and Masha had both been overly curious about anything to do with me.

Crap.

Masha.

I groaned to myself. Masha wouldn't appreciate losing her friend to mysterious circumstances. She'd had it in for me before, but now she'd be laser focused, waiting for the chance to wrap that bullwhip of hers around my neck.

She'd be watching me even more closely than she and Trinity had before. Watching. Waiting. Wanting to catch me in the act. Catch me breaking the rules. To catch me in a compromising situation—like sharing a secret blood bond with a renegade vampire.

The other girls were right—Carden would've had every reason to want to remove Trinity from the picture. If she'd discovered our bond? The Directorate wouldn't look too kindly on Carden secretly hitting on a first-year Acari. They killed for much less around here.

I had much to think about as I walked back to the dorm. Thankfully, Yas had to run off to some Trainee thing—more and more such mysterious events seemed to be claiming his attention this semester. But I was glad for the alone time.

It didn't last long.

I felt Carden before I saw him. A vibrating power at my back. I felt those eyes consuming my body, boring into me. I imagined I even *smelled* him. Rich, heady, like earth and man.

I wanted to turn and fling myself into him. To know a second kiss.

But instead I balled my hands into fists and sped up my pace.

I didn't know why. It was stupid. There was no running from McCloud.

I didn't understand our bond. For all I knew, he could read my every thought. He probably knew where I was going better than I did.

I felt his presence even more strongly now. My skin turned hot, awareness pounding through me. I had silly impulses—to wonder what I looked like from behind, to slow my stride and sway my hips to match the low pulse in my belly. I fought my urges.

He laughed, a low rumble behind me. "You can run, my pretty wee Acari. . . ."

I was being ridiculous. This was a chemical bond, pure and simple—like a drug addiction. I refused to act like a silly, lovesick girl.

I sucked in a breath through my teeth. "I know. I can run, but I can't"—I stopped short to deliver the line. It'd been so sassy and careless in my head. But Carden was right behind me, and his body walked right up against mine, a hard, hot wall pressed at my back. "Hide?" I finished weakly. Lamely.

"Aye, and best you accept it, young one." He traced a single finger along my shoulder blade.

I took a defiant step forward. "Just because you've got a few hundred years on me." Determined not to cower, I planted my hands on my hips and turned to face him. "It's not like you were so ancient when you became a vampire. You can't have been much older than—what?—nineteen? Twenty, max?"

He looked amused. "As you say, little Acari."

"I am *not* little."

He was grinning now, and my words hung in the air, preposterous. Because next to Carden, I *was* little. I was tiny and delicate and frail.

It cast my mind back to when we first met. He hadn't seemed so large, dying of thirst in a dark, dank cell, imprisoned by a bunch of evil vampire monks.

He'd been dying, and all I'd known was that I couldn't fail on my mission. I had to help him survive. And so I'd fed him. My blood had pumped into his body, engorging muscles and flesh until he regenerated into this strapping hunk of a man before me.

Just the memory gave me a shiver.

I had to stop thinking of him as a man. He was a *vampire*.

"So?" I demanded.

He raised his brows, looking aggravatingly amused. "So, what?"

I scowled. "Don't patronize me. So . . . how old *were* you?"

"You had the right of it the first time."

I rolled my eyes. "Can't you just answer the damned question like a normal person?"

He rubbed his thumb along my lower lip, stealing the breath from my lungs. "Careful, my wee dove. There are relics on this island who'd kill upon hearing such language."

"Dove?"

"Oh, aye." His laugh was easy, but the dark glint in his eyes made me shiver down deep. "And how I'd love to watch you fly." He licked his lips.

My body buzzed, the yearning for him pure anguish. My blood demanded more of his. My lips burned to kiss him once more. I had to fight to control my breath. "What have you done to me?"

He ignored the question, answering a different one instead. "I was indeed nineteen when I was turned," he said calmly.

I thought my head might explode—the guy was impossible. "What are you doing even talking to me? You're Vampire; I'm Acari. We're not supposed to—how do you say it?—fraternize." I shook my head. Since when could I not remember a simple word?

I glared. "What did you do to me? What's happening to me? I can't think straight." I lowered my voice to a hiss. "And who killed Guidon Trinity?"

"Questions, questions." He pinched my chin, studying me. "What I did to you," he mused. "It's what *you* did to *me*." His pinch grew firmer. "You fed me, girl. And now we're stuck with each other."

But then he let go, easy Carden once more. "You made the bed. And now we must sleep in it." He winked.

I flushed from head to toe. "Fine. Whatever. What about Trinity? You didn't kill her, did you?"

He parted his lips, revealing the barest glimmer of fang. "Yours is the only nectar I've a taste for."

Vertigo spun my brain as I began to fall into those eyes. They were golden brown, like honey.

I gritted my teeth. I would *not* lose myself. I was Annelise Drew, and I was stronger than that.

"Does that line generally work for you?" I turned from him, and it took everything I had. "Look, I've gotta go."

With a gentle hand on my shoulder, he stopped me. "Little one."

"I told you not to call me that."

"Ah, but if you'd *asked* . . ."

Maddening. Why didn't he act less like a cocky guy and more . . . *vampiric*?

"Fine," I said. "Please don't call me that."

"As you wish, my wee dove." He pressed on before I could get out more than an outraged squeak. "But before you go, for the record, I do not savage young women." He gave my shoulder a final squeeze. "At least, not without their consent."

I stormed off, the sound of his rumbling laugh at my back.

All I wanted was peace and quiet, and I couldn't get back to the dorm quickly enough. As much as Lilac's empty bed creeped me out, at the moment, I was thrilled at the prospect of a single room.

Carden's scent lingered in my head. I exhaled sharply but couldn't rid myself of his memory. He was branded into me.

I jogged up the stairs, anxious to get back before I ran into anybody. I didn't even want to see Emma. If I saw her, I'd have to pretend nothing was going on for me. I didn't think I could do it.

I passed her room without event. The hallway was oddly silent. Of course. It was lunchtime. The thirst for Carden was so consuming, I hadn't even realized I was missing a meal.

His eyes were in my head, staring. One minute playful, the next minute smoldering. I knocked my head against the doorframe, resting it there as I slid the key in the lock. I actually shuddered with relief as I turned it.

Almost there. I'd crumple onto my bed, roll into a ball, and wait for the throbbing in my belly to stop.

I opened the door, and for one surreal moment, I thought I'd entered the wrong room. But no. It was Lilac's bed, with its gray mattress ticking and neat stack of white and gray linens.

Only now a slim figure sat at the edge. I registered a sheet of shining black hair. Slim shoulders.

The figure turned.

My new roommate.

CHAPTER THREE

———∞∞∞———

D ammit to hell.
        She was here. My roommate. I'd known this day was coming. Was actually kind of relieved it had. But still, I made it a general rule not to trust girls on principle.

As she turned, I sized her up. Asian. Pretty. Young looking. Younger than me. I tried to guess what flavor of badass she might be.

I muttered, "How young do they take them now?" Even though she was new, part of me braced for her to pull a weapon on me. But nothing happened.

Her cheeks were blotchy. *Crap.* "Are you crying?"

She gave me a curt shake of her head. Perfectly cut layers swished into her eyes, and she swept them away again.

"Oh, okay. Because it looked like you were crying."

She cleared her throat and said firmly, "I wasn't crying."

"Fine. Got it. Not crying. I'm Drew." I waited, but she just looked at me blankly. "Well? What's your name?"

"Mei-Ling." I watched her slim throat convulse. There'd been some definite crying. "Mei-Ling Ho."

"Pretty name." I slung my bag onto my desk. Making idle chatter was the last thing I felt like doing.

Carden preoccupied my whole mind and body—I didn't have time to deal with anyone else, much less some kid.

I realized it was past time for her to speak. I probed. "Mei-Ling. That a Chinese name?"

She nodded.

I was getting impatient. "What's it mean?"

"Beautiful and delicate." She turned her back on me.

Great. "My advice, best change your name. What's Chinese for ruthless and savage?"

She ignored the question. Was she in shock? I thought she'd been crying when I came in, but she seemed utterly emotionless now. I watched her long fingers repeatedly smooth the sheets, the nervous gesture the only thing telling me she was in there somewhere.

I could *not* deal with this right now. I had to sort out my bond with Carden.

Carden. My breath caught, just remembering the feel of him.

I fisted my hands and shook them out again. I needed to get ahold of myself. There was no way I could function in this place with all the obsessing I was doing. I had to figure this bond out before someone figured *me* out. Which meant I couldn't trust anybody in the meantime. Especially not a new roommate who could be in my face—and maybe even in my stuff—24-7.

I looked at her, trying to figure out how to go about laying down the ground rules, and took a step closer. Was she even sixteen? "How old are you?"

"I just turned fifteen."

"Damn." No wonder she was proving hard to read. She must've come from a seriously messed-up place to land here so young. "So you were in, what, ninth grade?"

"I just started at the performing arts school," she said in answer. "My parents relocated to Long Island so I could go."

"Fancy." How I would've loved parents who supported me. What a different world I'd live in now. "Does that mean you're some sort of prodigy?"

To my surprise, she nodded. I wanted to snark that I was smart, too. On this island, special meant nothing. *Special* got you a shooter of blood and a knife in the back.

"I'm a violinist," she said, "but I can play a lot of things."

Was that why the vampires had placed her with me? Put the musical genius in with the genius-genius? Because my room wasn't the only one with a sudden vacancy. "Well, now you're an Acari. Fights to the death seem to be the only performing art we've got going around here."

She gave me a flat look. "When do we receive our syllabus?"

"Our *syllabus*?" I choked back a little laugh.

"Yes." She looked at me like I was a moron. "Otherwise, how will I know where I need to go?"

Oh God, the poor thing was being serious. She had no clue what she'd agreed to, and it dismayed me. "Don't worry—they'll let you know. The vamps go for drama. They'll probably slide some ancient piece of parchment under the door at some ungodly hour, and if you can parse the old-school calligraphy, that'll be your syllabus."

I watched her riffle through her stack of books, even though I was sure she'd done plenty of riffling before I came in. What weapon had she been assigned? Because surely there was a weapon hidden in one of her dresser drawers.

Would Mei-Ling be a threat to me? Maybe smother me in my sleep? Most important, would she find out about me and Carden and narc on me?

I had no clue, and knew I needed to get one fast. I rested my foot on my desk chair to unlace my boots and kick them off. "So why'd you wanna up and leave your fancy new school for a place like this?"

"I didn't want to leave," she said.

"Wait." Surely I misheard. The vampires recruited us onto the island. Maybe they sometimes used little hypnotic tricks to persuade us, or seduced us with fancy private jets and hot Tracers, but they didn't resort to outright kidnapping. "Back it up. What do you mean, you didn't want to leave? You're here, aren't you?"

Her jaw tightened. "He made me. He killed my boyfriend and said if I didn't go with him he'd kill my parents and my sister, too."

I could say that I sat on the chair, but it was more like my knees gave out. I dropped. Thankfully, the seat was there to halt the progression of my butt onto the floor. "You didn't come of your own will?"

"I tried to fight back, but he was too large." Her expression changed, and she looked at me like I'd just told her I drowned kittens as a hobby. "Why? Did you?"

"Yeah." Her tone had put me on the defensive. "The guy was pretty persuasive, though." I thought back to that day—Ronan, sexy Ronan, in a Florida parking lot. He'd used his hypnotic touch to help convince me. But honestly, the guy was so good-looking and my world had been such crap, it hadn't taken much.

I bristled at the memory. Suddenly, I felt eager to explain this to Mei-Ling and her judgmental eyes. "I had no place else to go. I had nothing but thirty bucks in my checking account and an abusive dad waiting for me at home."

She gave me a look that said she didn't fully understand me, and worse, that she found me pathetic. My defenses locked even more firmly into place.

It made me think with cold reason. "Hold on." She was brought in against her will—which Tracer would do such a thing? "You said *he* made you come. He *who*?"

She shrugged. "He . . . he had an accent."

"Scottish?" I held my breath.

"Not like that," she said.

Not Ronan, then. I felt more relieved than was good for me. "You mean English was his second language? Could it have been a German accent?"

She shrugged again.

The one-sided interrogation was tiring me. "Blond?"

Finally she nodded, and I said, "Sounds like Otto." I could picture him doing it, too. He was the badass Tracer who'd been strong enough to bring my pal Yasuo in.

Mei studied me, and it made me uncomfortable. She looked like she was evaluating me, and evaluations made me feel vulnerable.

I struck out in defense and said, "If you were taken against your will, that means your parents are probably looking for you." I regretted the words the moment they were out.

An expression of acute misery flickered in her eyes then was gone again. "You're right."

I'd noted the tiniest waver in her voice. "Damn," I whispered, aghast. Why had they kidnapped this girl? This nice, normal, fifteen-year-old girl?

And even better: Why on earth had they put her in a room with *me*?

I felt bad for mentioning her parents and found myself volunteering, "You're lucky. My dad wouldn't have cared. And my mom is dead."

It took her a moment to roll with my topic change. "I-I'm sorry."

"Thanks," I muttered, the response feeling rote. I should've felt relieved. I could definitely write off my concerns about what Mei would do if she were to find out about me and Carden. This girl didn't know up from down. "But it's not me you should worry about."

Mei-Ling wasn't a runaway. She wasn't a gang girl or a meth addict. She was a fifteen-year-old musical prodigy from Long Island.

She wouldn't survive a day.

I knew it meant that Carden and I would probably be safe from her prying eyes. But instead of feeling relief, it needled me. This poor kid.

Bastards. The vampires had abducted her against her will, which meant they wanted her here for a reason. A really big reason, if they were willing to risk kidnapping. What were they going to do to her?

I went over and sat next to her on the bed. "Look, I'll help you out. But you need to be strong."

She stiffened. "I *am* strong."

"No, I mean really strong." Amanda had told me much the same when I'd arrived. The girls on this island, if they scented fear, like wolves killing the weakest member of the pack, they'd turn on you. And worse. "Because if you're not, they'll kill you."

CHAPTER FOUR

———∞∞∞———

I stared at my class list.

The dining hall's mealtime hum swirled around me—the clanking of cutlery and chattering of teens as they snarfed down a dinner of bread, potato soup, and mystery fish. We ate a lot of mystery fish. The only thing separating this cafeteria from that of any other boarding school or college was the side shooter of vampire blood.

It was only the first day of classes and already it was shaping up to be a banner semester. A Guidon was dead, and everyone thought I had something to do with it. I shared an inexplicable bond with a vampire. I had a mysterious roommate whose very presence here was wrong. And now *this*.

I reread the schedule, as if maybe it'd changed in the past twenty-four hours. All in all, there were some cool things, taught by some cool teachers (creepy Alrik Dagursson notwithstanding).

It was all good, or as *all good* as it could be. Except for the last item on the list. That was what made my stomach do a flip-flop.

CMD 101   Combat Medicine
          MWF 9–12
          Tracer Judge

MUS 103   Intro to Medieval Musicianship
          TTh 3–6
          Master Dagursson

COM 201   Expeditionary Skills Training
          MWF 3–6
          Watcher Priti

IND   Independent Study in Fitness
          TTh 7:00
          Tracer Ronan

Yasuo leaned over my shoulder. "Is that seven *a.m.*?"

I flinched away, feeling grumpy. "What else?"

Yasuo shrugged. "*Trainees* have classes after dark."

I peered hard at him over the sheet. The guys who were brought here as vampire Trainees kept much of their instruction pretty secret. Yas didn't talk about it a lot, but I got the sense that few survived the transition into full-fledged vampire.

I'd seen what could happen to Trainees who didn't. They turned into mindless flesh-hungry Draug, lurking in the shadows off campus, waiting for people stupid enough to break the rules and stray from school grounds, or for those of us punished and dropped far from school grounds—whichever came first.

Not that being an Acari was such a cakewalk. Training to

become a Watcher was intense, and first-year Acari were sub-jected to humiliation, torture, and, oh yeah, death.

So I totally wouldn't have put it past them to schedule late-night classes.

Emma leaned around Yas to give me an encouraging smile. "Beats seven p.m., I guess."

I didn't smile back, though. Em was my bestie on the island, but she was currently sitting closer to Yasuo than she should've been. I was sure their knees were touching under the table. I didn't care how crushed out they were on each other—playing kneesies and footsies was not the brightest thing. Vampires didn't seem to hang with any relationships beyond the ones that re-volved around *them*.

Yasuo grabbed a corner of the paper and tilted it his way. "Did you make him mad or something?"

"Who, Ronan?" I asked, knowing the answer was very com-plicated. I did, in fact, make Ronan mad all the time. But I got the sense it was because he cared about me.

If I angered him, chances were it was because I'd done some-thing reckless. I'd pulled a few idiot maneuvers in my time on the island—rule breaking, back talking—and though some of it had been necessary, some of it had been just plain stupid.

But Amanda's death had sobered me. That, and my bond with Carden—I was in such a panic over our bond being discovered, I vowed to keep a low profile this term.

Really, I would.

"Ronan's gonna kick your ass," Yasuo said. "An early-morning independent? Dude will have you swimming to Iceland or something."

When I'd first arrived on the island, I hadn't known how to

swim. It was Ronan who'd browbeat me into learning. He might've been the Tracer who brought me in, but his instruction and support was one of the main reasons I was still alive—I'd bet on it.

Our relationship was complicated, to say the least.

Yasuo did something under the table that made Emma giggle, and I glared. They needed to be more careful. I lost Amanda—I wouldn't lose her, too.

Emma saw my expression. Blanching, she scooted over, putting a little more space between her and Yas. He gave her a wink to make her feel better. It was a slow, owlish, and very affectionate little gesture.

I felt a stab of envy. Not that I resented my friends' relationship. And I wasn't jealous that Emma was with *Yas* in particular—I'd asked and answered that question myself when I'd first arrived on the island. He was cute and nice and one of my closest buddies, but that was where our relationship stopped.

No, it was more than that. I wished *I* could find a nice, normal guy to crush on—the place was crawling with new Trainees—but apparently it was only the bad boys, the dangerous, and the mysterious who gave me a quiver in my belly.

I frowned, spinning my empty cup around and around on the table. A red film covered the sides, tiny red ropes of vampire blood clinging to the glass. I craved the drink—couldn't imagine life without it—and I'd downed it first thing.

Only now, the desire I felt for my cold shooters of blood seemed like child's play compared to the aching need I knew for Carden.

I put my glass down, slamming it harder than I'd meant to.

Carden consumed my thoughts. Just the memory of his

mouth—picturing the curve of it in my mind, remembering the feel of his breath hot on my cheek—gave me The Quiver.

I blamed the bond. My biggest problem at the moment was Carden.

But.

In the beginning, it'd been Ronan. Only Ronan.

I'd known loss in my life, but Ronan was still around. So why did a dull ache clench my chest at the thought of him?

I stared again at his name on the bottom of my course list. *Independent Studies in Fitness. TTh 7:00 Tracer Ronan.*

Today was M. Tomorrow T. I'd see him then. I hadn't seen him much since returning from my mission off the island. In fact, I hadn't really spent much time with him since I won the Directorate Challenge at the end of the first term.

But somehow I didn't need to see him much to know he was out there somewhere, on my side. Or so I suspected.

Between sharing swim lessons and secrets, against all odds, Ronan and I had forged a sort of friendship. We'd grown as close as two people could when one had suckered the other onto a plane bound for a deadly vampire training ground. At the time, I didn't know which had felt like more of a betrayal: that he'd brought me to this godforsaken place, or that he'd used his persuasive powers to do it.

But still, there was something about him that tugged at me. A recognition that he had a living, feeling heart in his chest—a heart that saw something good in me in return. It was nice to feel there were people around who perceived some decency inside me. Sometimes it was the only thing to remind me that I still had some humanity left.

Ronan and I had grown as close as a student and a teacher

dared get. Not that he was so old and, well, teacherly. He couldn't have been *so* much older than me. Early twenties, max, with that head of tousled, black, just-surfed-in-the-sea hair and a pair of haunting forest green eyes.

But those eyes weren't what currently unnerved me. The problem was, Ronan really saw me. He really looked and always saw into the true me. Which meant, if anyone could sense this bond with Carden, it'd be Ronan.

Which was why *TTh 7:00 Tracer Ronan* was freaking me out.

It was impossible to think of Ronan without a tinge of panic. Of regret. The thing of it was, I got the sense that Ronan gave a damn. That he cared about me, and I'd never had a lot of people in my life care about me. If I were to be honest, *I* cared right back. I cared about him and I cared what he thought about me. That alone made me vulnerable to him. And that made him dangerous.

And, okay, I admit. Those killer green eyes were pretty dangerous, too.

"But I don't get it. Seven o'clock until when?" Emma asked, calling me back from my thoughts. "Why didn't they list an end time?"

I flopped back into my chair. "Because it *never ends*."

"Check it out." Yasuo fake-punched me on the arm. "Blondie made a joke."

We laughed, and I savored the feel of it. This whole friend thing was new to me, and their acceptance was powerful. Enough so that I felt it as a physical sensation, like a warm balm.

I was still riding that high when my eyes caught on my new roomie.

I flagged her over, and my friends gave me appropriately

shocked looks. "Yo, Miss Congeniality," Yasuo mumbled to me. "Who put a nickel in you?"

"New roommate?" Emma guessed.

"Two points to farm girl." I scooted over to make room for Mei-Ling at the end. I wasn't about to make her sit next to the posse of statuesque Valkyrie at the head of the table.

Yas took the opportunity to snag an uneaten roll from my tray. "You gonna eat this?"

I waved it away. "Take it. And, how are you not, like, five thousand pounds?"

"Growing boy," he said, chewing over a mouthful of bread.

I greeted Mei as she sat down. Her eyes looked puffy from crying, and I asked earnestly, "How are you?"

But the tone of her reply was all business. "Fine," she said, "thank you." Her expression was unreadable as she nodded a cursory hello to my friends.

I suspected the vampires wanted me to look out for Mei-Ling, but it sure seemed like she needed more of a sense of urgency if she was going to look out for her own self.

With a shrug, I did the introductions. "This is Emma and Yasuo."

They were looking at me as if I'd grown horns, and I had to suppress a smile. There were two things on this island that I loved: eliciting emotion from Emma and catching Yasuo off guard.

"This is Mei-Ling," I said. "I'm showing her the ropes."

Yasuo finally closed his mouth. But then he quickly opened it again to ask, "Isn't that your Proctor's job?"

Our new Proctor. *Shudder.*

Emma and I exchanged a charged glance. Then I looked at him with a raised brow. "Have you met Kenzie?"

"She's no Amanda," Emma said.

"Nobody is," I agreed quietly.

Mei gave us a flat look. "Is that one of our instructors?"

"No," I said. "Kenzie Samuels is the Proctor on our floor. It's sort of like . . ."

"Like a dorm mother." Yasuo guffawed at his own joke.

I ignored him. "She keeps an eye on things. There's one assigned to each floor."

Emma leaned in. "I heard the Guidons call her Killer Kenzie."

That was the last thing Mei needed to hear, so I rambled on, explaining, "Proctors are always older girls. After Acari, you become an Initiate, and then comes Guidon—"

"If you live that long," Yas muttered, and I kicked him under the table.

"Then finally you become a Watcher. You'll meet some of those, too."

"How long will that take?" Mei-Ling asked.

Yasuo laughed at that, and I cut him off. "A few years, maybe. I've never really asked."

Mei's eyes were void of emotion. Was she registering all this, or was she about to snap?

"You'll probably have a class taught by a Watcher," Emma chimed in brightly. She might be quiet, but she didn't miss a thing and, undoubtedly, had sized up Mei and got what I was trying to do.

I gave her a grateful smile, nodding and adding, "You see them around—they have much better uniforms than we do."

"I saw some of them when I was looking for a phone," Mei said, and after a moment's hesitation, added, "There isn't one in the dorm."

"A phone?" Yasuo sounded incredulous. "No phones here, kid."

"I'm sorry." I squeezed her arm, but she ever so subtly flinched away.

This Mei-Ling was remarkably steady for someone who'd seen her boyfriend killed, was abducted, taken to an island in the middle of the sea, and learned about the existence of vampires all in the space of, what, a few days? She might look like a sip of water, but she had an inner strength—that was for sure.

"So, Mei-Ling." I leaned my elbows on the table, acting casual. "Did you have other hobbies in New York? Like martial arts or something?" Because why else would they have brought her here?

She gave me a frown. "Because I'm Chinese American?"

I put my hands up in surrender. "Because most girls here have some experience with kicking ass, and you don't strike me as the shotgun type."

Her frown cleared. "I'm not supposed to go to gym class. I need to be careful of my hands."

My eyes flicked to those hands, with long, graceful fingers that I could picture flitting over piano keys or across violin strings. If she was this calm on her first day at a vampire training academy, I imagined she'd have been cold steel on a symphony stage.

She picked up her glass and drank the blood—that right there explained at least some of her composure. The drink brought a false sense of calm that, after enough doses, eventually became real calm. They must've been dosing her from the get-go.

Such careful treatment on the part of the vampires—it was baffling.

I studied her. If it weren't for the extra consideration on their part, she'd obviously not survive. It wasn't that Mei looked weak.

She had the stiffest upper lip I'd ever seen. No, it was more that she looked tended. Cared for. *Loved*.

She didn't want to be here, but not in the same way that we didn't want to be here. So many of us Acari didn't want to be anywhere. If she were a musical prodigy, she obviously worked hard and had a competitive edge. But there was another sort of edge that was lacking. It was the one that'd been shoved, starved, stymied, and slapped into the rest of us in our lives before *Eyja næturinnar*.

So what was her deal? I wanted to keep her talking. "Have you met her yet? Kenzie, I mean. Blond bob? Kinda reminds me of an American Girl doll."

Yas snorted. "If American Girl dolls wore catsuits and carried sai knives."

My eyes lit. "Is that what those things are called?" Our new Proctor's weapon of choice was a pair of daggers, each one flanked by two sharp, short spikes. They looked like something you might see wielded by some manga badass.

Yasuo made a little hissing noise, slowly sweeping his hands in front of his face like a ninja. *"So desu ne,"* he informed me in Japanese.

The guy had been born in Japan and prided himself on knowing his native weaponry. And I had to give him credit. He was one of the only people who'd respected the power of my throwing stars—and known their true name, *shuriken*—before I'd even learned to use them.

Still, I couldn't let Yasuo get too smug. I nudged him. "Okay, sensei. Cool your jets."

"You're welcome, grasshopper."

"Hush. Both of you." Emma silenced us in her North Dakota

prairie girl way. She was the only person I'd ever met who was capable of using the word *hush* without irony. I think it was because she could do things like skin a wild animal with just three flicks of her Buck knife. She turned her attention to Mei. "What classes are you taking?"

My roommate pulled a neatly folded paper from her jacket pocket.

"Hey, you finally got that syllabus you've been wanting." My attempt at humor fell flat, so I just I leaned in to study her schedule. It was a weird one.

> SCI 101 Intro to Phenomena
> TTh 9–12
> Tracer Judge
>
> IND Independent Study in Combat
> MWF 9–12
> Watcher Angel
>
> IND Independent Study in Fitness
> TTh 2–5
> Tracer Ronan
>
> IND Independent Study in Advanced Musicianship
> MWF 3–6
> Master Dagursson

"Ohhkayyy." I shared a quick glance with Emma. This was Mei-Ling's first term, and already she had *three* independent studies? "Well, Phenomena is cool."

"Watcher Angel is her combat teacher?" Yasuo piped up, clued out as usual. "That's the girl with the arms, right? Isn't her nickname the Angel of Death?"

Watcher Angel had some seriously cut biceps. But Mei-Ling didn't need to hear that right now. I narrowed my eyes, giving him my best STFU look. "Not helping."

"Advanced Musicianship?" he went on, ignoring me. "What do you play?"

Something flickered in Mei's eyes—it was an enviable mix of pride and self-knowledge. I imagined it was the thing that'd given her strength to get her this far. "Violin . . . or at least I did play the violin. I can manage most string instruments." She shrugged. "Woodwinds, too."

Yas grinned. "Tiger Mom?"

Mei-Ling's eyes went flat with disdain. "What, you think you know the Chinese girl? You assume because I play the violin that I have a Tiger Mother and my sister is good at math? You just perpetuate your own clichés."

I braced, wondering how Yas would handle it. Instead of getting upset, though, he just smirked. "Hey, you don't give us much to work with."

"Fine," Mei said, sounding more clinical than angry. "I play the violin because it's a beautiful instrument. I also play bass guitar in a garage band. My mom is awesome. She makes killer handmade dumplings, but she also volunteers at the soup kitchen and can rock a pair of skinny jeans. I work hard because I like to." She gave him a teasing half smile. "You should try it."

I wasn't sure if this was still a charged moment or not—Mei wasn't the easiest person to read—but I chimed in, hoping to ease the tension if there was any. "Handmade dumplings, huh? All I ever got to try were those gummy pot sticker things they have at Panda Express."

Yas moaned. "I'd kill for their sweet-and-sour chicken."

I rolled my eyes. "You say that about everything. You'd kill for an extra pat of butter. For a soy latte. For a Snickers bar. You're losing your cred."

Emma nodded sagely in agreement. "It's true."

I smiled and looked over to catch Mei's eye, but instead of being cheered by our chatter, she sat silently, swirling a spoon in her congealed soup. Thinking about those handmade dumplings, no doubt. A thick silence followed.

Finally it was Emma who broke the ice and brought us back on topic. She peered at Mei's schedule and cleared her throat. "They certainly gave you a lot of independents," she said, stating the obvious in a neutral tone.

"What's up with that?" Yas said, already back to his usual self.

He snatched the paper out of Mei's hands for a better look. She allowed it, though, and even leaned closer to look at the paper in his hands. Apparently, the weird conversation had relieved the strain between her and the rest of us.

"What is up with that?" I agreed, though I had a feeling I knew. They wanted to protect her. "Maybe they're worried about her hands." I'd said it jokingly, but there was a kernel of truth there. The vampires had kidnapped her and wanted to preserve her.

And somehow *I* played a part.

"Oh," Emma chirped. "Let's ask Ronan."

I looked up, and there he was. I braced instantly, trying to put up shields I knew would be no match for those green eyes.

"Ronan," I said under my breath. "Speak of the devil."

CHAPTER FIVE

Ronan made a beeline for the table. There were many of us he taught, but a small part of me hoped that I was the one he was coming to see.

I checked that emotion. If anyone would be able to sense my bond with Carden, it'd be Ronan. If anything, I should be avoiding him. Besides, the vampire wouldn't take kindly to the quasi-friendship we shared. I had enough complications in my life without testing that theory.

I realized I was glaring at him when he glared at me back. I had to say something now. "Good evening to you, too, Ronan."

Sure enough, he stopped by my chair. "Will you be ready to work tomorrow morning?"

Why would he even ask me that? And why did I feel like his gaze could pierce right through me? I forced myself not to squirm under the scrutiny. "Do I have a choice?"

Then I saw it—the briefest smile flickered across his features and was gone just as fast. He'd told me once how I reminded him of his sister who'd been killed in Watcher training. What else did he see when he looked at me?

He glanced at my tray. "Are you finished here?"

Mei-Ling was eating quietly. I didn't want to leave her alone. I glanced at my friends, an unasked question in my eyes. Emma nodded. She'd keep an eye out for my mysterious roommate.

"Yeah, I'm done." I stood and gathered my tray.

"Walk with me."

"I need to get back soon." Curfew was coming, and it was time for all good girls to be nestled safe in their beds. "We Acari aren't allowed to roam like you guys." I chafed my arms, feeling as bitter as the wind that pummeled me even through the thick wool of my coat.

"I'll drop you at the dorm," he said.

It was September and the end of the dimming, which meant the sun was dipping low on the horizon. Full darkness was back—thank God. I thought I'd never see it again. And I thought I'd never want to. But the body craves darkness. There was a metaphor in there somewhere that I didn't want to spend too much time analyzing.

My mind went to Carden. Would I see him one more time today? I told myself it didn't matter.

"How are you?" Something about Ronan's tone was stilted.

Why did he want to know? Had he already guessed about my bond with Carden?

Impossible. I was imagining things. Interactions with me were always stilted. If he sounded weird, it was just more of my own social ineptitude. So why the inane question?

"I know you better than that, Ronan." I attempted a smile

over my chattering teeth. "I don't think you pulled me from the dining hall just to ask how I was doing."

The strained look on his face told me I was right. "I wanted to ask you what it is you think you're doing."

"What do you mean?" I asked, instantly on the defensive.

His expression softened. "You're in danger, Annelise."

"I heard about the killer. I know . . . I'll be careful."

"It's not the killer that concerns me. It's Carden McCloud."

My every sense went on alert. "Why would you say that?"

He cut a look at me. "Do not pretend naïveté. I see how he favors you. The other vampires have noticed it, too. Your name has been on many a vampire tongue, and it's a concern."

Something deep inside me deflated. A secret part of me had hoped maybe Ronan was having a guy's reaction to Carden— that maybe he was jealous. Instead, it was just a concerned-teacher reaction.

Ronan was one of my primary instructors, not to mention the Tracer who'd brought me in. If my bond with Carden was discovered, would Ronan get in trouble as well? He'd warned me not to trust Alcántara. Given time, I'm sure he'd warn me against Carden McCloud, too. And if he ever found out I'd bonded with McCloud? Fellow Scotsman be damned, Ronan's head would probably explode.

"Just keeping an eye out for me?" I asked.

My tone had been cynical, but Ronan's reply was serious. Heartfelt, even. "I am looking out for you. Is that such a surprise?"

I just shook my head, needing a moment to rid my throat of this tight feeling. I spent so much time armored against my solitude. To be reminded that there might've actually been some people out there who cared . . . it sideswiped me with emotions I couldn't afford.

"You must be careful," he continued, slowing his pace. He lowered his voice and looked around to make sure we were alone. "Vampires have their own agenda. You must always be wary. And if you ever need help, you can come to me. Don't wait until it's too late."

I swallowed hard, the ache in my throat too thick. I'd already ignored *careful* and had flown right past *too late*. "Thanks," I said, mustering a weak smile. "But there's nothing to worry about between me and Carden."

Guilt crushed my chest. I'd assumed the worst of Ronan, and now, by underplaying my relationship with Carden, I was lying to him, too. "I've been staying away from him these days anyway," I added, consoled that at least that part was true.

Then I thought of a problem I could bring to Ronan. If anyone could give me insight as to why the vampires had abducted Mei-Ling, it'd be him.

"There is something I do need help with," I said. "My roommate. I don't get why she's here. They took her, you know."

"I know," he said, his voice tight.

"I thought only girls who'd hit rock bottom ended up here. Your hoodoo-juju powers aside, it was me who walked up the steps into that plane."

"What you say is true."

"So now they're kidnapping girls for their little Watcher army?"

"Mei-Ling is the only one," he said.

"But she's just a kid from Long Island. What can she do for a bunch of *vampires*?"

"She's not entirely helpless."

I stared hard at him. "You sure are being mysterious."

After a moment, he conceded, "She tried to fight back."

I pictured Mei-Ling. Slim. Young. With a name meaning *beautiful, delicate.* The image of her fighting back made me ill. She'd had some fancy school and parents who loved her. She shouldn't have had to learn to fight back.

I flashed back to those times I'd tried to fight back at fifteen— and I'd only ever faced off against my father. Mei had been up against Tracer Otto.

I made a mental note to kick his ass someday. Him and so many others . . . It was getting to be one long list.

"How'd she possibly fight back against *Adolph?*" I sneered, using my pet name for the detested Tracer Otto.

"Caution, Annelise." Ronan cut me a look, then glanced around to make certain no one was close enough to overhear. "Otto came for her after school. As I understand it, she stabbed him in the throat with her violin bow."

I chuckled, surprised and more than a little amused. "Go, Mei, go. Maybe she'll last more than a week after all."

Ronan smirked. I got the impression he wasn't the biggest Otto fan. "She caught him by surprise."

"Fighting spirit or not, she's just a regular kid. She's not saying much, but I'm sure she must be terrified. How's she even going to make it through the week? Once the other Acari get wind of her, they'll chew her up and spit her out."

"I believe her placement with you was intentional," Ronan said evenly.

I stopped short. "What?"

"*You* are how she's going to make it through the week. I believe that's why she was placed with you."

"Wait, you're saying they put her with me on purpose? Why me?"

Ronan shook his head, frowning like I was a puzzle to be muddled out. "Have you heard how you've been speaking? Have you heard your own outrage? All you have said to me is true. Other Acari would've met a younger girl, sensed weakness, and struck. But not you. Look how you've reacted."

He was right. The moment I saw how young and scared she was, I went into protective mode. Apparently I had some shreds of humanity left inside. I guess that was heartening. Heartening and stupid. "Are you saying the vampires hoped I'd bring her under my wing? Why would they care whether or not she's safe?"

"I don't know for certain," he said quietly. "What I do know is, it would probably serve both of you well should you use your best efforts to help keep her alive."

"As in, if something happens to her, I'm toast?" As if I didn't have enough on my mind. He'd paused but began walking again, and I did a little jog to catch up.

We reached the dorm, and I bobbed up and down on my toes as we stood there. I was chilled, and it wasn't entirely due to the weather. "So, tomorrow. Did you *have* to make our class at seven in the morning?"

"I have many students."

"Couldn't you have made *them* get up at dawn? What are we doing that can't wait till, I don't know, nine a.m.?"

"It's time to bring your swimming to the next level."

Not this again. "What else is there? You already taught me how to swim in the sea."

"Now we'll acclimate you to its rips and undertows. *Ejya* has a low-tide break. And tomorrow, low tide is at seven fifteen. Meet me here. I'll drive us."

"Wait, wait, wait." I put up my hand. "What do you mean, a low-tide break?"

"Tomorrow, we surf."

Gooseflesh shivered up my arms. I dreaded the water, but I told myself surfing was cool. I tried not to whine or moan, and my voice sounded strained with the effort. "What on earth will surfing teach me?"

"Surfing has many lessons to teach."

"You're talking like Yoda again."

He surprised me by laughing. "Try it, Annelise. You'll learn about balance. Fear. Patience. Inconsistency. Unpredictability."

A feeling seized me out of the blue, a shiver rippling across my body. I sucked in a breath.

Ronan's gaze strayed over my shoulder, focusing hard on a spot behind me, and a muscle in his jaw pulsed. "And it will teach you *trust*," he added, his voice heavy.

I knew who I'd find when I turned. I'd felt him coming even before Ronan had seen him. *Carden.*

I braced. But I could do all the loin-girding in the world and I'd never be prepared to face my blood-bonded vampire.

Yes, *my* vampire.

I tried to be cool as I peeked over my shoulder, but what I really wanted to do was fling myself into him.

Carden's eyes were pinned on me, but his words were for

Ronan. "Tell me, Tracer. How is it that every time I see you, you are with our Acari Drew?"

"I'm her teacher," Ronan said tightly.

"Yet she always seems so distressed in your presence. Odd, that." He stepped closer, close enough to cast me in shadow.

Easy on the testosterone, guys. I glanced at Carden to give him a quelling look, but what I saw stole my breath.

Like a peacock spreading his wings, Carden had plumbed some serious vampire mojo. It wasn't that he'd changed his appearance in any way, but suddenly he radiated power. He seemed about ten feet tall, all broad-shouldered, fierce Vampire.

Carden reached toward me, and I fought to stand upright. It felt as though there was an invisible cord connecting me with the vampire. I felt its pulse low in my belly. I fought not to sink into him.

I inhaled with a hard sniff, gathering myself. It was the blood bond. What I felt for Carden wasn't true attraction.

Right?

He brought a gentle fingertip to tilt up my chin. Carden was big, and my eyes had a long trip up that buff body to his face. He studied me, and it felt like a caress. "What lessons have you to teach this gifted creature?"

Gifted creature. He'd meant *me.* My mouth went dry.

Ronan's response was brisk. "I teach her fitness. Ann— *Acari Drew,*" he quickly corrected, "did not know how to swim when she arrived. We have been spending a lot of time in the water."

Carden's lips curled into a smile. "I'd like to see that."

I'd rather die.

I almost said it—I *would* have said it if Ronan hadn't been

VERONICA WOLFF

standing there. But something told me I couldn't let him see how informal I'd gotten with Carden.

"You are welcome to join us anytime, Master McCloud."

That cleared the fog from my brain. I jerked my head to look at Ronan, dragging my chin from Carden's grasp in the process. *Wow.* He had to call Carden by his formal title, *Master McCloud*.

I could tell by the furrow in his brow that Ronan had noticed me noticing. "Curfew is soon," the Tracer told me. "Be careful. Until we learn who killed Trinity, there is a killer on the loose."

There was an unspoken challenge in the words, but Carden didn't rise to the bait. Instead, he gave Ronan a jaunty smile. "If you're done here . . . ?" He waited for Ronan to get the hint.

Ronan gave a curt nod. "Of course. Tomorrow at seven, then, Acari Drew." And then he left me alone with my vampire.

CHAPTER SIX

I felt a peculiar twinge in my chest as I watched Ronan walk away. He was one of the few people on this island who cared about me, and I wasn't entirely sure why. Would those feelings change if he discovered I'd bonded with a vampire?

It was a wonder he hadn't figured it out already. Carden's posturing wasn't exactly subtle. "Way to keep our bond secret," I chided him. "Maybe you should just brand me."

Carden scoffed at that. "He's but a boy. He doesn't see what's right in front of his face." The way he traced his finger down my cheek implied that I'd been what was in front of Ronan's face only to be ignored.

The notion stung. I lashed out. "He behaves better than you do." I bit my tongue, regretting the words at once. I'd seen how angry these vampires could get.

But Carden shocked me with a rollicking laugh. "You're pretty when you're peevish, little one." With a glance right and left, he tugged my hand. "Come, *eilean mo chridhe*, let me feed you. It will ease your mind."

I felt the tug of his hand like it was on a direct line to my lady parts. I flashed to a fantasy of going with him, disappearing into the shadows, where he'd kiss me like he'd kissed me before. I'd melt into him like a pat of butter on a hot skillet.

And then we'd be discovered, and I'd be killed.

Or *he'd* be killed, our bond would be severed, and I'd realize I was never truly attracted to him in the first place. Then some other vampire would try to bond with me and I'd be back to square one.

No, thank you.

I tugged back, reclaiming my hand. "Was that Gaelic? What ridiculous thing are you calling me now?" *Honeybun? Sugarbear maybe?*

His normally lively expression grew quiet. "Isle of my heart."

I swear, I felt an actual twang in my chest. Because that was how I felt. . . . I was an island, choked by my solitude. Did this reckless, inscrutable vampire actually see inside me? We had a blood bond—I'd assumed it was a purely physical thing. But had it attuned him to the ways of my heart? Could he sense my deepest secrets? Had he noticed just how lonely I was?

I felt vulnerable, and it made me wary. "I'm not going with you until you tell me what's going on."

"What's going on?"

"Why can't I get you out of my head?"

"Because I'm a handsome devil?" He gave me a naughty smile, knowing the truth of the matter was that my head had nothing to do with it—I couldn't get the feel of him out of my *body*. "What's going on is you need blood."

"I have a shooter of the stuff with every meal."

"*My* blood," he said with a sexy growl. He got that look in his eye again—that twinkly, beckoning look—and nodded his chin away from the dorm. You'd think he was merely suggesting we sneak around back to make out like real teenagers would.

I crossed my arms at my chest, closed for business. "Not until you explain this. Do other Acari have bonds like this? Why can't anyone find out? Is it permanent?"

"Perhaps. Because. And not necessarily." He snatched my hand and began to walk. "Now come. Your peevishness is wearing."

I dug in my heels and snatched away my hand. "If you're not going to answer my questions, then it looks like we've got nothing to talk about. I'm going inside."

Anger flashed in his eyes, sharp and crystalline. Adrenaline dumped into my body as I saw what rage smoldered beneath that carefree surface. "You're a foolish child to deny me," he snarled. "To deny yourself. It was foolish what you did to us. Now, more so, what you continue to do."

Terror sent my heart galloping. I'd gotten too relaxed with him. With all of our flirty banter, I'd forgotten—this was a *vampire*. He might be easy, sexy, devil-may-care Carden, but he was a creature who could turn on me in an instant, flaying me. Sucking me dry, if he chose. He was ancient, with the strength of ages.

I wouldn't forget again.

"You only want me because of the bond," I said, trying to sound reasonable. "Not because of *me*."

"Just let me take care of you," he said through gritted teeth.

But I didn't want to feel like I needed a vampire. Especially not *this* vampire. Until I figured out why Alcántara seemed to have it out for Carden, the last thing I needed was for the Directorate to think I was with him.

"I can't go with you," I said quietly. Technically, I didn't have to agree to go with him. I supposed he could just take me. Grab me, throw me over his shoulder, and do what he would. The way he stepped closer made me think for a second that he might.

"Then I have two things to say to you." His jaw was clenched, as though he was restraining himself from doing something bad. "First, Tracer Ronan is correct. Stay in your room. There is a killer out there, and no, it's not me."

I mustered my willpower. It was the hardest thing I'd ever done. Putting space between me and Carden felt like walking away from an ice-cold glass of water while dying of thirst. But I swallowed hard and made myself say, "And the second thing?"

"The second thing," he announced, biting out the words in a glacial tone. "Stay away from me. If you won't accept me, it is the only way."

Maybe I was stubborn, or afraid, or cautious, or just a romantic hoping for more. . . . Whatever my reasons, I hadn't wanted to go with him. But now that he forbade me, well, that was a different story. It felt so final. I laughed nervously. "I thought I was your wee dove."

His eyes narrowed, his desire grown fierce. The quiver I'd felt in my belly shot through my whole body, heating me, weakening me, until my knees went shaky. He wanted me, and it was a heady thing.

"I grow hungry," he said, his voice hoarse, "and yet you wish to sever our bond. To be this close is to be too tempted."

This was the most he'd ever said about the bond, and it gave me strength. "You can break a blood bond?"

"With effort," he said through gritted teeth. "But there must be distance."

He leaned down, and I froze. His lips were perilously close to my neck. "You're catnip, you know." The air tickled across my neck as he inhaled. "I was your first kiss. It's not too late for me to be your second, too."

I flinched back. "How'd you know you were my first kiss?"

"I know many things." He lightly swept the back of his hand down my arm, leaving a ripple of goose bumps in its wake.

How easy it would be to let him scoop me up and carry me away. How much I wanted him to.

But I also knew I didn't trust the bond. If we could sever it, we had to try. My reaction to Carden was too powerful, and I didn't believe it was real. I didn't know him, but in our short acquaintance, I'd sensed the tension between him and Alcántara. What was Carden's history with the Directorate? Until I understood this island more, I wasn't ready to hitch my wagon to any vampire.

"No." I took a step back. "So is that it? If we stay away from each other, we can break the bond?" My voice came out sounding more bereft than I'd intended.

His eyes lingered on me. Finally he turned from me.

It felt like saying good-bye to a lover. Carden was my first and only kiss, so I supposed I *was* saying good-bye to a lover.

He spoke over his shoulder, his voice cold. "This will be difficult for you. You must steal extra doses of the blood. But for now it's late. Curfew is soon. Get inside, Acari Drew. And watch your back."

CHAPTER SEVEN

———— ∞ ————

I was trapped. My limbs grew numb. I was helpless. Held captive.
I was sitting in an audience, pretending to appreciate
some early medieval musical stylings, played with almost comical
solemnity by an ensemble of effete vampires.

Master Dagursson was kicking off our semester of Medieval
Musicianship with the Boringest Concert Ever. It seemed like the
entire campus had gathered for the recital, and we were trying to
be good students and sit silently, but the music was monotonous,
to put it mildly.

"What did Beethoven have as a snack?" Josh whispered in
my ear.

I didn't answer, but that didn't stop him from delivering his
punch line, intoned to the tune of Beethoven's Fifth. "Ba-na-na-
naaaa."

I elbowed him hard. "Shhh . . ."

Boring didn't begin to cover it.

And uncomfortable.

I'd glimpsed Carden from the corner of my eye as I walked in. My pulse pounded at the sight of him, a dull throbbing along the surface of my skin. It felt like ages since I'd fed from him, and just the thought of it had me shaking like a junkie.

I didn't need to look to know he was standing near the exit. Probably glowering at the back of my head for talking to Josh.

"You all right? You're looking pale, D." Josh had leaned close to say it, and the back of my neck prickled.

There. My Scottish vampire was definitely glowering at us.

Thoughts tumbled into my head. Snapshots of Carden's mouth. The touch of his hand. His breath on my neck.

Sweat broke out on my forehead. "There's a vampire out there who's mad at me."

"Ah. But I'm not mad at you." He edged even closer, and our shoulders touched. "No need to be cranky with *me.*"

Little did Josh know he was in very dangerous territory. I wouldn't be surprised if Carden was the jealous type.

The piece ended and the room swelled with applause. I took the opportunity to scoot away. "Yeah, well, *I'll* be mad at *you* if you don't give me some space."

He snickered. "So what's with these music classes, anyway?"

I tried to take my mind off my abject thirst. *Music.* We were listening to and discussing music. I'd actually wondered about the music thing before myself. I grabbed onto the topic. "Who knows? Though somehow Emma was spared."

"I heard she gets to hack computers this term instead."

"So jealous," I said, and I was.

He shrugged. "But not your roommate. Yas said they have her in a bunch of independents." Josh's Australian accent made *Yas* sound like *Yeahz.*

"She's some kind of musical prodigy." I grew quiet. There were lots of music prodigies in the world, so why did the vampires want her so badly? I sensed she was more upset about it than she let on, but the kid was a vault, sealed tight. I couldn't get much information out of her to begin to piece it together. At fifteen, she was younger than the rest of us, and she didn't seem to have any extraordinary physical gifts.

Another group of musicians arranged themselves onstage— they were empty-handed, which meant we were about to be serenaded. The chatter in the room slowly died, and we settled back, shutting our mouths, too.

This was a form of torture. I rubbed my belly, which was starting to cramp. It was an empty, needful feeling . . . beyond mere hunger and thirst.

As the men took their places, I distracted myself with an internal debate over which was worse: surfing with Ronan in the bitter-cold sea, as I had that morning, or sitting here, trapped and uneasy, listening to this god-awful music.

At least now I was sitting down. This morning on my borrowed surfboard, I'd paddled and paddled, and still hadn't been able to get past the break. I'd panicked, feeling how I'd grown weaker. I'd tried to take my mind off it by eyeing Ronan, looking hot in his wet suit, but not even that had been enough to distract me. My arms ached so badly afterward, I'd barely been able to shampoo my hair.

I needed Carden's blood. I was growing weaker and clumsier without it. The refrigerated shooters just weren't enough.

A shrill trilling startled me from my thoughts. A particularly pale vampire was currently rocking his woodwind.

Josh chuckled, and I was grateful to have him there, always a willing cutup. "Who knew the recorder was such an instrument of passion?"

"That's not a recorder," I said, though I really should've shut up. If I were smart, I'd act as grave as those vampire musicians, but anything to get my mind off my hunger. The accompanying harpsichord was a surprisingly loud instrument—it was amazing what it drowned out. "I think we're enjoying the magic of the pan flute."

Josh snorted, then turned it into a cough.

But a starchy-looking Watcher in the row in front of us had heard. She peered behind her to see who had the gall, and I stared straight ahead using my best serious face. Thankfully, we sat far enough toward the back to escape anyone else's notice.

They'd begun a chanting number, and I cringed as a vampire singer hit a particularly shrill note.

Josh's shoulders shuddered with silent laughter. He leaned toward me to whisper from the corner of his mouth, "You think that mate's a castrato? Like with the—" He made a little snipping motion with his fingers.

Unexpected laughter bubbled in my chest, dying to burst free in a fit of the giggles. My intense thirst was making me slaphappy, but I was going to get both of us in trouble if I couldn't pull it together. I hissed at him, "Shut up."

He slouched back in his seat with his legs kicked out and arms tucked at his chest. If someone were to glance at him, he'd just appear to be really laid-back, but the pose put his head closer to mine, enabling more whispering.

We clapped at the end of the number and he muttered, "This is killing me. Do you think they know any classics? 'Free Bird,' maybe? Can't you just hear it chanted?" He made a low humming sound, not unlike the chanting men. "Hohhhhhh . . ."

An Acari in front of us turned and glared, and I gave her a prim smile. Placing a discreet hand in front of my mouth, I muttered, "I'd settle for anything *tonal*. What kind of mission will they send us on that we need to be familiar with Gregorian chant?"

Thinking about it, I supposed the possibilities were endless. Especially considering that our enemy vampires were once monks who lived on another island in an abandoned monastery.

As I whispered to Josh, I felt the hairs on the back of my neck stand on end. *Carden.* Why was he even there? He didn't strike me as a big music fan, nor was he the monastic type—particularly as *unholy-goddamned-sexy* could be counted among his qualifications.

What did this preoccupation with him mean? Was it permanent? Did I feel him out there, looming nearby, because he was focused on me, or was it that I was obsessed with him? Not to mention the fact that he was so hot in a roguish, careless sort of way. But again, was that purely the bond talking?

Regardless, I leaned away from Josh—I didn't want to get him in trouble. I'd already been his downfall once before, when he'd intervened and stopped Masha and her cronies from hazing me. Her cronies . . . including Trinity.

He'd had hell to pay for it, too. I still didn't know who'd beaten him up. All I knew was that he'd put a stop to their torture and had shown up the next day with a battered face. He still had a scar cutting through his left eyebrow—a little jog where the hair hadn't grown back.

Did that mean that he also had a motive to see Guidon Trinity dead? Did he even have the ability to drain a body like that? His vampire Trainee baby fangs weren't all the way grown in yet.

I thought I knew him, but couldn't say for sure. He'd been

friendly with my nemesis, Lilac, and although it was probably just because Josh was friendly with *everyone*, that fact stuck in my craw and prevented me from really trusting him.

I felt myself beginning to nod off and I stretched my legs, squeezing life back into my butt cheeks. "Is this going to last the full three hours?" Class went till six p.m., and I wouldn't put it past Dagursson to regale us with zithers and lutes for the full period. It was a grim thought.

Josh shushed me, canting his head to listen. When I cut my eyes to glare at him, I realized he hadn't shut me up because he was listening to the music. A low murmur was traveling through the room, and he was straining to hear.

Two Acari in front of us began to whisper. I picked out bits and pieces. One girl's eyes widened. "Another one?"

I opened my mouth to speak, but Josh held up a finger to silence me. He turned to the girl next to him and turned on the old Joshua Nash charm.

When he leaned back toward me, his expression was unreadable. "Angel, I hardly knew you."

I cut him a quick look. "What are you talking about?"

"You know Watcher Angel?"

I gave a slight nod, gluing my eyes back to the stage, pretending to listen to the music. "Angel of Death, you mean?"

"Yeah, the chick with the arms."

What was it with guys and her arms? It made me impatient. "What'd she do?"

"She got herself killed."

My mouth dropped open. There were lots of different ways to be killed on this island, but only one would cause this much gossip. "Like . . . ?"

He shifted uneasily in his seat. "Like, drained killed."

My eyes shot back to him. "Like Trinity." I went numb.

"I also heard there was another one they didn't even tell us about. Before Trinity. But you didn't hear that from me."

Suddenly, everyone around us was clapping. It jarred me to attention, and I clapped right along, but my gaze didn't budge from Josh.

Everyone began to stand and gather their things. And even though the burst of activity made it safer to talk, Josh kept his voice low. "Careful, little D. It's looking dangerous to be a sheila around this place."

With a sigh, I stood. "What else is new?"

We exited and a male figure stood waiting, silhouetted in the half-light. I sucked in a breath.

Alcántara.

His lips peeled into a smile. The setting sun was a dull white orb on the horizon. Its light caught and glimmered along one long fang. "Good evening, *querida*."

CHAPTER EIGHT

———

Master Alcántara was waiting on the steps as I walked from the Arts Pavilion. He leaned against a pillar, looking every inch the dark, seductive rocker. One would never guess that he was actually an ancient Spanish vampire who'd served as a mathematician in the royal court.

For a moment, I hoped he was there for some other reason, but his gaze didn't budge from me. He pushed from the pillar to approach, his movements lithe like a deadly panther.

"I'm outta here," Josh mumbled under his breath.

I shot him a scowl. "Thanks."

But then I smoothed my features to something bland and proceeded to ignore Josh entirely. Alcántara had expressed an unnatural interest in me—and lately it felt like I was the focus of *a lot* of unnatural interest. The last thing I wanted was for him to suspect Josh and me of fraternizing. I'd lost enough people in my life.

And where was Carden? I'd felt his presence practically

vibrating through the room earlier. Fear for him speared me. From the start, I'd seen only animosity in Alcántara's eyes where my Scottish vampire was concerned. I suspected that vampire rivalries were more ruthless than anything a mere Trainee would be subjected to.

"You are looking as lovely as the evening, *mi cariño*. Might I escort you to the dining room?" He reached his hand out to me, as if I might need help descending the stairs. It was a courtly gesture, and he wore it well.

I clearly had no choice. Suppressing a shiver, I responded how I imagined any good fourteenth-century lady would have and accepted his cool hand in mine. Besides, I wanted to get out of there before Carden came out to find us talking. "That would be lovely."

He stroked my palm, easing way closer to me than was comfortable. "Did you enjoy the concert?"

I lied—of course. "I did. Baroque music is so evocative." The wind gusted, and I was grateful when my hair blew into my eyes—tucking it behind my ears gave me an excuse to reclaim my hand. After getting my hair burnt off by my psycho roommate, my bangs were growing out in the most frustrating way imaginable.

But then Alcántara paused to bring his own hand to my face, gently pulling a couple errant strands from between my lips. "*Que rubia,*" he whispered. "*Tan rubia.*"

So blond. The sentiment and his touch made my skin crawl. Ever since I'd disobeyed his orders while on our mission and rescued Carden myself, our relationship had been different. I'd thought I was no longer his pet. Apparently, I'd thought wrong.

I couldn't pull away, so instead struggled to change the subject. "I particularly enjoyed the harp," I said, my voice chirpy. "It must be such a difficult instrument to play."

Nodding, he tucked my arm in his and continued to walk. "Master Heinrich studied in Vienna."

As much as I hated music with Master Dagursson, I supposed it could've been worse. I could've been made to study the harp with Master Heinrich.

Alcántara mistook my silence for contemplation. "Much has been written about the links between music and mathematics in the Late High Middle Ages."

"Your time period."

He gave me a satisfied nod. "Indeed. My time period. I'd be happy to tutor you privately in this matter, if you so desired."

Just what I needed. "That sounds great," I hedged. One didn't say no to a vampire. Especially this vampire. "I'm still figuring out my fall schedule, though. But once the dust settles . . ." I petered out.

I felt the slightest shift in Alcántara's energy—a stiffening, like that of impatience and disappointment. I hadn't sounded sufficiently enthusiastic.

Stupid.

My brain scrambled to figure out how to make up for it. I altered my tone, trying to sound *very* curious. "You served in the court of King Pedro. I can't imagine a man nicknamed 'Pedro the Cruel' could've been a big music fan."

"Pedro was a man of science," he said distractedly. "But that is not what I came to discuss."

Dread settled like a rock in my gut. My cheerful attempt at conversation had come too late—it was bait that might've worked for a fish, but Alcántara was a shark.

VERONICA WOLFF

He stopped on the path to face me. His pale features shimmered in the twilight, like polished marble.

Gooseflesh crawled up my arms. How had I ever thought Alcántara was attractive? I complained about many people on this island—Tracer Otto, Master Dagursson, too many Guidons to name—but at least they didn't terrify me, not like this.

Another sensation followed quick on its heels—that feeling again, of the hair on my neck standing on end, and a cramping, like hunger, deep in my belly.

Carden.

His voice came from behind, sounding cold and angry. "Preying upon young women again, Hugo?"

My eyes went to him at once. My body wanted to go, too—just the sight of him set my hands trembling. I had to fight not to walk mindlessly to him. He stood tall, holding his arms slightly askew, all coiled power.

Why had he come? He'd said we needed distance, but had he somehow sensed my distress?

Alcántara snarled, "Do you not tire of the self-righteousness, McCloud? I know I do."

"A man always has a choice, and he has but to choose the right thing," Carden said with a blithe smile, implying a whole universe of subtext that was beyond me.

His proximity seared through me, quickening my pulse, my breath. My throat was parched . . . thirsty. I was so thirsty. Too late, I realized that while I was watching Carden, Alcántara was watching me.

He turned to Carden with disgust. "You speak of the right thing. Learned men call such statements ironic." Alcántara directed his next words to me. "McCloud buys into chivalric nonsense."

"A man must prove his worth," Carden said nonchalantly.

"His worth?" Alcántara scoffed. "I find the idea barbaric. I suppose you'd call a man unworthy until he's done battle."

"Unworthy?" Carden's expression was dismissive. "Untested is perhaps the better word."

Alcántara shuddered. "My father had such brutish notions. The real test is how one wields words, for they can be fiercer than any sword. But that is something you savages don't understand." He touched a finger to my chin. "You and I, however . . . We are of like minds, are we not, *querida*?"

I'd thought Carden might be the jealous type, but never had I imagined this. He looked ready to go ballistic.

I was certain I must've looked like a gaping fish as I fumbled to think up a reply that would keep me alive and the two vampires from shredding each other to bits.

But Carden saved me from answering—and if that was chivalry, I was all for it. "Words as swords? Is that what this is?" He smirked. "Some might say words are the tools of cowards who won't do their own dirty work."

There were clearly more layers of history in this conversation than I could deal with. I began to back away slowly.

"Stop." Alcántara halted me in my tracks. He stared at Carden with pure loathing. "Are you quite finished with this vulgar rant?"

But Carden only laughed at him. By the look on Alcántara's face, he didn't join in the amusement. It was a dumb move that could get McCloud killed, and I braced for some form of retaliation.

"Have you urgent mathematical issues to discuss instead?" Carden raised a brow. "I'll leave you to your triangles then."

He was stupid and gutsy, not giving a care for what anyone else thought. And God help me, watching his strong back as he walked away stole my breath. Carden was all courage, and suddenly it wasn't a stretch to picture him riding around on a horse, waving a sword.

The moment Carden was out of earshot, Alcántara spun on me, his black eyes boring into me. "As you may have heard, another young woman was exsanguinated."

"I—I did hear," I stammered, worried what the abrupt topic change might indicate.

"This time, the victim was not merely a Guidon. She was a Watcher. Those who ascend to Watcher are the cream of the cream. The elite. Such young women are not often caught unawares. Our Watchers do not die easily."

"Yes," I said carefully. "I know." Every alarm in my head shrilled; every shield slammed into place. Why was he discussing this with *me*? He couldn't seriously think I had anything to do with it.

"We are very curious as to Master McCloud's whereabouts yesterday evening. Do you know, *querida*?"

He'd torn the ground from under me. He suspected Carden. Not only did Alcántara suspect him—I could tell by the look in those coal black eyes that he was after him, guns blazing.

But was this an investigation to discover if McCloud was guilty of murder, or was he also investigating whether he was guilty of being with *me*?

For all I knew, Alcántara had seen us talking last night, and this was a test to see if I'd lie for Carden. It was a stunt he'd pulled before. "Yes, actually," I replied as calmly as I could. "We exchanged words in front of the dorm after dinner."

He put a finger under my chin, like he needed a better angle with which to peer into my traitorous eyes. "Are you certain?"

"Yes, sir," I replied, trying to sound blasé. "I'm certain. In fact, Tracer Ronan was there as well." I cringed instantly. Why had I brought *him* into this?

Alcántara tilted his head as if to say he found all of this deeply fascinating. "What a compelling trio. Whatever did you discuss?"

"The importance of swimming," I stammered.

"How peculiar."

Relief set in. We were on to a new topic. "Ronan—I mean, *Tracer* Ronan—will be my swim instructor again this term."

"I see." He nodded. "Do you know where Master McCloud went after your little tête-à-tête?"

Every muscle in my body seized. Which was worse—Alcántara suspecting that Carden and I were close enough for me to know his comings and goings, or that Carden might have something to do with Watcher Angel's death?

"I . . . I don't know where he went." And I didn't. I didn't know where he went, where he rested, how he spent his time. Carden had told me to keep my distance, and even if I wanted to defy him, I didn't have the first clue as to how I'd find him.

"I cannot help but note that these unfortunate incidents have coincided with the arrival of McCloud," Alcántara said, adopting a pose of elegant thoughtfulness. "I wonder if something happened to him in that dungeon. If our enemies poisoned his mind somehow."

"I couldn't begin to say." My words hung, and Alcántara did nothing to fill the silence.

We stood frozen, locked there on the path, but footsteps coming from behind pulled both of us from the moment.

I looked over my shoulder. Who knew I'd be so glad to see my mysterious roommate?

"Hello." Mei was calm, neither overly formal, nor overly casual. You'd have thought the vampires were an everyday occurrence in Long Island.

"Hey." I edged from Alcántara to insert myself between them. I'd gathered I was supposed to protect Mei-Ling from outside forces, but at the moment, I wanted to protect her from this vampire the most. "You headed to dinner?"

Her eyes shifted from me to Alcántara and back again. Her expression remained flat, sizing us up like some young Chinese-American Terminator. "Yes."

"Cool. I'll be right there." The perfect excuse to flee. "I saw on the board that it's pasta night. A girl's gotta get her carb on. Save me a seat."

Mei nodded and walked on.

"You must look after her," Alcántara said to the back of my head.

"So I've gathered." Alcántara, out of everyone, saying I needed to look out for some girl? It was ludicrous. "But why?"

"Acari Mei has promise, and we'd like to nurture that promise."

"I see." My voice was calm, but my mind was racing. My suspicions had been correct—*Alcántara* had been the one behind her kidnapping.

"She has a great musical gift," he went on, "but her extreme youth does not lend itself to the same physical adeptness as the older Acari."

I wanted to snark, so why'd you kidnap her if she's only fifteen? But I only nodded. "I understand."

"We like to give every guest of the island a fair and equal shot."

Yeah, right. Seeing as they'd killed her boyfriend, threatened her family, and simply plucked her from some New York suburb to take her for their own, these vamps had a pretty weird concept of protection.

He began walking again. "You are both so gifted, after all."

I shuffled to catch up, thankful to see the dining hall peeking in the distance.

I'd been right. The vampires had stuck Mei-Ling with me so I'd protect her. But why? Did *she* know what she was doing here?

Before this went any further, I needed to get to know her better. And quickly, too. Because on the Isle of Night, watching out for someone just as easily meant offering your life for theirs.

CHAPTER NINE

─────◦◦◦◦◦─────

He came for me in the night. I woke to his touch. Gentle pressure stroking up and down my leg.

I stretched, rolled onto my back. The pressure increased until I sensed his individual fingers splayed along the side of my thigh. A light grip, then release. Grip and stroke.

I sucked a breath in through my mouth. Arched my back. I felt languorous, like a cat. I wanted that hand higher. Lower. *Something.*

Why was he teasing me like this? I wanted him to peel away my blankets. Why didn't he?

The frustration made me angry. My body pulsed now, needing him. I tried to speak. I wanted to tell him. Why couldn't I—?

I sat up, clutching the blanket to my chest. My heart pounded, its pulse echoing through my body until I throbbed with it.

Carden—where was he?

I widened my eyes and looked around in the darkness. Mei-

Ling was in her bed, her breathing deep and even. The clock read 3:02. It was the middle of the night. A dream.

No Carden.

I flopped back, breathing like I'd just sprinted a mile. It was only a dream. I pulled the covers tight under my chin, but it didn't make me feel any less vulnerable.

I measured my breathing, forcing myself to calm down. *A dream, stupid.* Carden was out there somewhere, but he wouldn't know I'd dreamed of him.

Would he?

No, he wouldn't. It was a silly notion brought on by the vivid sensuality of it. There was a simple explanation: I was coming off the bond and it was giving me fever dreams.

I rolled onto my side, clutching the blankets snugly at my chest until I felt cocooned. It was no good, though. I'd never feel safe.

My throat felt so dry it ached. Hunger clawed at my belly. I curled into a fetal position around the cramping.

My bedside clock ticked. No digital readouts for us, just old-fashioned clock faces with glow-in-the-dark hands, and I watched their slow progress. Tick: 3:12 a.m.; tock: 3:47. Time crawled, but I was too jangled to sleep. And way too uncomfortable.

I tried to think peaceful, meditative thoughts to relax, but it was no good. My mind raced.

Mei-Ling. I needed to help her, but I couldn't get a bead on the girl. Did she hate me? Or was she just too proud to accept my help? Maybe it was that she somehow knew more than the rest of us about the island, and her stoicism was actually disdain.

Was she shy and longing for a friend? I could think about it all night, but I wouldn't be figuring that one out anytime soon. So around 4:14, my mind skittered on to the next topic.

The killer. Who was killing girls on the island? A rogue vampire? A Draug? A clever and vengeful Acari?

But all the girls had been drained, and only a few creatures could manage that. Could Trainees do it? Or had one of our vampire enemies come from another island to terrorize us?

Whatever was going on, I had the sinking suspicion that I was getting pulled into the drama. Alcántara was overly curious about Carden, and to know Carden was to discover our bond.

I had to find the killer.

And why not? I was a walking, talking weapon. In several short months, I'd learned sabotage, secrecy, and worse—I'd become one of the world's most elite killing machines.

I lay there with the thought, trying to muster up fear for my own safety. Investigating the murders would be stupid and dangerous. But it would be even more dangerous for me if something were to happen to Carden. We were tied together now, whether I liked it or not. The need clawing at my belly told me as much.

I rolled onto my side, curling into that empty feeling. At the very least, looking into the murders would be a good distraction.

Planning soothed me, and the next thing I knew I was being shaken awake. I peeled open my eyes. My alarm was ringing. Mei-Ling was saying, "Acari Drew. Wake up." I'd have sworn I'd been awake just fifteen minutes ago.

My head was throbbing. A dull ache, like a caffeine headache. Or a Carden one.

I moaned. "All right, all right."

I remembered my dream. It came back full force, bringing with it the ghost of a throbbing between my legs. I threw back the covers. The room was freezing, but I embraced it. Anything to get rid of this heat in my body.

Carden had been right. I needed to stay away from him. I needed space. We needed to sever the bond, because any more dreams like that and I'd be walking in my sleep to find him. I had no doubt I'd be able track him down with my eyes closed.

Scowling, I swung my feet onto the floor and tried to push away the last of my sleep and focus on my day. Monday morning. I'd survived my first weekend of the fall term, and, man, it'd been a rough one. But I had a plan now, and plans were good.

But dressing myself was a struggle. My hands trembled, my body clamoring for Carden. I fumbled with my bootlaces, and it took forever to get them tied. My head felt ready to split in two, my headache a steady pulse in my skull, pounding out my need for him. "I'm going for breakfast."

Mei studied me. "You're not going to shower."

I couldn't tell if it was a statement or a question. I scraped my hands through my hair, willing the throbbing to subside. "No shower. I've got expeditionary-something class today. Sounds dirty."

It was with Watcher Priti. She had the looks of a Bollywood star and the ferocity of a ninja—I *loved* Priti. I should've been looking forward to it. . . . I *tried* to look forward to it. "What do you have today?" I forced myself to recall Mei-Ling's schedule. It was mostly independents—not much dirt for her, I bet.

"I'm supposed to have my independent study in Combat this morning, but . . ."

"But Watcher Angel is dead." I pulled on my fleece—my teeth were chattering now. "Don't know what to tell you." I almost left it at that, but remembered I was supposed to be helping her. Besides, I was aching and feverish. There'd be no investigating anything without food in my belly. "Come with me to the dining hall—we'll figure it out. I need to eat."

I needed more than food—I needed Carden's blood. I had to touch him. I was going to crawl out of my skin if I didn't. But I couldn't. So instead I'd get a shooter of refrigerated blood. Maybe sneak a second one. Anything to take the edge off.

I steeled myself, waiting with gritted teeth while Mei-Ling pulled on her uniform.

This wasn't *real*. This was the bond ruling my body. He wasn't my boyfriend. This wasn't real attraction. It was a chemical reaction. I'd gotten hooked on a drug and was detoxing. My drug was Carden.

I almost knocked on Emma's door as we passed it, but the silence on the other side told me to leave her alone. Maybe she was showering. Maybe she'd been up late and was sleeping in. Maybe she'd already left. I had no clue. I was psyched for her and her relationship with Yasuo, but it had also inserted the smallest, vaguest bit of distance between us.

It was just as well—Emma would see that something was wrong with me, and I didn't have the energy to lie.

Mei-Ling and I were walking down the path toward the dining hall when I saw her. *Masha*. And she had two of her Guidon pals with her.

"Oh shhhh-sugar." I didn't even get the pleasure of a real curse—I dared not while I was outside and vampire ears could be listening.

I panted a few quick breaths. *Focus*. I needed focus.

"What is it?" Mei asked, her eyes uncharacteristically bright.

The girl might've been quiet, but at least she had good instincts when it came to danger.

I didn't have time to answer. We'd been spotted. "Acari Drew," Masha purred. "Who's your little friend?"

I sensed Mei standing tall next to me. *Good.*

"Mei-Ling Ho," she announced in a clear voice.

Speaking openly to a Guidon. *Bad.*

Masha's face lit as she glommed on to the name instantly. "Hohhh." She walked a circle around her. "Ho, ho, ho. You having fun . . . *ho*?" Her friends snorted and snickered.

Oh crap . . . Here we go.

But Mei didn't respond. It struck me that she must've heard that joke a million times growing up. Did she even register the taunts? Did she care? Either way, her nonresponse riled the older girls.

Masha stalked up from behind, one hand stroking the bull-whip she kept looped at her hip. She leaned close to Mei's ear and said in a menacing whisper, "Would you like to play, little ho?"

A dump of adrenaline cleared my mind, and I reveled in it. I pushed away my hunger, but I could almost sense it in the back of my mind, like a Pandora's box, waiting for me.

I shifted my weight, parting my legs into a more solid stance. It was a subtle move, not so much that the Guidons would notice, but just enough to brace myself. At five two, I didn't have as much weight behind me as the other girls and I liked to take extra precautions.

I flexed my calf, feeling the leather boot pull. My stars were strapped in there. Finally, I'd found focus. Like a battle calm.

But wait. I glanced at Mei. Where was her weapon? This

damned headache—I hadn't been thinking properly. I'd been so preoccupied, I'd forgotten to ask what her weapon even was.

"She's a *ho*," one of the Guidons said with a snorty little laugh. She was rewarded by a bunch of snorty little laughs from her friends and so she added in a lower tone of voice, "Ho, ho, ho."

What was this, sixth grade?

But then my roommate shocked me—shocked me more than I think I've ever been shocked.

Mei-Ling turned to me and in a cold, clinical voice asked, "Does she have a tic? She keeps repeating my name."

I momentarily forgot my chattering teeth and felt my eyes bug out of my head instead.

The Guidon stepped forward. Her cheeks were blotchy with outrage. "What did she say?"

I'd been wondering the same thing. I opened my mouth to speak, but had no clue how to de-escalate.

But then Mei piped up again, in a tone so flat she might've been discussing a specimen in a lab. "There are disorders that result in repetitive speech. You kept repeating, *Ho, ho, ho, ho.* I was wondering if maybe you had that problem."

I almost laughed. I was *dying* to let loose a hysterical half giggle. But this fire was lit and burning, and the slightest smile from me would only throw gas on it.

The Guidon stepped into Mei's face. I tried desperately to remember her name so I could talk her down. Pamela, Paula, Patty . . . it was a P. "*You're* my problem," she snarled at us.

A thin switchblade appeared in P-whatever-her-name-was's hand. As amusing as Mei was, I needed to bring this down a notch. I took a step toward Guidon P (Penny?) and put my hand on her arm. "Easy, cowgirl."

She flinched away.

It struck me that it was overly quiet, and I glanced at the other Guidons. "Let's all stand down, ladies."

Masha's expressionless face was completely unreadable. *Weird.* Usually she was the one front and center in the brawling, but something had her just as wary as me.

Mei said, "I can handle this, Acari Drew."

Was she *totally* clueless? Or would she turn out to be the gutsiest girl on the island? Either way, she took a notch up in my opinion. Though I did get the sense that this "look out for Mei" gig was going to be a whole lot more challenging than I'd originally thought.

Masha broke her silence and took a step forward. "I think I would like to see how you handle it."

Crap. This was going to escalate after all.

But then I noticed how Masha's bullwhip was still holstered on her hip. Something had her feeling cautious. She usually took every chance she could to sling that strip of leather around.

I decided to take a gamble. Mei-Ling was about to get herself all kinds of messed up. I was supposed to protect her—even Alcántara had said so—and at the moment, I *wanted* to protect her. I didn't have the stomach to watch these girls have at her.

"Hey, Masha," I called. "I know you've got a big old girl crush on me, but there's no need to take your fixation out on my roommate."

It'd come out more brightly than I'd intended, my grin wilder. What was wrong with me? I had a bad habit of being reckless, sure. But had the bond added *volatile* to my list of flaws?

Masha's eyes zoomed in on me like two little lasers. "You wish."

"Here's what I wish," I said calmly. "I wish you'd go away." I regretted the words immediately. They somehow invoked Trinity and how she'd conveniently *gone away*.

I was tired of dancing around the subject. The ghost of Trinity was out there now—I could see it in their eyes—so I faced it head-on. "You're just pissed because you think I had something to do with Trinity. News flash, girls. I don't give a crap about you, and I certainly wouldn't bother to sneak around killing any of you."

The Guidons arranged themselves before us, forming a half circle. *Damn, damn, damn.* My little head-on plan wasn't working at all. Weapons were in hands, and they were all pointed at me. I guess I did succeed with one thing: I'd called their attention away from Mei-Ling.

I had one last shot. "That's cool," I said, keeping my poker face. "You can have at us, right here in the middle of the quad. But first you should figure out which one of you is going to explain it to Master Alcántara. He seems *very* interested in Mei-Ling here."

Masha got the hint. She hooked the bullwhip back on her hip with one hand and held the other out to stop Guidon—Paige! Paige was her name—to stop Guidon *Paige's* approach.

"Another time, then," Masha said. "But be warned, Acari Drew. If the vampires are interested in *Ho*, then maybe you're losing your status as their little pet. I wonder how concerned they still are about *your* well-being."

They walked on. Thankfully, it was away from the dining hall, because I was still starving, dammit.

Mei was silent beside me. I guessed she'd want to talk about what'd happened.

"Are you okay?" I tried to sound sympathetic, and really, I guess I kind of was, even though she'd escalated that scene herself.

"Yeah," she said, sounding more annoyed than scared. "Fine."

"Didn't that upset you? The *ho, ho* thing?"

She just shrugged. "Those girls are simple. Probably jealous."

"Wow. Okay. Maybe. Wait, do you mean uncomplicated simple, or simple as in dumb?"

Her mouth flinched. A nascent smile? "Right," she said, not really answering my question.

"Well, either way, you were pretty funny. I mean, you were trying to be funny, right?"

"I guess."

I realized I'd seen no signs of tears since that first day. If she had a problem, would I know it? "You can totally let me know if you ever need to talk. You're always so quiet."

"If I'm quiet, it's because I listen. Unlike you."

Whoa. Get back. I actually laughed. Was that an insult or an observation? It didn't piss me off, though. On an island of secrets, I liked her candor. "What do you mean, *unlike me*? I'm just trying to help. I wasn't sure if you understood what was going on back there."

"I grew up in New York. I speak English." Though the words carried a sting, there'd been no animosity in her voice when she'd said them.

I stopped on the path. "Wait, Mei. Do over. I *know* you understand English. Jeez. I meant, you're not used to the Guidons." I rubbed my temples—the headache was back with a vengeance. "God, I can barely think straight." Inhaling deeply, I faced her. "All I meant was that those girls would love to kill us—and they will if we're not careful. They could make your life serious hell."

I'd lost Amanda, and keeping Mei-Ling safe felt like righting that wrong. Besides, I liked odd ducks, and Mei was shaping up to be pretty massively odd.

"Hey," I added, trying to lighten the mood. "We've gotta watch out for your hands, right?"

She held out one of those hands, studying it. Then her eyes met mine, and she smiled. A real, genuine smile. "Right."

CHAPTER TEN

———❦———

Mei and I met up again for lunch, but this time I made it a quick one, claiming I wanted to go for a swim. She believed it, which was obvious proof that she didn't know me at all.

I jogged south along the coast. I had to find clues to the killer before people began looking too closely at me. I had a small window before Priti's class and figured there was no time like the present.

Food had done nothing to ease the gnawing in my gut. I was light-headed now, my hands shaking like I hadn't eaten in days. It looked like my investigation would be just like everything else on this island: performed amidst the worst of circumstances. But I rolled my neck and fisted my fingers, powering through.

I tried to focus on the real issue at hand, namely, that I had no clue how to go about investigating a murder. But I'd seen *CSI*. It wasn't rocket science to deduce that, in the absence of a body, one began at the scene of the crime.

I didn't know about Watcher Angel's death, but Headmaster had let spill some clues about Trinity's. He'd said her body was found not far from the cove. That'd be Crispin's Cove, where I'd weathered so many swim lessons. No wonder they all thought I had something to do with her death—I knew that stupid inlet better than anyone.

I'd since heard that, like Amanda, her body had been dropped, and I decided the jagged bluffs due south to be the likeliest spot. I slowed my pace as I approached. Any worries that I wouldn't be able to find the murder scene were for naught. Judging by all the footprints crisscrossing the area, the place had been visited more times than Disneyland. Most of the prints were larger versions of my Acari uniform boots. The morbidity of my peers never ceased to amaze me.

I bent, then squatted, then finally lay on my stomach, peering along the rocky dirt, searching for clues. I saw none—just a few dozen sets of footprints. Like a TV detective, I wanted to rail about all the civilians messing with my crime scene.

I stood, brushing myself off. My grand investigation would fail before it even had a chance to begin.

With a sigh, I looked across the rocks and down to the cove, inching as close to the ledge as I dared. I wanted a better look at the site of so many of my cursed swim lessons. It was strange studying it with a bird's-eye view, yet somehow, just then, it didn't feel like a bad association. Rather, that cove and Ronan's steel-jawed persistence were probably what'd kept me alive so far.

He'd taught me so much, and I hated to admit that those damned surfing lessons had already taught me a lot, too. About patience, how to watch and wait. How, when opportunity finally arrived, to seize it with courage. I'd found it nearly impossible not to panic at the first giant wave that'd come crashing toward me. But Ronan had taught me when to act on instinct and when to act on intellect, and intellect had told me the wave couldn't have been more than three feet high.

He'd shown me how to see what was truly there.

I looked away from the horizon, clearing Ronan from my mind. And it was then that I saw it. A thin smudge of brown along the thick green moss that carpeted the ridge's outer edge.

I inched closer, then finally just dropped to my hands and knees. Falling off a cliff would really put a damper on my investigation.

Once, I'd had to rely on my basic tracking skills. Ever since, I'd treated it as valuable a skill as combat, keeping a frequent eye to the ground, learning how to read it as I would a story.

And what a story these marks told.

The deep scuff that'd called my attention was thin and deep, a dark brown slash in the thin carpet of moss. That slash represented a slender boot heel that'd been dug in violently—and recently—its owner clinging to life.

"You fought him," I murmured, knowing instinctively we were dealing with a *him*. Sympathy and an odd sadness choked me. Trinity had fought, but she'd been too weak. We all were against the vampires.

Scooting closer, I divided the area into a grid in my mind. The evidence was faint, and to the untrained eye it would've looked like a normal landscape. But I'd been practicing. I read where the grass was torn, where moss had been scraped, where darker flecks of earth and displaced gravel spoke to a scuffle.

The exsanguinations suggested the killer was Vampire, but vampires were strong. Strong enough to kill with a single snap of the neck. This predator hadn't just murdered his victims—he'd toyed with them. This killer liked to play.

"Right along the edge," I marveled. She'd fought for her life while balanced on a high precipice.

The sight brought home just what we were up against, and heaviness swept my chest till I felt my chin sink into twined fists.

"Nice ass."

The male voice shattered my reverie, and I lurched up like one of those suction cup toys, instinctively springing forward so as not to tumble down.

It was a Trainee. Rob the Trainee, to be precise. One of the clowns who'd once almost peed on me, thanks to a particularly degrading Masha hazing episode.

If he'd come with friends, I was toast. I scanned the area behind him. Luckily there was no one else in sight. "What the hell are you doing?"

He gave me a slow, slack-jawed once-over. "I said, nice ass, Acari."

"Unlike yours," I snapped. "I've hated the sight of your gangly ass from the first moment I laid eyes on it."

"They said you were an ice queen." He nodded knowingly, but kept his eyes half-lidded and leering. Was he trying to look sexy? "I say you just need a good thaw."

"What is your problem?" Standing tall, I stepped forward, figuring a good offense was the best defense. "What are you doing here?"

"I could ask you the same." He took a lazy step toward me. "Thought you'd return to the scene of the crime?"

I sidestepped him. He didn't scare me. I might've been smaller and weaker, but surely I was smarter than Rob-the-Trainee. "I had nothing to do with any of this."

"That's not what I heard." His hand darted out, petting my hair.

I flinched away, shuddering at his touch. "You heard wrong."

But then—boom—he was back, standing in front of me. Was he further along in his training? His movements seemed faster than normal. That was my cue.

"It's been great catching up," I said. "But I gotta run. Class time." I tried to dart by him.

He grabbed my arm, stopping me, and his hand brushed against my breast. "Not so fast."

I tugged, fighting a growing panic. "Seriously, Rob. This has been a real treat. But I'm leaving." I made another move to scurry around him—I refused to run away—but with another sidestep, he remained in my face.

"Not till I tell you it's time to leave." He traced a brazen finger down my cheek. "I liked what I saw that day," he said, referring to the Guidons stripping me down to my underwear. "I think I'd like to see it again."

If he was trying to scare me, it backfired. I'd been messed with by far worse, far older, far scarier creatures than this d-bag. All my recent stress, all the uncertainty, it all fueled me. I snatched his finger, wrenching it hard till it cracked. "So not going to happen."

He howled and shook out his hand.

I smiled. "Don't hurt yourself, Rob."

"We vampires heal fast." He was glaring at me with pure hatred in his eyes, prowling back toward me with hands poised like he might attack.

I snatched a throwing star from my gym shorts. "You're not a vamp yet."

He smirked at my shuriken. "What do you think happens to girls who mess with Trainees?"

Now, there was something I'd never considered. "I'm all too happy to find out," I lied.

He laughed. "You'd risk your life just to keep the ice queen status?" Seeing my flat stare, he said, "Yeah, that's right. Your life. As in, I don't think the vamps will let you mess with one of their own."

"Get over yourself." My scorn was thick, despite my creeping doubts. "You're just a Trainee."

"Sure. And a Trainee is far more precious a commodity than you bitches."

I had to laugh at that gem. "Oh, *really*?" Was the guy actually trying to make me angrier?

"Yes, really." Rob didn't like being laughed at. He adjusted his pants suggestively. "Time for you to take one for the team, Acari."

I almost snorted a laugh. Maybe he thought he was menacing, but I wasn't taking anything for anyone. I had an idea, though, so instead I gave him a pretty smile, playing along. "You think you're that cute, do you?"

A smile flickered on the edge of his lips. "I know I am."

I shot a glance to a grassier spot away from the ridge. "Let's at least move away from the ledge."

He headed toward it, saying, "I knew you'd see the light." The idiot sure had bought my line quickly.

"You guys always know best." I knelt, like I was ready to get comfortable.

He chuckled, and it was a perverted little satisfied sound, like he was about to get lucky. "That's right. You relax."

He began to unzip. It marked the second time in my life I'd seen Rob's hand on his zipper.

I was sick of it. "Let me help you." I sprang up and around him, gripping my star between fingertip and thumb, and in one swift flick, I slashed his pants front to back.

"What the—?" His voice was a high-pitched squeak.

I backed away, watching in amusement. "By the way, you touch your pants one more time in front of me, I swear to you, it'll be your last."

He patted at his crotch, making sure everything was intact. "What the fuck?"

I let myself laugh. "You seemed so anxious to air it out. I thought I'd give you a hand."

He reached around, and I saw the moment he realized there was a giant gap where the seat of his pants should've been. "You little bitch."

"Relax," I told him, mimicking his earlier instruction to me. "You said I shouldn't mess with Trainees." I gave him an innocent shrug. "You're not hurt. I'm better with my shuriken than that. Besides, you helped." I flicked my eyes toward the seat of his pants. "Small target and all."

"You'll pay."

I had problems so much bigger than Rob-the-teenaged-Trainee, I found it hard to muster a care. "Will I?" I began to jog backward away from him. "I'm not the one returning to campus with a giant hole in my pants."

I was in a grand mood as I headed to Watcher Priti's class. I passed Tracer Otto on the path and bit my lip not to smirk at the sight of his bandaged throat. Mei-Ling had stabbed the guy with her violin bow as he abducted her. I hadn't fully believed Ronan when he told me, but the proof was right in front of me.

"Is there a problem, Acari Drew?" Otto's German accent was thick when he was angry.

"No problem," I quickly replied, darting my eyes down.

Getting myself back under control, I kept my head down the rest of the way. I'd endured quite enough interaction with my peers for one day—there was no need to go looking for any more.

Expeditionary Skills Training was held outside, on a stretch of sandy beach, and by the time I reached it, I'd pulled myself together. I'd handled the Masha incident. I'd investigated a murder scene and put some boneheaded boy in his place. I'd even gotten in a bit of roomie bonding. Maybe this was how normal college girls felt.

I hadn't yet found any clues to the actual identity of the murderer, but I'd taken the first step, and first steps felt good. First steps were empowering.

I was in a halfway decent mood for the first time in a while, but it did a nosedive when I felt him. When I saw him.

Carden. Standing next to Priti on the sand.

And he looked ready to teach.

CHAPTER ELEVEN

C arden spun his head, his eyes fixing on me the moment I stepped from the rocks onto the beach. Instant longing thrummed through me at the sight of him. The gnawing in my belly became hot fingers, twining and teasing through me enough to falter my step.

He looked about as pleased to see me as I was to see him.

My feet carried me toward him. It was stupid, but I couldn't help myself. Like breathing, it was something I couldn't have stopped if I wanted to.

Every muscle in his body seized taut, the evidence of which was obvious—not only was he super-buff to begin with, but he wasn't wearing a jacket over his tight white T-shirt. I'd have sworn his pecs actually cast their own shadows. It did nothing to help my addled state.

Sand had spilled into my sneaker, and I concentrated on the cool, damp grit. "Hi," I said, my voice impressively calm.

He gave me a tight nod. "Acari."

His voice echoed through me, and all my hard-won calm of a moment before shattered. "I didn't know you'd be here." The words spilled out of me. Anger, desperation, relief—competing emotions made my voice crack. *Oh God*, had I really just spoken like that to a vampire in front of everyone? I quickly tried to amend it by saying, "That is, it's a pleasure to see you again, Master McCloud."

The silence around us seemed infinite as I felt people's shocked stares boring into me, though it was probably only a moment that passed before Watcher Priti said, "Acari Drew, are you well?"

I forced a neutral expression. "I . . . Yes . . . I'm sorry. I have a headache, is all. I missed lunch," I added quickly, lying to explain it away.

That seemed to mollify her. She peered hard at me. "How many meals have you missed? You look pale."

"Just the one." I fisted my hands to stop the trembling. "But I've been working out more."

"You know how important our meals are," she said with equal concern and scold in her voice. I was a Watcher Priti favorite. She really, honestly liked me.

I liked her, too. But just then that meant nothing to me—all I was able to register was how close she was standing to Carden.

It was jealousy to the nth degree and it felt like madness, like acid was searing a hole through my insides. I feared the throbbing in my head would make my skull shatter. I fought to keep my face bland.

Thankfully, Priti seemed clueless as to my sudden, over-whelming urge claw her eyes out. "I gather you met Master McCloud on your mission," she said. "I've asked him to be our special guest today. He'll be taking us rock climbing."

"Yes, we're acquainted." I smiled, sure it looked more like a teeth-baring.

Carden's eyes were on me, intense and unreadable, like they might peer into my soul. Was he paler than usual, too? I thought he might be. I had to look away.

My gaze went to the horizon, gray and vast, interrupted only by the gigantic pillars of rock that rose from the sea like chimney stacks. Here, the sea churned, black water and white froth that pummeled and roiled, powerful enough to have punched ruts into the ancient granite over the centuries.

One thing reassured me: At least we weren't going to have to go in the water. People didn't go into *this* water.

There was a reason Priti used this particular beach for her classes, and it was the same reason Ronan never surfed here. Inlets like Crispin's Cove were protected—land cradled the water on either side, making for more manageable surf. It also meant rocky beach.

But this bit of coastline jutted bravely into the sea, fully subjected to the punishing waves—waves that, across generations, had battered the shoreline into sand. It was the favorite spot of many teachers, and good for things like wind sprints or hand-to-hand combat while knee-high in the breakers.

Ronan wouldn't surf here. The waves were erratic and unpredictable beasts, cresting and smashing into the sea stacks. Not a great ride if you're on a board.

"Good afternoon, my little birds, and welcome to Expeditionary Skills Training." Priti's voice brought me back to reality. She always sounded so shiny, a lethal fighter with a sunny disposition. "Different missions demand different skills. As Acari Drew can tell us"—she gave me an appreciative smile that I didn't deserve—"some missions require a facility with language or disguise. Others require no more than the simple ability to survive in the wild, and those are the skills we'll be addressing this term. Basics like shelter, navigation, and"—she smiled brightly at Carden—"rock climbing."

Carden took over. Or rather, he bowled me over.

I was used to the flirty, naughty-boy Carden. This Carden was different. This Carden was pure Vampire.

He stood, arms crossed at his chest and legs slightly parted, straight and solid, like an echo of the granite pillars behind him. He commanded the class, and every eye on that beach was glued to him. "In a survival situation, there are three things you need to address above all others. I call them the three H's. Heat. H_2O. Hunger."

"Don't forget *hatred*." Some Acari had said it in an attempt at humor or flirtation—I wasn't sure which. She looked impressed with herself and her own bored superiority.

Carden slowly swung his gaze to her, like a wolf sizing up prey. "Aye. Hatred—an easy answer. But it's the easy answers that kill you."

The girl's face fell, her superior look replaced by a mix of contempt, resentment, and fear. In a few words, he'd turned her sass into a deficiency. Like she'd made a joke, and now we could cross her off the list because she clearly wouldn't survive the week.

Seeing Carden now, I thought it miraculous that I'd found myself in his good graces. Was it only the bond? Would he have been just as disdainful with me if we didn't have this chemical connection?

"Hatred is easy," he continued. "Anyone can feel it. It's the rare person who'll face a life-or-death situation without emotion. Without panic."

Just then, it felt like he was the one without emotion. He was utterly removed from me, more like *them* than he'd ever been.

"You need to get your mind right," he said calmly, "if you're to survive *this*." He pointed to the water at his back.

Oh God. Were we going to go in the water after all?

I tuned in to the roar of the sea, a raging hum that filled my head. Its power was so great, it'd punched holes through those towering granite pillars. It had ground boulders into the sand beneath our feet.

"Sometimes you have control over your situation. Sometimes you can find water easily. Sometimes shelter presents itself." He began to walk around us, catching our eyes, addressing each one of us. "But sometimes you'll have no control. Sometimes your situation will control you. Forget food or heat; sometimes all you'll have is your will to survive.

"Every one of you has faced a competitor in the ring and *you* were the ones who walked out alive. Facing nature is no less than that. When on a mission, you must view the outdoors as you would an opponent. See your natural surroundings as a threat. Because if you let nature catch you unawares, she will kill you as surely as any enemy."

He stopped in front of me and touched a finger just above my left breast. My heart leapt. The feeling of perfect connection was so profound it made my vision waver.

"You must know this in your heart," he said in a voice hoarse with intensity. His touch was a brand, burning through the flesh and bone, straight to my heart. But it wasn't a sexual thing. In that instant, I felt how he was trying to communicate something to me. Something that might keep me alive someday. "You must believe you can master every situation. Or you will be finished before you even begin."

I gave the slightest nod. He gave the slightest nod in return. I knew a peculiar sensation—it was the feeling that I'd found something.

With a sharp breath in, Carden turned from me. "Watcher Priti has asked for a climbing demonstration."

Climbing. Not swimming. Relief swelled through me as he headed inland, toward one of the cliff walls lining the beach. Anything beat swimming.

Priti interjected, "Today, Master McCloud will introduce you to the basics. And then we'll be mastering these skills over the coming weeks as I lead you on our own climbs."

Carden led us far along the beach—farther than I'd ever been—and stopped at the base of a modest-sized face. He slapped his hand against the rock. "The basics." He looked up, squinting against the glare. Sunlight picked shades of gold and red in his hair, and the wind whipped it into a tangled halo around his head. He was beautiful. "This wee rock should pose no trouble. I'll talk you through it as you go." He faced us. "Who's first?"

CHAPTER TWELVE

————✄————

"I can climb." A girl stepped from the group. It was the Acari who'd made the crack about hatred. I wondered if this was her way to prove herself.

Carden narrowed his eyes. "Can you, indeed?" He stepped aside so she could take her place at the base of the rock wall. "And I'd thought there was always something more to learn. But what do I know? I'm a lad of only . . . let's see . . . over two hundred and fifty years now."

The other Acari tittered at his joke, but I saw from the steel in his eyes that this was no laughing matter. Things rarely were where vampires were concerned. I was discovering that Carden's nonchalance was much more of an act than he let on.

"Your name?" he demanded.

"Acari Kate." Her eyes were fever bright. It made her look like a junkie whiffing a fix.

"All right, Acari Kate. You've climbed before?"

She nodded, pleased with herself. "A lot."

"Have you ever done a free climb, climbs-a-lot-Kate?" There was a hint of derision in his voice, like he'd seen her type before.

Her lip curled. "That's all I do. I'm from Colorado, and there we—"

"So you know to imagine your path before you begin," he said, cutting her off. Acari Kate didn't like it, but I did, guessing that it was for the benefit of those like me who'd never scaled a rock in their lives.

Shielding his eyes with his hand—the glare can't have been easy on vampire eyes—he pointed up the face. "Search for the shadows along the rock. Those are the cracks and ruts that will be your handholds."

"I know," she said, and took off.

Carden's smirk spoke more to his disgust than amusement. "This is not a race. If you try to compete with Mother Nature, you will lose."

We watched her climb, and she *was* impressive, scrabbling up the cliff side. I made a mental note to beware if I ever found myself facing her in a combat ring—the girl had killer fingertips.

She paused at a difficult point, searching for a handhold.

"See how she finds her center," Carden told us. "Her breath, her movements . . . She remains composed and even."

Kate bent her knee to her chest, nestling her foot in a crack, then lunged, stretching high for the next handhold.

"Ah, there. Did you see how she used her legs?" His gaze lingered on me as he said, "You must let your legs do the work. They're stronger than your arms." I felt his hand over my heart again, even though he was several feet away. A phantom caress soothed me. Reassured me. "You must never think your arms weak. You'll only panic. Trust your legs—they have all the power you'll need."

I believed he'd catered his comment to me, the person who'd just recently managed her first series of successful pull-ups.

When he glanced back up, Acari Kate was near the top. He shouted, "That's enough. You'll be unable to make it all the way."

But Kate upped her speed, calling down, "No, I can make it."

"My role is not to scold you like wayward children." He set his jaw in a grim line as he faced us. "The intention was to discuss climbing. I fear this has become a lesson about pride."

I'd been mesmerized by the sight of Kate scaling the rock like a spider, but Carden's tone demanded my full attention. What lesson would he teach Kate when she came back down? I didn't want to know. I didn't want to have to see this side of him.

I hadn't realized Priti stood behind us until she announced somberly, "Pride kills more surely than the fiercest competitor."

Dread prickled my skin. So sure they were. But why?

Pebbles crumbled loose, skittering down the rock wall, and we all swung our heads, looking up the cliff. What did this girl think she was trying to prove?

"Almost there," Kate shouted with satisfaction. More rocks trickled down. "Whoa." She laughed, a rolling, self-satisfied cackle that sounded crazy. I wondered what was wrong with her. The wind carried her laughter over our heads to the sea.

Carden stalked from the cliff face, looking disgusted. We parted to let him through. His arm brushed mine as he passed, and breath whooshed into my body, my traitorous lungs sucking in air, trying like an animal to catch his scent.

"I can reach the top," she shouted, sounding determined. Maybe she wasn't nuts—maybe she just had something to prove.

Hell, maybe she just really liked climbing. She was mere inches from the top now.

"Vanity outlives the man," Carden muttered behind me.

"Acari Kate," Priti called. "You will return. Now."

"A Scotsman said that," Carden went on, sounding as coldly impassioned as any vampire. "Robert Louis Stevenson."

"Okay, okay," Kate shouted. "I'm coming back down."

But she didn't. I squinted into the glare. Watched as her leg pushed her up. She reached an arm over the ledge. Hoisted herself higher. She froze.

And then Acari Kate screamed. A terrified, shrieking scream, like she'd looked over the ledge only to be faced with a nightmare. A large chunk of rock broke free and bounced down, and we had to jump back not to get hit. Tiny rocks dislodged, crumbling down around us like hail. She screamed again, and this time it seemed she barely stopped for breath. It was one long, uninterrupted cry.

Everyone gasped when her foot slipped. But then her arm slipped, too, and she began to fall, the image surreal as both her arms spun in the air like a slow-motion windmill.

I clapped a hand over my mouth, aghast, as she tumbled down, bounced once against a jut in the cliff wall, and landed with a chuff in the sand.

Her body was still.

After her screams, our silence was deafening. There was only the breathing of the girls around me, heavy like we'd just run laps. Waves crashed behind us, a loud, rhythmic thrumming reminding us that we were minuscule and meaningless and that life went on without us.

Finally Carden broke the silence. "This is enough." He

gazed out toward the sea, and what I saw in his expression was unexpected. Beneath the anger, I imagined I saw sadness, too. Had he really wanted to help us? Did he want us to succeed? To live?

Watcher Priti told him quietly, "Perhaps it is time for your demonstration." Her tone was that of one adult giving another a hint.

And then she turned and stepped away. But as she did, I spied her sliding a small device from her belt. She keyed something in. Was she *texting*?

I darted my eyes away so she wouldn't catch me staring. It was a shocker, that was for sure. Her device seemed too small for a phone, but who could guess? For all I knew, the vampires were more wired than Silicon Valley.

I heard her speak to Carden behind my back. She'd pitched her voice low, but the wind carried it to me. "They're coming."

It was a long, slow walk back to where we'd begun. What had Kate seen? What would Carden have done to her if she'd made it back down alive? Or had he known she wouldn't? There was still more than an hour left in class. I wondered just what this demonstration of his would entail.

He walked us all the way down to the surf. Foamy water rushed up to us, then back again, leaving the sand glassy in its wake. I hated swimming, but for once I wanted to slip off my shoes and feel the frigid water roll over my feet. Maybe the cold would shock my body out of this numbness.

"Acari Kate's foolishness teaches a valuable lesson." Carden's voice was hard. Whatever sentiment I thought I'd seen earlier was gone. He was pure Vampire once more. "Only when you master your emotions, will you master your surroundings. Today I will prove this by climbing"—he pointed to the sea stack far offshore—"that."

"Will *we* need to climb that?" Some panicked Acari had spoken without thinking. Had she learned nothing from watching Kate plunge to her death?

"No," he told her. "Not today. But perhaps someday. Someday you'll face your biggest fear."

I chafed my arms. I had a feeling there were fears that would dwarf even that giant chimney rock.

Carden stepped into the water. It swirled around his calves, the deadly riptide sucking at his feet already. He looked blasé about the whole thing. "The average temperature of the North Sea in winter is six degrees Celsius. That's forty-three degrees Fahrenheit." He paused. "It is not yet winter."

Easy for him to say—he was a vampire. Surely he didn't feel a thing. An Acari I recognized from my dorm put words to my thoughts. "But we're human. We'd freeze in that."

He crossed his arms at his chest. "A normal human can survive this temperature for thirty to sixty minutes before reaching exhaustion or unconsciousness. *You are not normal humans.* A normal human could stay alive up to three hours in this water. You have been consuming vampire blood since your arrival. *You are not normal.* So stop thinking you are."

He stepped deeper. "In a real situation, you won't have a wet suit. You'll be wearing clothing, and it will be heavy and cold. You must learn to manage the pain. The panic." The water soaked his jeans, the denim dark and clinging to his thighs. It mesmerized me.

"Situations have a way of taking us by surprise. There will come a day when you'll need to climb and you won't have gear.

You won't have a climbing kit or rope. You won't be able to hook in or rappel back down. I'm here to show you that it's possible. Because until you believe it, you won't be able to do it."

And then Carden simply turned and dove into an oncoming wave.

Priti chattered at us, droning on about the sea cliffs and stacks. About climbing kits. Free climbing. Bouldering. But I tuned her out, unable to do anything but watch his powerful strokes cutting through the water.

He disappeared under the surface, and concern nagged at me. I sent feelers out into the universe, trying to sense if he was safe. Somehow I knew he was. Somehow I knew I'd be able to tell if he were in danger.

"They call it the Needle," Priti said. Water churned violently at its base, and Carden burst from the surface, riding the crest of a swell. It tossed him a few feet above the water, and he found his grip with ease. He began to climb at once. "McCloud is a local. It's a particular favorite of his."

I detected the hint of a smile on her face, and I wanted to smack her. I chafed my arms, trying to get a handle on these crazy thoughts. Was this jealousy? That she'd known something about him that I hadn't? I was getting cold just standing there, and I hunched into myself, making myself watch instead of think.

The Needle dwarfed Carden, but his small figure clambered up until he reached a point where the rock forked into two. He swung like a monkey to the center and slipped between the cracks. The space was much larger than it seemed from afar, and he wedged himself in and began to hobble up, one foot braced on either side.

Near the top, he edged onto an outcropping. The glare off the water had a way of distorting scale and distance, and I hadn't seen it before. He stood, and I saw that, sure enough, a table of rock protruded from the side.

He walked to the edge. A collective breath sucked in, as loud as the ebbing tides. Then Carden dove off.

He swam back to shore. I'd expected to see giddiness on his face as he emerged, but he was grim. Sober. His white T-shirt clung to him, and I stared unabashedly. I didn't care anymore— I couldn't peel my eyes from him. He was magnificent.

Who was Carden McCloud, really?

Once more, the water churned and pulled at him as he returned to us, only now my heart felt as tossed as the seas.

CHAPTER THIRTEEN

⸺⸰⸺

I stayed after, sitting on the cold, damp sand, contemplating the Needle, reeling from what I'd just seen. Would I have been strong enough to complete Kate's climb? Would I have been brave enough to hold fast, seeing something so unsettling it'd made another girl lose her grip and fall to her death?

I'd thought I was alone with these thoughts, but then a heavy body plopped on the sand next to me, casting me in shadow. I knew at once who it was—his identity practically vibrated to me, echoing through my body with a pull stronger than the tides.

He'd said we needed to keep our distance, but Carden had sensed my distress before. Maybe he sensed my turmoil now, my need for answers.

I didn't even look at him. I just said, "The girl who died climbing. Acari Kate. Why did she fall?"

"Pride goeth before a fall."

"Please, Carden. I need to know—in English." His non-answer gave me the mental strength to angle my body to look at him, and I wished I hadn't. He'd wrapped his arms around his bent legs, and his shirt tugged against his body, outlining ropes of lean muscle. I looked down the beach, back to the scene of the accident. "She climbed to the top and saw something. It scared her enough to make her fall. What did she see?"

"Only Acari Kate knows what awaited her at the top." At my impatient look, he chuckled, but he continued. "You've seen the mysteries this island hides. What monsters lie in wait. Not all are as brave as you in the face of danger."

Had she seen a Draug? A vampire? How many creatures were hiding out there, lying in wait?

He added nonchalantly, "I believe Acari Kate must have bonded with someone."

My eyes bugged open. "Seriously?"

He shrugged. "It would explain much."

"With who?" I ran a mental catalog of all the vampires I'd seen on the island—the possibilities were endless.

"That, I do not know."

I remembered her mania, her recklessness. "Was that why she was acting nuts? Is that going to happen to me?"

"You're strong in mind and body. This island has made you forget, but it is time for you to remember: Your fate is not beyond your control."

I flopped back on my hands, stretching my legs before me on the sand. "I wouldn't be so sure."

"You must credit yourself. This leg, for instance." He smoothed his hand along my thigh. "You've worked hard to carve muscle where once there was none."

My flesh grew hot, buzzing where he touched me. "I . . . I thought we were supposed to stay away from each other."

"Ah." He pulled his hand back. "How quickly I forget. You are still anxious to break the bond."

"I am," I said, sounding more sure than I felt. "It is possible, right? To become unbonded."

"Aye," he said. "It's possible. Difficult, but possible."

"And you think Acari Kate had bonded with a vampire?"

He shrugged. "It would explain such rash behavior. It's the blood fever. Some who've bonded feel as beyond the reach of death as their vampire mates. Others bond, and when they cannot feed again, they grow mad with their need."

Mad with need. I had some experience with that. I remembered Kate's restless, fevered eyes. Was that how I appeared?

Clouds scudded overhead, stealing light from the sky and warmth from my skin. "You're saying my options are to stay bonded, be reckless, or go insane."

He gave me a sidewise look. "I don't recall saying any of those things."

"You're giving me more nonanswers."

"On the contrary," he said. "I've been more honest and more forthcoming than anyone."

Even though the wind had whipped his words from me, they reverberated in my head. Carden was right—he *had* been honest with me, from the moment I'd met him in that dungeon.

I had to ask another question and I feared the answer. "Will I become reckless?"

"Is that a bad thing?" he asked in a musing tone. "There are two sorts of reckless, are there not? There is impulsive and there is brave—you must decide which you will be."

"Strong and brave," I whispered into the wind. He'd told me I could be these things.

Then it hit me. I didn't need some vampire to tell me—I knew in my heart already that I was these things. Strength and guts—it was how I'd survived my childhood.

I became aware again of his body next to mine. There was another sort of reckless, and the blood pounded beneath my skin to consider it. Could I be the sort of woman who was strong enough to stay bonded with a vampire and remain sane? To be brave enough to lean over and kiss her bonded vampire? "So I can be whomever I want to be?"

"Are you so quick to think yourself incapable? Do you accept Vampire superiority so willingly?"

"No," I answered at once.

He gave me a thoughtful look. "Then why are you quick to doubt yourself? Perhaps *you* are in control. Maybe you have only to realize this."

How much was in my control? The longer I stayed on this island, the more mysterious it became. "The vampires have told us why they want us here. But why might they *need* us?"

Carden smiled. "You ask a good question, pretty one. You are strong, and the vampires recognize this strength. Now you must recognize it, too." He put a fingertip beneath my chin, ensuring I wouldn't turn away. "You must recognize your power."

Why was he telling me this? "You're a vampire. Why help me? Why be honest?"

"I was once a man. As not all men are good, not all vampires are evil."

CHAPTER FOURTEEN

I was in control. I was powerful.

I was also very, very stupid. I was heading back to Crispin's Cove. I'd need to do some climbing, and yet there remained just one tiny problem: I still didn't know how.

But ideas had woken me in the night, implanting themselves and not letting go. What if Trinity hadn't been attacked from behind? What if the killer had climbed up the rock face, surprising her from below? What if there was evidence lodged somewhere on the bluffs, waiting to be discovered? Or what if she'd wrested something from her attacker? A tuft of hair gripped in her hand, a bit of fabric torn free, someone's dropped knife. She'd put up a fierce fight; maybe something had tumbled down with her.

It was a long shot, but one I had to take.

Unfortunately, I was taking that shot before I'd had a chance at more of Priti's climbing instruction. But I had to act now—soon the infamous island wind would scour the rocks clean.

And besides, I did have that one climbing class under my belt, and thanks to Acari Kate's little exhibition, I'd learned two things:

1. I didn't need ropes and carabiners to scale rocks. (Good, because I didn't know the first thing about that kind of gear anyway.)
2. Ropes and carabiners helped you not die. (Bad, in that a plummet to my death wasn't exactly on my bucket list.)

I assured myself that this'd be different from Acari Kate's ascent. I'd be going down—surely that was easier, right? And besides, I wouldn't really be rock climbing anyhow. More like bouldering. Hiking, even.

Really, really steep hiking.

I headed straight to the ledge—it'd do no good to chicken out now—and tightened the straps of my bag. The thing had been thump-thumping across my back as I'd jogged along the coast, but I decided to keep it just in case I found something I needed to tuck away. And hey, maybe it'd provide padding in the event of a freak accident.

I edged closer, and the height gave me a moment's vertigo, sending a wiggly sensation crawling up the backs of my legs. "A puzzle," I muttered, parroting Priti's words. While Carden had been climbing the Needle, she'd lectured. I'd tuned her out but had tuned back in when she'd likened climbing to mathematics, speaking about angles, degrees, ratios. "Just a problem to be solved."

I squatted now, trying to decipher that puzzle and detect a

possible path. It wasn't a sheer drop here at the top. Instead, the upper ridge was graded, forming steep, mossy tiers.

I craned my neck to see. There was an outcropping roughly fifteen feet down and a few feet over. It angled away, not readily visible from above. If I could make it down there, it'd be a good vantage point from which to scan for some clue that might've lodged in the rocks and brush.

I sat on my butt, scootching past the spot marking Trinity's final footprint. What lay between me and that plateau couldn't have been called a trail, but it was horizontal enough to shimmy and slide down if I used the rocks and roots as handholds. I inched some more, tentatively scrabbling down like a crab—a lame, clumsy crab.

My boots met flat rock, and I pushed with my legs, testing the support. It was solid. It gave me a spurt of confidence. I inched to the left, over to where I thought I'd spotted the rock shelf below.

"Here goes nothing," I muttered as I eased onto my side. I had the sensation of being almost vertical now, and it felt more secure to have so much of my body pressed against the granite. I guess somewhere in my reptilian brain I also figured that if I started to slide, maybe I'd be able to stop myself using hands *and* legs *and* belly.

It took me about thirty seconds to realize my reptilian brain was a total idiot.

Getting down to the next tier was less a thoughtful descent than it was a controlled fall. I slid, and rocks scattered loose, clacking down the side of the cliff in a shower of gravel.

"Crap." I picked up speed and careened past the next tier without stopping. Rocks cut into my belly and punched hard along my rib cage as I bounced and slid down the face. "Ohhhh crap."

Panic choked me as the mottled brown, gray, and green of the cliff angled steeper, rolled by faster. I grabbed for all of it. Flailing now, I swatted for rocks, dirt, the tufts of grass that poked from between the cracks.

My feet slammed into something, and the impact reverberated up my body. *The plateau.* Relief.

But I'd hit it too hard. Time slowed as I felt my body propelling forward, like I was about to swan dive from a platform.

Carden appeared in my mind's eye, a vision of him diving from the Needle, all power and grace.

Power and grace. I could be that, too.

I refused to die this way. I'd see this through. I'd see *him* again.

I made a split-second decision. It was me or my knees.

It took a conscious effort to let go, to render myself limp as a rag doll, but I did, forcibly turning my legs to jelly beneath me. They buckled and I slammed hard onto my knees. I gripped the ledge, stopping myself before I tumbled from the outcropping.

I winced, immediately flopping back onto my butt, half cradling my bruised legs while skittering away from the ledge at the same time. *Made it.* And I refused to think on why, in my moment of near death, my mind had gone to *Carden.*

I dusted off my legs. I was here to investigate, to get my mind *off* the bond. I sat all the way up, and punishing wind instantly whipped the hair into my face, bringing tears to my eyes.

I squinted. Looking around, I saw how it wasn't just a shelf I'd landed on, but there was a little niche, too. Not big enough to be called a cave, but deep enough to shelter me from the wind howling off the sea, lashing the rock face. I pressed my body into it, feeling like a creature in a seashell, and let myself take a moment to gather my wits and pick the bloody bits of grit and rock from my tattered palms.

I was busily panting and catching my breath, so I didn't hear it at first. But as my heart slowed, I began to discern an alarming sound from above: men's voices. Two of them.

I mouthed a curse, instantly pressing as far into my little shelter as I could. Had the killer—or *killers?*—returned to the scene of the crime?

I curled in more tightly. If I was discovered, I'd be dead meat. Literally.

I tucked my legs, grimacing through the pain as I bent them. I quickly reeled my bag in, too, and clutched it close to my side, grateful that I hadn't stowed it at the top or anything stupid like that.

My sweaty undershirt clung to me, and I became instantly chilled leaning against the damp, hard rock. But I hunched closer, turning my back to the voices, praying that, if they happened to walk to the edge and look down, the gray of my Acari uniform would act as camouflage.

I huddled and stared at the rock wall, and that was when I saw it. Simple carvings. Old runes, like graffiti.

The sight made me smile despite myself. Viking carvings could be found all over the islands in the North Sea. It was amazing—the graffiti was thousands of years old and yet it was as unremarkable as the stuff you'd find in the bathroom stall at Applebee's. *Magnus red-legs was here*, that sort of thing.

I used my thumbnail to scrape away the fine layer of moss, peering at the letters.

ᚢᚠᛗᚲᛁᚱᚾ · ᛒᚱᚠᛏᛏᛁᛏᛏ · ᛋᚠᛏᛁᚠ

I imagined it was Icelandic, or Old Norse maybe. I could stare till I went blind and it still wouldn't make any sense. But it cheered me just a little. It was such a peculiar reminder of my humanity.

I wriggled heat into my fingers and toes, forcing my mind back into the moment. The men were still there, closer now.

Angling my head as far as I dared, I tuned my ear, trying to make sense of their conversation in the keening wind. Their words echoed down the bluffs, bouncing into my shallow crevice. *German*, I realized. They were speaking German. I didn't recognize the voices, but I could tell that one speaker was more deferential than the other.

The wind shifted, bringing me a phrase. *Hat er unter Kontrolle?* "Is he in control?"

Ja, Meister. I didn't need to rely on my years of study to recognize "Yes, Master" when I heard it.

The explosive cries of a flock of seabirds bursting into flight shattered the moment. I shifted, waiting for the flapping to subside, considering what I'd heard.

Is he in control? He who? A vampire? Tracer? Trainee? *He* could've referred to any number of people on this island.

There was more gruff murmuring, a pause in the wind, and then: *Sie werden unvorsichtig.*

"They grow reckless."

Again, *who?*

Reckless. The word harkened back to my chat with Carden. There were so many different ways to be reckless. There was reckless brave. Murderous recklessness. Or my favorite kind of reckless, disobedience. Then another wrinkle occurred to me: There was also the recklessness of pure instinct that was the Draug.

I hung on for more, but the voices dissipated and never returned. Even so, I dared not budge. I needed to make certain the men were far from here.

As I waited, I did several dozen careful scans of the cliff side, but found nothing. There were no clues. No murder weapon waiting for discovery, flashing "look at me!" in the twilight.

Bored of that, I stared at the runes for a while, discerning others carved along the moss-covered stone. But they quickly lost their power to comfort me. Soon, I was just cold.

I decided to give it fifteen more minutes, an arbitrary amount of time more to wait, and bided it by staring out at the sea. When thoughts of Carden and my need for him grew too piqued, I distracted myself by pulling a sheet of paper and pencil from my bag to take a rubbing of the runes. A little reminder of my humanity, of how tiny and meaningless we were. That time marched on, but the rest of us had expiration dates.

I thought about who might've left the graffiti so long ago. What would I carve, if given the chance? *Drew + Vampires 4ever*? I smirked at the thought. How fleeting our human dramas became when viewed through the telescope of centuries.

Finally, the sky turned the color of metal, and the air took on a bite too sharp to ignore.

I scrabbled my way back up the hill. Since I was able to leverage my body and control where I put my hands and feet, I found it much easier to go up than down. Carden had been right: Using the strength of my legs was the key. I scanned the rocks as I went, but saw no more evidence beyond that scuff left by Trinity's heel.

On the walk back, the pencil rubbing was an odd weight in my bag. Other people had been here thousands of years ago.

And who knew, maybe others would walk this same bluff a thousand years hence. I tried to feel a sense of connection to my fellow man through the ages, but instead all I could think was how those Vikings were long dead, and someday I would be, too.

CHAPTER FIFTEEN

———— ⚬⚬⚬ ————

M ei-Ling and I picked up Emma as we headed out the door. The week had limped along. I'd risked my neck to find clues, and all I'd found was a bunch of old Viking graffiti. Worse, I remained torn about Carden, feeling desperate to see him again but also hoping desperately that I wouldn't.

Emma sensed something was up with me. "Are you okay?" She'd asked it slowly, her words heavy with meaning. But then she flicked a glance at Mei. We needed to be discreet in front of this girl we didn't really know.

Between me having a new roommate and Emma joined at the hip with Yasuo, I wondered if we'd ever talk openly again. "Yeah, I'm okay, I guess."

"You haven't been the same since your mission. Ever since you saw . . . that girl," she said carefully. But I knew immediately whom she meant. I'd seen someone I could've sworn was my old roommate and nemesis, Lilac.

Lilac, who was supposed to be dead.

"I can't stop thinking about it. That, and—" We stepped outside to see Yasuo waiting for us.

"Yo, lovely ladies," he shouted in greeting.

"Never mind," I mumbled. The sight of him made me inexplicably grumpy. Sometimes a girl just wanted some girl time. "It's no biggie."

But I needed to be mature about this. Emma and Yas were my friends. I was glad someone had found love. I *would* be mature about it. "Yo, yourself," I called back. "Isn't this out of your way?" The guy's dorm was a creepy castle-looking thing on the other side of campus; it would've been much faster for him to have simply walked to class and met us there.

He clapped a hand to his chest. "It must be love." His goofy tone was meant to play down the meaning of his words, but I knew there was truth to them.

Emma's response was to look down and zip her jacket, the tiniest smirk the only thing to indicate that she'd heard.

Calm, cool, and collected—that was Emma. It was why I loved her. She wasn't one of those squeeing, melodramatic kind of girls, who got all weepy and huggy and ohmygod-I-love-you about things. It was what made her and Yasuo so easy to stomach as a couple.

Our friendship was the same way: smooth, steady, and drama free. I didn't need her to squeal and flap and air kiss to know she loved me. Emma would have my back till the bitter end. It was all the show of love I needed.

Except . . .

The image of Carden slammed into my mind. There was another kind of love that I'd be very open to. And I had a willing partner. I didn't know if the vampire offered love in any emotional sense, but I suspected he'd happily offer the physical part—which was not to be underrated. I was desperately curious about sex. The bond had given me a physical craving for him, but ever since watching him on the beach, spying the unexpected layers of sadness and anger at Acari Kate's death, I'd ached for him in a whole other way. I wanted him to kiss me again, sure. But now I had the weirdest urge to simply be held by him.

Only *I* would want a vampire hug. *Freak.*

"Earth to Blondie." Yas reached over Emma to scruff my hair. "What is up with you?"

I flinched away. "What do you mean?"

"I mean, you're wearing your crazy eyes this morning." He raised his brows, going all bug-eyed.

I didn't feel like playing along. I had big, round eyes to begin with—my dad had always called attention to them—and it was something I didn't feel like remembering at the moment.

Yas wasn't one to pick up on subtle cues, though. "Last time I saw you with those eyes, you were about to fight your roommate." He quickly looked to Mei-Ling. "Not you, Tiger Cub. Of course."

"Tiger Cub?" Emma and I asked in unison.

But Mei ignored him, asking me, "What happened to your last roommate?"

My pals and I exchanged a look. "Dead," I said.

"We hope," Emma muttered.

"That chick was crazy," Yas said with gusto. "There was some big competition in the spring," he explained to Mei. "One-on-one girl action. It was nuts. Princess here won the show." He scruffed my hair again.

I shot him a look. "Would you stop that?"

"Never," he assured me. Puffing with pride, he added, "Emma here saved the day in her own way. When she found out she was going to have to face D in the ring, she pulled out. Now, *that's* balls."

I rolled my eyes. "How romantic."

"That's how he sweet-talks me," Emma said quietly. "He accuses me of having testicles."

Yasuo snorted like it was the funniest thing ever. And it was true—her shy prairie manner had a way of turning simple statements into amazingly funny deadpan.

I stole a look at the two of them. They weren't holding hands—that'd be stupid—but I caught them bumping shoulders. He looked like a puppy dog.

What would it be like to walk along, doing the occasional shoulder bump with Carden?

Like that would ever happen. My excruciating hunger came back full force at the thought. I tightened my abs, pretending the pain I felt was simply muscular instead of this deep-down longing.

I shoved my hands in the pockets of my fleece, racking my mind to come up with more conversation. The best I could come up with was, "So much for summer. It's getting cold already."

Was I colder than usual, more susceptible to even the weather without Carden's blood?

Between my thirst for Carden and the memory of Lilac, I was tense, and Emma must've sensed it. She was never the one to break the silence with conversation, but she turned to Mei and asked, "Which class do you have this morning?"

"Combat," she said, her voice quick and tight. The girl was usually so hard to read, but just then it was like she'd used a neon sign to announce her anxiety.

I forgot about my own problems for the moment. "You're worried about your hands, aren't you?"

Her eyes flew to mine. "Yes. How did you know?" She sounded unsettled that I'd guessed.

"Don't freak out." I gave her what I hoped would be seen as a casual nudge. "You mentioned it before, remember? Besides, you keep fisting and unfisting them."

Yas added, "Girl, you look like you're secretly fantasizing about strangling someone."

She looked from her hands to me, and I saw the flicker of vulnerability in her eyes. Mei was showing me just a little bit more of herself than before. "It's just . . . everyone looks so bruised."

"Wait," Emma interrupted.

I was on instant alert. A tide of Acari was headed toward us on the path. It was time for class, and yet they were headed back to the dorms, away from the academic buildings. "What's up with *that*?"

"Class is canceled," said one of the older girls as she walked by. I recognized her as the first-floor Proctor. "Everyone is ordered back to the dorms."

"Why would they cancel class?" asked Mei.

She and I shared a weighty look. That was a very good question.

Then weird got weirder. As the students passed, we spotted a vampire standing off the path in the distance. A cluster of Trainees stood behind him, like a bunch of glowering pups.

My gaze was drawn to one in particular—Rob, staring the hell out of me. I glanced away, unsure how to play it. If I stared him down, he'd see it as a challenge, and I had quite enough of those at the moment.

Yasuo's attention went to the group instantly, as though summoned. "I've gotta roll, guys."

"Should we—"

"Like now," he said, cutting Emma off. He broke into a jog, headed away from the path.

I frowned, watching his long, loping stride. Unlike the girls, Trainees were sometimes allowed off the path. "That's such bullshit."

Emma grabbed my arm, pulling me close. "Watch your language, Drew."

"I know, I know. But"—I lowered my voice—"I don't get why the guys are allowed to do more than we are. Am I the only one who has a problem with that?"

There was a lot on this island we had to put up with. Every girl's seemingly imminent and likely death was at the top of the list.

But the thing was, that made a sick sort of sense. If the vampires were training us to be an elite corps of agents, then obviously our training would be ruthless. Only the strongest, the most clever, survived to ascend to Watcher status.

But going off the island had given me a new perspective. Looking around and picking it all apart, some of these rules struck me as pure whimsy. "It seems pretty arbitrary, if you ask me. And in a totally sexist kinda way."

When Emma and Mei-Ling didn't answer, I looked from one to the other, giving them probing looks. I could see by their furrowed brows that if they hadn't considered it before, they were now.

CHAPTER SIXTEEN

⸙

"Wow," I said. "Grab it."

One end of the corduroy couch was miraculously free, and Emma dove for it, claiming space enough for the three of us.

I plopped down, then smooshed closer to Emma to make space for my roommate. "What do you think is going on?"

Girls were trickling into the common area. Our entire floor was jammed in, Acari leaning against walls, draped on couch arms, sitting in chairs. Some of the girls didn't take a seat; they just stood rigidly, as if they were waiting to be taken to the firing squad. Those were mostly the new Acari.

Mei-Ling wasn't the only new girl, not by a long shot—a whole new crop of Acari had arrived, and new Trainees, too. There were no surprises—it was the usual gaggle of outcasts. I did my best to ignore the lot of them.

Gooseflesh crept up my arms. More than half of these girls would be gone by December.

Emma leaned close. "What's *she* looking at?" We dared not use any names. One thing the blood was good for was amplified hearing.

I tracked Emma's line of sight till it landed on our Proctor, Kenzie, who stood staring out the window. I shrugged. Every Proctor was holding her own meeting on her own floor. As ours waited for people to arrive, she looked pretty checked out. "Who knows? I make it a point not to think too much about Kenzie."

In fact, I purposely steered clear of our Proctor. For all I knew, she might've been the nicest person on the island, which was all the more reason to steer clear. I'd lost one friendly Proctor already. Losing another would be harder even than dealing with yet another cruel Initiate.

My weight was jostled as someone else dropped onto the couch. I felt all expression fall from my face. *Masha.* She wedged herself next to Emma, then caught my eye. "Sad," she said, shaking her head with mock grief.

"I'll bite." I crossed my arms, bracing for it. "What's sad, Guidon Masha?"

"I hoped maybe it was *you* who died."

I looked at Emma. "Don't the Initiates have their own dorm to go to?"

Maybe it was a dumb thing to say, but I was getting more and more fearless with girls like her. Stupid, maybe, but a big part of me thought maybe, just maybe, it wasn't. This island had a lot of posturing, and I'd come to the conclusion it was a good idea to set yourself up as someone to be reckoned with.

Emma wasn't dumb, though, and she gave me a warning look.

"I take any excuse to keep my eye on you," Masha told me in her Russian-accented snarl. "One day very soon you will go down. It would be a shame to miss it."

I gave her a grim smile. "I'm not out of the game yet."

She took her whip from its little holster and began to slide it through her hands over and over. She peered around us to look at Mei-Ling. "Acari Mei," she said slowly. "How do you like your new friend?"

"I just arrived. I have no friends."

A naive person might think Mei-Ling was selling me out. I was not a naive person. That was the smartest thing my roomie could've said.

Masha gave her a sly smile. "Pretty answer, Acari. But you will need someone to watch your back if you are to live through the month."

I pressed my thigh against my roommate's in a silent show of solidarity, and though Mei didn't so much as shrug, she nudged her leg firmly against mine.

In that moment, I decided my roommate's stoicism was the awesomest thing in the world. Her face was utterly emotionless, and the nonresponse was aggravating Masha. The Guidon loved nothing more than terrifying her peers—what would she do if she were no longer scary?

Masha cut her eyes at me, then back to Mei. "Who is your combat instructor now that Angel was killed?" She was digging for something, I was sure of it. She thought I had something to do with the murders.

"Watcher Clara," Mei said evenly.

Masha snorted a laugh. "Good luck to you. Clara trained Trinity, and she's eager to see her killer found. She will be *very* interested to hear that you spend so much time with this." She stabbed a thumb my way.

"Watcher Clara's trained a lot of girls," Emma pointed out.

"I've heard much about my roommate's feats," Mei said. "Are you suggesting she's under suspicion for this as well?"

Masha gave a little shrug, a little innocent tilt to her head. "She had the motive and maybe the friend to help her."

Was she implying Carden? Did she suspect something was going on between me and the Scottish vampire? Either way, it sounded to me like Master Alcántara's words coming out of her mouth.

I narrowed my eyes at her. "Dangerous words, Guidon Masha."

Emma bristled, and her arms flexed, practically vibrating with tension beside me. "Are you saying *Drew* had something to do with the murders? You're nuts. It's impossible."

"I thought Guidons were stronger than the younger girls," Mei-Ling said, her tone innocent and matter-of-fact. "Are they so easy to overpower after all?"

Masha's face hardened. Even with Emma sitting between us, I could feel waves of anger wafting off her.

"Quiet," Kenzie said, and her timing was impeccable. I suspected I was one comment away from a thrashing.

"This isn't over," Masha growled under her breath.

"So you've said."

Kenzie banged on the window. "I said, listen up. I'll make this brief. Another body was found. A *human*. He was drained."

The room exploded with questions. This was *huge*. There was a small human community on the island, and though they sometimes worked for the vampires, driving cars, operating boats, or farming I don't know how many bushels of those godforsaken turnips the vamps were always feeding us, there was an unspoken pact. They didn't bug us and we didn't bug them.

We certainly didn't *exsanguinate* them.

She raised a hand to silence us. "The Directorate is investigating. They are actively searching for the killer. The punishment will be death."

Mei looked at me. "Vampires can die?" In her surprise, she hadn't lowered her voice.

Kenzie heard and answered for me. "In a staking, they can."

I sank low on the couch. Wow. The vampires must be pretty pissed if that was the message they were communicating to the masses.

"Who do they think did it?" someone asked.

I shivered. I knew who they *thought* did it. Alcántara had seemed suspicious of Carden from the moment I'd sprung him from that prison cell, making me wonder more than once how much the Spanish vampire had really intended to rescue him in the first place.

Carden was Vampire; I'd seen it firsthand. But I'd also seen something else in him—those flickers of concern for me, shreds of his old humanity that told me that, although he might be physically capable of the killings, Carden wouldn't murder for sport.

"They don't know," Kenzie replied, sounding exasperated. "That's the point. They're escalating security island-wide. Until then, classes today and tomorrow are canceled. You're in lockdown until further notice."

The questions exploded again—"What *lockdown*? Can we eat? We can't leave at all? What if I want to go to the gym?"—but Kenzie ignored all of them. "No more questions," she said brusquely. Then she wove her way through us and left the room.

CHAPTER SEVENTEEN

E mma and I plopped on my bed, and Mei-Ling on hers. I flopped backward, staring up at the ceiling. So much for my ill-fated investigation. How could I hunt for evidence if I wasn't even allowed to leave my dorm? "I am so sick of these four walls."

When we'd heard the news that we were basically being quarantined, my first thoughts had been, *When will I see Carden?* It was as if I'd already decided I'd feed from him again. It was pathetic.

Mei-Ling misunderstood the reasons for my misery and gave me a sympathetic look. "We could sit in the lounge."

"Nonstarter," I said. The common area was plagued with girls angling for a fight. "The lounge is crawling with people. This is our only option."

Emma turned onto her side to face me. "Sorry we can't hang in my room."

"Does your roommate ever leave?" I asked. "I'm so sure she was transcribing our last conversation. It creeped me out."

"She did seem suspicious," Mei said.

"Oh, totally," I agreed. "I think she probably assembles her notes into little reports for the vampires." The girl was so into life on *Eyja næturinnar*, she'd changed her name from Audra to Frost, and spent all her free time studying Icelandic and brushing up on her Norse legends. I thought the new name made her sound like one of the X-Men.

"She's just an eccentric, is all." Ever-forgiving was our Emma.

"Eccentric?" I rolled my eyes. You'd have thought Frost's study habits would make her prime friend material for me, but the slavering look she got in her eyes whenever she came near a vampire was enough to turn my stomach. "She's Master Dagursson's pet. 'Nuff said."

I put my arm over my head, covering my eyes. Most normal teens got to spend their free time talking on the phone, texting, or downloading stuff to their iPods. Not us. For all we knew, a whole new iPod had been invented since we'd arrived. "Nope. We're stuck here, and I'm dying of boredom."

"We could play Gin Rummy," Emma said.

With a moan, I rolled onto my stomach. I wriggled, trying to get comfortable around the permanent ache in my gut. "Not again. I'm sick of cards." But then I laughed, hearing how ridiculous my tone of voice was. "Sorry, guys. I'm sounding like a brat. I'm just cranky." Cranky and in pain.

Emma smiled. "You're not the only one."

She had no idea. She thought she did, but if she was cranky, then I was *raging*. It was only day two of lockdown, and my Carden detox was in full swing, worse now that we weren't even having chance encounters. I felt like I was dying without him.

The vampires gave us supplements—lockdown didn't mean

starvation—but the refrigerated blood they served wasn't the same. It was a weak substitute, like craving coffee and getting something old and watered down instead.

With a sharp inhale, I sat up. My friend was trying, and so would I. I would have a good attitude.

Emma sat up, too, and patted my back. "It's totally understandable. We're cooped up in here while there's some crazy murderer out there."

That wasn't my problem, but I nodded just the same. She had no idea what I was going through, but this was one misunderstanding I was happy to embrace. Anything to get my mind off Carden.

Mei stood and pulled down the window shades, looking creeped out, as if the killer might be standing just outside. "It is disturbing."

I caught her eye and gave her a nod. "Disturbing is exactly the word for it." The vampires employed a few humans to do menial tasks and there was Ronan who actually had family on the island, but otherwise everyone kept to themselves. "A regular human person, drained of blood? It's an aberration."

"Drained and then just left there." Emma shuddered.

Her words were a revelation. The fact that the bodies were left behind was in some ways the most shocking thing of all. "This breaks every rule they've got," I said, feeling good to be engaged in something other than my own problems. "Any normal vampire would make the dead body disappear. For the killer to leave the bodies in the open to rot . . . it's like he's bragging."

"Or *she's*," Mei amended.

"It's gotta be a guy." I ticked the reasons off on my fingers. "A vampire did this. Vampires are guys. Ergo the killer is a guy."

"The vampire could've had help from a woman," Mei said, defending her point.

"True enough." I thought of Masha and her preoccupation with Alcántara. It wasn't hard to imagine her or many of the other girls doing anything to earn vampire brownie points. But did she want vampire attention badly enough that she'd help kill her friend to get it?

Emma shrugged. "It could be a Draug." She knew Draugs as well as I did, having fought one with me.

"We can't rule it out," I said, though I had a hard time believing it was anything but a thinking, scheming vampire.

"From what you learned on your mission," Emma began carefully, "it seems like . . ." She looked from me to Mei and back again. "There might be other stuff, on other islands, that we still don't understand." She gave me a pointed do-you-understand-my-hint look.

She was hedging around one of my least favorite topics: Lilac. Subtle, Em.

Mei shifted to the edge of her seat. "Would you like me to leave?"

"No," Emma and I said at the same time.

"No," I repeated, rubbing my temples. Thoughts of Lilac did nothing to help my killer headache. "You can hear this." I needed to trust my new roommate. What would my life be if I never trusted anyone ever again? Besides, I had a good feeling about Mei-Ling, and one of us had to take the leap. Who knew? Maybe if I confided in her, she'd open up a little more to me. "Look, this isn't for public consumption, but . . ."

I proceeded to give her the full download. Lilac, the crazy pyromaniac roommate. How I'd supposedly killed her in the

Directorate Challenge. The weird tension between me and Al-cántara on our mission together. The mysterious sighting of someone who looked exactly like her.

"Wait." Mei stopped me, confused. And of course she was—I was confused, and this was my story. "Didn't you see Lilac's body? How could she be alive?"

I remembered back to that day. By the time our fight was over, I was covered in bruises, slashes, and third-degree burns. Not a lot else registered. "I thought she was dead."

Emma spoke for me. "They took away the injured girls. They always do. We don't know what happens to them."

"Maybe it wasn't her you saw," Mei said.

"I thought I was hallucinating, but then I mentioned it to Alcántara and he wigged out."

She looked alarmed. "Wigged how?"

"Nothing crazy. You know, he got all . . . focused. Distant."

"Strange," she said, frowning.

All I could do was nod at that, the understatement of the year. How or why Lilac could be alive and living with a bunch of crazy Germanic vampire monks was a mystery. And rather than put it behind me, it loomed out there like something that might come and bite me in the butt while I slept.

We were all quiet then, considering what it could mean, when Kenzie startled us out of it. She was walking down the hall, banging on doors as she went. "Lights out."

Mei-Ling glared at the door. "She's like the warden in a prison movie."

I felt Emma's hand on my shoulder. She whispered, "You going to be okay?"

I considered her question. I had a new roommate, and not

only was she *not* a psycho, she might end up being a friend. I gave
Emma a true smile. "Yeah, I think I just might."

After Emma left, Mei flicked off the lights as I got into bed. I
chuckled in the darkness. "Talk about overwhelming you with
information on your first week, huh?"

But her response was somber. "We could investigate."

I edged up onto my elbows. "My thought exactly." I weighed
my words. How much could I trust her? I decided it was all or
nothing. "I've already tried a little. Investigating, I mean."

"What'd you find out?" Eager excitement tinged her voice.
I'd been right—despite our age difference, Mei was total good
friend material.

"Nothing really. Trinity fought her attacker and ended up on
the rocks near the cove. We already knew all that."

"Well," she began, "next we could . . ."

"Next we could . . . what?" I'd hit a dead end. "Anyway,
we're locked in."

"We could investigate without leaving the dorm. I'm sure we
could find out more about the latest killing if we asked around.
Gossiping is all anyone has been doing since lockdown." She was
showing me a whole new side. Apparently her stoic act masked
total unflinching guts. "It's possible."

I gave her idea real consideration. I was beginning to dig my
new roomie, and it could only mean trouble. As it was, I had a
sinking feeling the day was coming when the powers-that-be
would drop Emma and me into some vampire coliseum and force
us to go gladiator on each other. No, I had to protect her. "Possible, but too dangerous."

"If there were three of us, it'd be safer."

"Emma, you mean? Even if we convinced her, she and Yas

are inseparable, and I don't know if she'd do it without him." I loved Yasuo, but until I understood what was really going on with those Trainees, I wasn't ready to have one hundred percent trust in him.

"Then it'll be just you and me."

I laughed outright at that. "You and me?" I gave it a moment's thought. But then I dismissed the notion—I needed someone who'd watch my back, which I doubted Mei had the skills to do. "I don't even know what your weapon is."

"I don't have a weapon."

"What do you mean?" I sat up in bed—there'd be no sleeping anytime soon—and the rapid movement amplified the pounding in my head. "We all have weapons. Everyone's assigned one on the first day."

"I wasn't."

"Didn't they have something waiting for you in your drawer?"

"All I had was this." She stood and rifled through her dresser, pulling something out.

I hopped out of bed and pulled aside a corner of the shades to let in the watery moonlight. She held something long and thin, and I snatched it from her to make sure there wasn't a blade concealed in there somewhere. I hefted it in my hands and peered down the length of it. "They gave you a *flute*?"

"It's not a flute."

"Masha is gunning for us. There's a killer on the loose. You're jonesing to go play Nancy Drew. And all you've got to protect yourself is a *flute*." I crawled back into bed, suddenly overwhelmed. No wonder the vampires needed me to look out for her—they'd given the girl a *flute* as her only protection.

"It's a D'Tzu," she said, sounding amused.

"Okay, fine. It's a . . . that. But trust me, call it what you like, but it won't kill any Draugs. It's not even metal."

"It's bamboo." She held it to her mouth. "Shall I play it for you? It'll relax you." The way she'd said it—all calm and sure—sounded so culty.

"You're scaring me, Mei."

"The infamous Acari Drew is afraid?"

Laughing, I punched my pillow into shape and flopped my head down. "You don't scare me, Ho. Go for it. Play your little flute."

I heard her suck in a breath, then immediately winced at the sharp, high-pitched sound her instrument made. It reminded me of a cheesy kung fu movie soundtrack—like something that might play as an old wise man emerged from the mist.

I lay in the dark, patiently waiting for her to finish, wondering which would happen first, glass breaking or Kenzie knocking on the door, telling us to shut up.

But then something changed.

The music triggered something in my brain. There was a shift. A wave of calm. My headache subsided. I began to register a song where before there'd been only shrill, atonal notes.

The music became hypnotic. It surrounded me, filled me, enveloped me. As that high pitch hummed through my skull, memories swamped me. Mental snapshots of my mother, simple and random.

She unloaded groceries from the car, hitching a bag on her hip.

She put on lipstick and caught my eyes in the mirror.

She snapped her clutch shut with a laugh.

She widened her eyes, chugging soda as her Coke bottle fizzed over.

She hugged me, enveloping me in her lemony scent.

The images faded, but the scent lingered as I became aware of my bed again. Mei-Ling had finished playing. My pillow was damp. I touched my face—I was crying.

Mei had managed to reach deep into those parts of myself that I'd buried and forgotten. It was the most cathartic experience of my life. And it was the most terrifying.

That was Mei's secret. And her weapon.

And her talents would only be enhanced over time as she consumed more of the blood. I lay there, unable to speak. The possibilities were endless. Could she hypnotize people? Trigger reactions in entire crowds? Would she be powerful enough to influence even the vampires?

If vampires could harness her gift—gaining the ability to hypnotize with music, influence emotion, manipulate memory and thought, to *control* those around them—it would be a powerful weapon indeed.

"Would you like to sleep now?"

I felt a jolt of alarm. "Can that thing put me to sleep?" I had no doubts it'd work in the euthanizing sense of the word.

She sat at the edge of the bed, seeming calmed. When I saw her smile in the moonlight, I realized she hadn't given me many true smiles. I liked the sight. "Relax, Acari Drew. You'll wake up again. I promise."

"Mei, it's just Drew. You *gotta* call me Drew."

She began to play again, quietly this time. For the first time since the bond, the gnawing in my gut subsided. In the moment before I drifted off, I hoped I'd get to feel my mother's embrace one more time. But the black void of sleep was all that waited for me. Cold sleep and dreams of vampires.

CHAPTER EIGHTEEN

———⊶⊷———

I was climbing.

All I knew was the rock in front of my eyes and my own breath reverberating in my head. My fingers found handholds without effort. My legs pushed me up—just as Carden had said they would.

Suddenly my perspective telescoped outward. A moment of vertigo as my head adjusted. I was climbing the Needle.

I saw the rock and heard my breath, and now I was aware of the sunlight, too, warm on my shoulders. It almost soothed the permanent throbbing along my neck and in my skull—*almost*.

The sun was warm, but the wind was cold, whipping against my legs. I realized they were bare. I wore my favorite old pair of cargo shorts.

A dream, then.

Smiling, I climbed faster. I couldn't fall—this was a dream.

Carden was waiting for me, seated on the plateau near the top. I wondered for an instant why he was there if we were supposed to remain apart, but then I laughed, understanding. "Anything can happen. I'm just dreaming."

He smiled down at me, reached out his hand, and pulled me up and over to join him. "Anything can happen."

I sat and dangled my legs. They were so small in comparison to his muscular thighs, thick like tree trunks swathed in plaid wool.

"Wait, is that . . . is that a *kilt*?" The wind was cold on my smiling cheeks. "You didn't wear that when you climbed. The wind . . . I would've noticed."

He leaned down, speaking close to my ear. "You're saying you would've peeked up my plaid?"

The way he'd nudged his shoulder to mine set my heart pounding. I nodded to the preposterous scale of our legs, side by side. "I look so tiny, compared to you."

"You're just right, compared to me." His broad hand covered my thigh, squeezed, warm on my chilled skin.

My body crackled to life. Thirst clawed me, and I rubbed my belly. Desire robbed my words. I opened my mouth to speak, but nothing came. I wasn't good at this—not even in dreams.

"Do you know what your problem is, little flower?"

My problem? I pulled back to meet his eyes. "This is supposed to be *my* dream."

"Your problem is that you underestimate yourself."

"Oh, that." I sighed. "Some people think I *over*estimate myself."

"Those people are fools."

"You don't mean it. This is just a dream."

He leaned closer until his face filled my vision. His eyes—they'd reminded me of honey, and in the daylight they looked golden. "Then we shouldn't waste it talking." He fully cupped my chin and tilted up my face. He brought his mouth a whisper away from mine. "I've wanted to taste you again. If this were my dream, I'd not waste it talking."

I sank into the warmth of those eyes.

Carden was so close now, close enough to shelter me from the wind. Close enough to kiss. I *could* kiss him. I could fall into him, and what would it matter? After all, it was just a dream.

I *wanted* to kiss him. I'd wanted it ever since the moment our first kiss ended. This was just a dream, after all. It wouldn't count.

"Just a dream," I whispered. I closed the distance between us.

There was pounding. I gasped.

My heart?

Again, pounding. Was it the headache?

Carden faded. The rock disappeared.

Knocking. The sound was *knocking*.

Mei-Ling mumbled a complaint from the next bed. She was asleep, and we were in our dorm room. I was lying in bed, face crushed into my pillow.

I actually had been dreaming. Disappointment swamped me. Disappointment and need. If I ignored the knocking, could I fall asleep right back into the same moment? I needed to kiss him again, even if it was just in my dreams.

The person knocked again. That roused me. I quickly hopped from my bed. Whoever it was would wake the whole dorm and it'd be seen as my fault.

I swung open the door. "What the—"

A dark figure loomed in the doorway. The ambient moon-light made his eyes glow. *Carden.*

Stepping inside, he closed the door and pressed his body against mine. His voice was a hoarse rasp in the darkness. "You called me."

CHAPTER NINETEEN

"What are you doing?" I shot a look at Mei, still sound asleep. I couldn't risk her seeing us. "You're going to get us in trouble."

He laughed quietly. It was a low, seductive sound. "Vampires don't get in trouble."

Instantly, I became aware that all I wore was my nightgown. Granted, it was flannel and came below my knees, but still, I was braless, cold, and after that dream, feeling very, very vulnerable. "You were banging hard enough to wake the dead."

His eyes swept me from my head to my bare feet. "And you're lovely enough to rouse them."

I hastily grabbed my fleece and zipped it up to my neck. "Well . . . it was too loud."

"I barely knocked at all." He raised a finger, pointing into the darkness. "Listen."

I paused. Sure enough, the dorm was utterly silent. It was the middle of the night. "I don't get it. It was so noisy in the dream."

He took a step closer. "You dreamed of me?"

I stepped back, babbling nervously. "Why are you here anyway? Because you're not supposed to be here." I shooed my fingers at him. "Turn around." I snatched my leggings from the edge of my bed and quickly stepped into them. I felt too exposed, though I feared clothing wouldn't do much to rid myself of the feeling. "We're not supposed to see each other. I thought we were . . . you know . . . severing."

"Are we truly?" He snuck a look, peering at me in the darkness. There was a question in his eyes. "Because you just summoned me."

"I can summon you?"

"It's more that I felt your need for me. Felt your desire to preserve our bond."

Preserve the bond?

"I don't," I stammered. "Didn't."

His lips peeled into a naughty smile. "Tell me about this dream."

It was fresh in my mind, how badly I'd wanted to kiss him. My body *still* wanted him, my blood pulsing hot just beneath the surface of my skin.

"Ah. Even now, I sense your desire." Inhaling deeply, he took my arm and gently tucked it in his. "What did we do in your dream?"

His proximity wasn't helping the whole break-the-bond thing. I tugged my arm. "You should go before you wake Mei."

Because I did want to break the bond. *Right?*

He must've sensed my hesitation, because even though he let go of my arm, he gave me a wink. "You're right, of course. We shouldn't wake her. I'll take you elsewhere, little turnip."

"Turnip?" I squeaked. "I thought *little flower* was bad."

He beamed. "In this dream, I called you little flower?"

I glared. "Maybe."

"Would you *like* me to call you little flower?"

"Of course not."

"Come with me, little flower."

I edged back. "I thought you wanted to stay apart."

"*You* wanted it." He stepped closer, only this time I didn't step away—I was too mesmerized. He was focused only on me, his eyes hooded and so intense in the shadows. "I can stay away from you no longer," he said in a husky whisper. "My need for you is too great. *Your* need is too great." He traced a single finger down my cheek. "I feel it calling to me across this island, all day and through the night. I'll no longer bear it. I must take care of you."

Care. It sounded so good. Was that my secret desire? I was so tired and so alone. . . . But those weren't good enough reasons to be with someone.

When I took too long to say anything, his expression turned grim. "You're uncertain."

"I just don't know if this is . . . right." The moment I said it, I felt how cold the room was.

"Please tell me, Annelise. And consider your answer well." He stood straight, and it put distance between us. "Do you wish to break from me? You have but to say the word and I will leave this island and we will be severed."

"You mean like a temporary thing, to break our bond?"

"More than temporary," he said grimly.

"Would you come back?"

"I am done with Hugo and his kind."

"But where would you go?"

"There are places for such like me."

I couldn't wrap my mind around it. "So you're saying I wouldn't see you again? Ever?"

He gave a solemn shake to his head. "You will not be bothered by me again."

It felt like the floor dropped from under me. But I made myself stand tall. I made myself consider it. I had to let my mind go there. I'd said I wanted to break the bond. This had been my idea.

Practical considerations occurred to me. "How would you, you know, feed?" If Carden was nothing to me, then why did my head fill with a flurry of random worries? His safety, his feeding.

He gave me a flat look, and I put up my hand, aghast. "Oh no, never mind. I take it back. Don't answer that." The thought was too unbearable. Him with another girl. And Carden was charming and handsome—if we parted, there *would* be other girls.

If severing from him was really what I wanted, then why did the prospect make my heart hurt worse than any ache I'd known these past days?

I pictured being alone again. Carden cared for me—it was the first time since my mother that someone cared enough to put me before anyone else. Could I let that go? Let him go?

Something in his eyes shuttered, closing from me. "I apologize for the trouble this has caused you. In the past, I have blamed you for our situation, but you had no way of knowing. You came to me an innocent, and the blame lies solely on me." His attitude became businesslike. "You will find the severing difficult. There will be days hence of pain, but you are strong and will bear it as you have borne so much else. Be on your guard against all who would harm you. You will survive our parting—"

"No," I cut him off. The thought of losing him, just the

thought of him leaving this room, made my gut clench. I knew what I wanted now—the truth of it rang through me. I tried to remember why I hadn't wanted to be bonded to him.

I feared the vampires, but how could I fear the one who'd given me honesty? How could I not trust the one who'd made me smile? Who wanted to protect me. Whose honor made creatures like Alcántara scoff. Now that I knew Carden better, all my old hesitations seemed mistaken. The wrong answer to the right question.

"No, Carden." I leapt into his arms as I'd been longing to do, and his low laugh reverberated through me. "No. I don't want to sever the bond."

I squeezed him harder. I didn't want to break from him. Carden had become comfort when I needed it. Ease where I had none. The long-dreamed-of man who smiled just for me.

He shifted, tucking my arm in his, and his broad smile told me I had indeed considered well. "Then come with me. Just for a short time."

Was such a thing truly possible? Could I have someone who cared for me? Someone to sneak off with and share secrets and kisses? It had the whiff of hope, and I didn't believe in hope. Hope died with my mother—the last person who'd cared about me.

I pushed away from him, my shoulders slumped. "I shouldn't. I can't. We're in lockdown."

"I told you. I can't get in trouble."

"But *I* can."

"I'll allow no harm to come to you. Ever." He reached for my hand. "Come. I need you close. I want you close. I mustn't be discovered here, which means it's time to go. I'll have you by my side now, as much as I can. I *will* protect you."

My pulse was throbbing a drumbeat. . . . *Carden. Carden. Carden.* I could go with him. We could be alone together. He said he'd protect me—nobody had ever wanted to protect me. "I want to"—oh God, he was so close—"but I'm afraid." And getting caught wasn't what scared me.

"Come," he whispered again, sliding his hand in mine. He gave me a wicked smile. "Or I *will* wake the dorm."

Suddenly, schoolgirl nerves overtook me. What would he do? What would happen? "Why should I go?" Even as I asked it, my body clamored the answer. The pulse was deep in my belly, in my skull, my chest—my whole body pounding my decision.

He twined my fingers with his. "Because you want to." His voice was deep and hushed, resonating into my core.

He was right. I looked at him, really looked at him. My want for Carden had grown deeper even than this need, more powerful than thirst.

"Please," he whispered.

I trusted him. I liked him. I wanted to be close to him.

What else mattered anymore?

But there *was* something else. "Why me?" I asked in a voice no louder than my breath. I wanted to sneak away with him— now that I'd made my decision, I wanted it so badly. But I couldn't see why he'd want someone like me. "Is it just the bond that makes you want this?"

"Dear one," he scolded. "I need you. You, Annelise Drew. I want to be with *you*." He slowly brought my hand to his mouth, eyes locked with mine, and placed a gentle kiss at my wrist. "It appears I've grown fond of you." He gave me a gentle nip. "And more than fond, aye?"

It felt like the sun rising on my face, I smiled so wide. I gave his fingers a squeeze. "Yes. Let's go. Let's get out of here."

We walked downstairs and outside, hand in hand. "I need to ask you a question," I began shyly. My dreams of him had been so vivid, I couldn't get them from my mind. "Did you have anything to do with my dreams?"

"How many dreams were there?"

I nudged him with my shoulder. "Just answer the question."

He laughed. "Are you saying you think I somehow came to you in your sleep?"

"Didn't you?"

"Trust me, love. When I come to you in the night, it won't be a thing you'll sleep through."

A shiver of anticipation rolled across my skin.

He patted my hand as he pulled me to a faster walk. "Make haste now. We must move before we're discovered." He gestured away from campus.

I hesitated, joking nervously, "Leaving the path?"

He gave me a reassuring smile. "I promise, you'll like where I take you."

CHAPTER TWENTY

H e led me to a place I'd spotted before, a break in the
foliage that I'd always assumed fell into a sheer drop on
the other side—but there was a trail. It was steep and slow going,
with only the light of the moon to guide us. As we descended,
the crashing waves grew louder.

A thrill shivered up the backs of my legs, and I worried that
Carden was right. Maybe I did like going off the path. Maybe I
was a natural-born rule breaker. It didn't bode well for my time
on the island.

As we neared the bottom, I had to use my hands to keep my
balance on the sharp incline. Water shimmered along the horizon, moonlight picking silver along the waves.

Carden jumped the rest of the way. From the sound of his
landing, there was a small sliver of rocky beach below. Turning,
he wrapped his hands about my waist and lifted me up, his grip
sliding ever so slightly up my torso. "Come, dear one."

The sensation of being held by Carden, of him floating me

up in the air and setting me gently down before him, was rapturous.

I felt on the precipice of some new relationship, and it made me feel vulnerable. I was more aware than ever how Alcántara was gunning for him.

When he put me down, I didn't give myself a moment to second-guess it, I just asked, "Why does Alcántara hate you?"

He took my hand, and waves of pleasure rippled over me, enveloping my body in warmth. "If I answer your questions, will you do a favor for me?"

I gave him a wary look. I've had experience with vampires and favors before. "It depends."

"So coy you are." He chuckled. "I see I have still to prove myself. All right, little dove. I'll answer you in good faith." He leaned close to whisper in my ear, "But I'll expect something in kind."

My skin tightened over my body in anticipation. "Alcántara?" I reminded him.

He began to lead us down the beach. "I've known women before, and I can say, you are one of the most tenacious."

Jealousy mowed through me. I stopped short, feeling gutted. "You've known many women?"

His smile gleamed in the moonlight. "Are you jealous?"

"No," I lied.

"Ah. Because I'd hoped perhaps you might be jealous."

I did a little jog to catch up to him. "You're trying to avoid my question."

"I don't recall hearing one."

"Do you have special knowledge Alcántara wants?"

He laughed. "No, nothing so clever."

"Then did you double-cross him way back when?" When he shook his head, I continued to rack my brain for why the Spanish vampire might be so interested in him. "I'm trying to figure out why he has it out for you. He wants to pin these murders on you, you know. Do you have some sort of . . . special powers or something?"

"We, all of us, have our talents," he replied mysteriously.

"*All* of us?" I slowed my pace, considering. "Even Acari?"

"Even Acari." He tugged my hand, pulling me forward again. "The blood merely intensifies these talents."

"How do I know what my talent is?"

He reached over and patted my bottom. "You strike me as a most talented woman."

I grunted and hopped away. I wouldn't let him distract me. "Your accent gets thicker when you're being . . . improper."

"Improper, is it?"

"Inappropriate."

"Indelicate?" He waggled his brows just before he rounded a corner, disappearing into shadows. It was a cave—I hadn't noticed the opening until he ducked inside. "Then you may not want to follow me in here," he called out to me.

The opening was narrow and sheltered from sight, but once I followed him in, I saw how the cavern opened up, tunneling deep into the rock. It took a moment for my eyes to adjust, and I peered into the blackness, unable to tell just how far back it went. "Cool."

"It's a sea cave. There are several throughout the island. Viking marauders once hid here."

"And now it's favored by vampire marauders?"

He laughed, and it was a deeply satisfying sound. "Are you accusing me of plunder and pillage?"

I caught my breath. I'll just bet he knew a little something about pillaging. I wondered if he'd try anything tonight, in the seclusion of our hideaway. "Time will tell, Carden McCloud."

I sat next to him, looking out of the cave mouth onto the beach. I resisted the urge to lean in to him and rest my head on his shoulder. Head resting would lead to other things, things that made me nervous, just a little.

Besides, before our precious time got away from us, I needed to understand the Alcántara rivalry. "So," I said, picking up where we'd left off, "what's *your* talent?"

He stroked a slow finger up my leg. "I have great talents at my disposal."

My body felt like it was on fire. I shifted away, feeling shy that he might kiss me, yet scared that he might not. "You said you'd answer my question."

His hand rested heavy on my thigh. "Such focus, love. If you must." He sighed, a world-weary sound. "To understand Hugo's recent . . . attentions, you must understand my history. The Clan McCloud descends from an ancient Celtic line. My ancestors were priests of a sort, of the old religion."

"Wait." I watched his profile in the shadows, trying to follow. "You mean like the Druids?"

"I mean like the Druids. These men had an ability for what they called the second sight."

I tried to picture him in a long brown robe, sleeping in the woods, chanting, and living on berries. I shook my head. . . . I couldn't wrap my mind around it. "You were a *Druid*?"

He laughed. "Not hardly. I was a soldier."

Now, that I could picture. He'd have had a sword or musket slung over a gritty, sweat-stained shirt. His eyes would be hard, his walk sure and powerful. I wished I could've seen it.

I felt a pang of loss, of all that I'd never know about Carden—his long-ago past, his unending future. I had to glance away, squinting hard at the moonlight dancing on the waves.

"My ancestors merely passed their gifts down our family line," he continued, oblivious to my reverie.

I cleared my throat, focusing. "So before you were a vampire, you had this second sight? Like premonitions?"

He shrugged. "Perhaps I was a more intuitive man than most. It was only when I turned Vampire that my gift became amplified." His hand grew still on my thigh, his thoughts lost to another time.

I asked quietly, "Is that why you knew to come to me when I dreamed of you?"

He became present again, life snapping back into those eyes. "With our bond, my mind is open to yours. I felt . . . needed by you, yes."

"So we really are sort of connected?"

He began to stroke again. "Mm. And hopefully other parts are engaged, too, aye?"

I swallowed hard. Stay on topic. "Do the other vampires know you can do this?"

He pulled his hand away. "There is no *doing* of anything. I merely have insights others lack, and that only sometimes." With a tired exhale, he reclined, resting his head in his hands. "But aye, the vampires have their suspicions. I believe it's why the Spaniard keeps me around."

"So, Master Alcántara doesn't like you, but he's too worried he might need you, so has kept you around just in case."

"He's not your master," Carden snapped, pinning his eyes on me.

"Hey, I don't trust him, either."

He softened his words, pulling a hand from behind his head to stroke my lower back. "These things I tell you . . . it's important you not discuss it with others."

I trusted Carden, and hearing his words made it clear how much he trusted me, too. "He suspects you of the murders, you know."

His laugh was jaded. "Suspects me, or merely wishes to conveniently pin them on me?" His hand stroked up to my shoulder, and he eased onto his elbow to pull me down beside him. "Fret not, petal. He cannot touch me."

I rolled onto my side to face him, the move natural, me drawn to him. My whole body throbbed, aware of him lying so close. I'd never been with a guy before. It was all so new, so overwhelming. How was I supposed to act? I rested my hand on his hard chest and longed to stroke up and down, to explore every inch of him, but was feeling oddly shy.

This close to him, my thirst nearly overpowered me. But something else overcame me, too—it was the urge to make him smile. I told him, "I can hang with dove, but you *cannot* call me petal."

He laughed, and the faint moonlight picked out the white of his eyes and teeth. "But it got your mind off Hugo; did it not?"

I tried my best glare, even though it was probably wasted in the shadows. "It did not."

"I'm flattered by your concern, but truly, Alcántara and I were sparring for centuries before you were born."

Sparring. The notion gave me a chill. I'd seen how Alcántara dealt with his enemies. I couldn't bear to see Carden hurt. I *wouldn't* see him hurt. "You're obviously not the killer," I said, growing serious. "We need to find out who is. I'm investigating."

"The killings?" Carden cupped my cheek, his tone suddenly intense. "You'll do no such thing."

"I have to prove your innocence."

"I'm flattered, Annelise." He swept his thumb along my lower lip. "You do me an honor even to think it. But I cannot allow you to put yourself at risk."

"Look," I continued quickly before his touch could distract me, "I'll be careful." I could make headway, especially now that I had Mei-Ling helping me. And I knew exactly where I'd look next— at the cliff where Acari Kate had fallen. She'd seen something before she died; I couldn't get that scream out of my head. "I'll go in daylight. I'll bring friends. There's strength in numbers."

"You'll get hurt."

"Alcántara told me that the punishment is death. If he pins this on you, and *you* get killed, how hurt do you think I'll be then?"

"Dearest one," he said, his voice gone hoarse. He twined his hand through the hair at the base of my neck, sending a delicious shiver up my body. "Pray it doesn't come to that."

I furrowed my brows, trying to keep focused. "It won't. Not if I find the killer."

"I'll find the killer," he said definitively. He was stroking my neck now, and his touch seared me like a brand. "You need only do two things."

I resisted the urge to rub against his hand like a cat begging to be pet. "What things?"

"You must swear you'll keep yourself safe."

"I swear I'll be careful," I told him, and it felt like I was mentally crossing my fingers behind my back. Because swearing to be careful and swearing to not investigate were two different things.

He studied me, looking for the truth, and I met his gaze unabashedly. After all, I hadn't lied, not really.

Satisfied, he began to massage the base of my neck. His fingers were deft, and the pressure finally, blissfully, began to ease the pounding in my skull that'd plagued me for days.

I sighed with pleasure. "And what else do I need to do?"

"You must kiss me."

CHAPTER TWENTY-ONE

I didn't take more urging than that. My eyes fluttered shut. I wet my lips. I waited, desperate to feel his mouth touch mine.

I'd waited so long, agonizing over just this, wondering about the bond, what it meant. All those questions seemed so useless now, faced with the total rightness of this moment.

There was more to our connection than just some chemical reaction. I trusted Carden. I wanted him. I wanted to spend time with him. And I wanted the bond, too. I wanted this feeling I got when he was near . . . this feeling that I wasn't in it alone.

This feeling that somebody cared and was brave enough to do something about it.

Carden was Vampire, which meant he was unfathomably powerful. He could be cold and callous. He seemed weary of vampire politics and gamesmanship, bored of the banal and brutish slog of humankind.

But he was also honorable. Wise. Strong in heart and body.

I'd sensed it in his reassuring touches—in the brush of a finger, a grazing hand. Touches that were small enough to seem like afterthoughts, but potent enough, with intent enough, to shore me up and make me feel like I wasn't forgotten. Those had been the moments when I'd felt like he'd not just looked at me, but had looked *for* me. Seen me.

"This is it," he whispered, and I felt the brush of his lips against mine. "This will sustain the bond. Are you certain it's what you want?"

I'd never before experienced a perfect moment, but this came close. The sound of the waves reverberated through our cave, and the crashing echoed my heartbeat. It was dim and cool, the air briny and fresh. It invigorated me, renewed me.

"I'm sure," I told him. His fingers scraped lightly along my scalp, raking through my hair, and my body shivered with pleasure at the sensation. The muscles in my neck slackened as I let his hand take the weight of my head.

But still the kiss didn't come. His lips were a whisper away from mine, and I longed to feel the pressure of his mouth on mine. Longed to give myself to him.

He'd been more forthcoming than anyone on this island. I could tell he had a history with Alcántara and probably with others of the Directorate, too. Was he fighting a secret battle with them? Did he court me as an ally or as a woman?

It might have been a little of both, but right here, right now in this cave, I felt all woman in his arms. I waited for the kiss to come, but he teased me, nuzzling my cheek and brushing his nose against mine.

"You can kiss me," I whispered. Then I said it again, my voice louder, more demanding. "Kiss me, Carden."

That was all he needed. His tongue swept along my lower lip, and *oh God*, it felt so good. He was so good. My lips parted on a moan, quickly taken by his kiss.

Fire crackled along my veins, burned through me until I was alive with only one sensation—his touch on my body. The crashing waves, the *drip-drip* of water in the depths of the cavern, the cold sand beneath me—all these things fell away. All I knew was his mouth on mine.

I couldn't get close enough and pulled him closer. Then I pulled him closer still, and when I did, I felt his low laugh vibrate through my body.

He parted from me. "Such passion," he whispered, kissing along my cheek. "I knew," he said, his breath hot in my ear. "I knew you were a dove with wings of fire." He kissed his way down to my neck, and I felt the scrape of his fangs.

We flinched apart at the same time.

I'd mocked the girls who were so beholden to these immortals. I had detested the feeders and disdained the vampires, and yet here I was, with a vampire—there was no more vivid a reminder than the brush of those fangs on my neck.

"I'm sorry," I said, "I— It's just—"

"Hush." He placed a gentle finger on my lips. "In time, sweet. When you're ready." He kissed me again, more gently this time.

But this long and tender kiss drove me wilder than I could've imagined. I began to writhe with frustration, wanting a kiss like we'd shared before. Stronger, firmer. "Please." I cupped his cheeks and pressed my mouth to his. "Really kiss me."

"I dare not." His voice was ragged with a desire that amplified mine.

I longed to be a part of him. We would remain bonded—it

was all I wanted now. I turned my head slightly, exposing my neck. I'd made my decision. I was ready. "It's okay."

"I mustn't leave a mark." He nibbled me, but didn't break the skin. "They mustn't see."

I squirmed, anxious for him to do it. "Who cares wh—"

In an instant, his mouth was back on mine, silencing my protests, and this kiss was different. It seared through me, my yearning of moments ago drowned by something more acute. The flames had become wildfire, consuming me. I craved him, desperate now for Carden to mark me, for his teeth to score my skin.

I tangled my hands in his hair and pushed his face away from mine. "You can bite. I want you to. I don't care who sees."

"Soon, love." He kissed me again, ducking his mouth to mine over and over, murmuring, "Soon" and "Someday." Then he growled, "But first . . ." He took me in a deep kiss, his tongue sliding against mine. He took the kiss deeper still, until I felt the nick of his fang.

I drew in a sharp breath, exhaled in a slow shudder. I tasted him on my tongue. Felt my breath go into his lungs.

He chuckled again, and the deep, masculine sound made my heart soar. In that instant, I could imagine nothing more gratifying than being the one who made Carden smile.

"We must get back," he told me some time later.

I was finally, finally sated, and it was better than I'd imagined it could be. Far better than the last time. Last time, when we'd first kissed, we'd been strangers. Now I knew Carden. We had a bond that was emotional as well as chemical. The aching had disappeared so completely it was as though I'd never even been in pain. I'd tasted him again and was at peace.

"Must we?" I held his cheeks in my hands, wishing it weren't so dark. I wished I could see those honey eyes and that they might tell me some truth about what was between us. "Why did you go with me that day in the dungeons? When I first got there, it seemed you'd rather die than return with Alcántara."

"You were too much for my defenses." He swept a finger down my cheek. "You are too bright a light. How could I help but bask in you? Even if it did mean going back to Hugo." He cupped a warm hand over mine, pressing it to his cheek. "We could run away now. I could take you from here. Something is happening on this island, but I could take you to safety."

Yes, I wanted to shout, but I thought of all the people I cared about. I couldn't leave Emma, or Ronan, either, I realized. And then there was Mei-Ling—she wouldn't survive without me. She'd last a week, maybe more, but she'd eventually get eaten alive. In my heart I said yes, but the word I spoke was "No."

He gazed deep into my eyes, a quiet smile on his face. "Then perhaps someday we will. But first there are larger battles to fight."

"And let me guess. A McCloud doesn't run from a battle?"

He swooped in, landing a grinning kiss on my cheek. "Precisely, love. And now we really must go. It will be light soon."

I peered hard, trying to read those eyes in the shadows. "Can you see in the dark?"

"Aye, well enough."

"How is it you can see in the daylight?" I wanted to know more, to know everything. About vampires, but especially about Carden.

He laughed. "You put off the inevitable. Come." He stood and held out his hand to help me up. "We will talk as we walk. If anyone sees us, you may tell them that we were out performing terribly onerous, dangerous maneuvers along the cliffs."

"Our *maneuvers*, huh?" I caught his eye with a sparkle in mine. "That was far from onerous. As for dangerous . . . that remains to be seen."

His laugh was genuine but low, and I realized I needed to lower my voice as well. The sky had faded from black to a deep gunmetal gray. We were cutting it close—we had only about an hour to get back before the campus began to rouse for the day.

"You still didn't answer me," I whispered, wanting to get every last bit out of our time together.

"About how vampires can see in daylight?"

"About how *you* can see in daylight. It seems like it's harder for Alcántara than it is for you."

"He's older than I, for one. But I've spent much time outdoors. I've become acclimated, of necessity."

"Outdoors. Are you from here?"

"Near enough. I've been here for many years. But I was born on the Isle of Skye, long ago."

I heard such sadness in his voice. How many generations of McClouds had lived and died while he still walked. I asked quietly, "Is Skye a lot like this?"

"Greener. It's spectacular. It's rocky and cold and beautiful."

I reached out and slipped my hand in his, needing to touch him, to take away that melancholy. "Is that where you learned to climb?"

"Aye, I learned on the Black Cuillin, climbing cliffs when I was just a lad."

We were cresting the top of the hillside, back to the point where the trail had dropped off so suddenly. He wrapped his hands about my waist, helping me up, making my ascent effortless.

His touch on my body made me breathless. I caught his gaze and held it, fantasizing that we weren't returning to campus. That instead we were running away into the sunset. He could return home, and I would go with him.

His eyes narrowed on mine, focusing as though he'd guessed my thoughts. Carden leaned down to steal a breathtaking kiss, and when he pulled away, his voice was a raspy whisper. "Someday, *mo chridhe*."

CHAPTER TWENTY-TWO

I rolled over, blinking sleep from my eyes. Faraway shouts had woken me. I eased up onto an elbow, trying to get my bearings.

Mei was wide-awake and sitting cross-legged on her bed. She held a book in her hands, but had a distant look in her eyes, listening.

"What's going on?" I mumbled, tuning in to the distant hubbub.

She put her book down. "Good morning, Acari Drew."

"I told you to—" I began to insist she call me Drew, but seeing the humorous light in her eye, I grinned right back. "Okay, okay. Good morning to you, too, Acari Ho."

I swung my legs out of bed. The floor was frigid, but I didn't care. I didn't even feel it. I was bulletproof again. I'd fed from Carden. I wasn't thirsty or jittery or achy. I was just *happy*. "God, I slept great."

And I was in a brilliant mood. Not only was I physically sated, but I was nursing a big old crush. I smiled to myself as I dressed, thinking of Carden. Already I'd thought of more things I wanted to ask him. More I wanted to tell him.

He'd snuck me back in the dorm before dawn, where I'd grabbed what I estimated was a few solid hours of sleep. I'd woken up hungry, only this time it was for food, not blood. It felt fantastic.

I patted my belly, thinking of the omelet I'd have, and some warm, buttery toast to push it around. I'd maybe even add a glop of marmalade. I'd have a yogurt, too, with fruit if they had any, which they probably wouldn't, but this morning I'd settle for the dried stuff, dates and tiny shriveled berries stirred in. "What time is it? I'm starved."

"You slept through breakfast."

"What?" I hunched, pouting. "Why'd you let me sleep?"

"Let you? I tried to wake you." The shouting was getting closer. There were lots of voices now, calling out. Mei-Ling shoved aside her book and stood. "What do you think is happening?"

"I don't know, but I'll take it." Something was definitely going on, and after days of lockdown, I welcomed the excitement. I finished pulling on my uniform as quickly as I could. Food would have to wait. "This is better than Christmas morning."

It sounded like people were gathering in the common area, and Mei was halfway out the door when I told her, "Meet you there."

By the time I ducked into the bathroom and jogged down the hall to join her, everyone had assembled.

"Come on, girls," Kenzie said sharply. "Let's get this show on the road. I know a bunch of teachers anxious to kick all your butts back into gear, so I'll make this quick. Lockdown's over."

Chatter exploded in the small space. "It's over?"

"If you shut up, I'll tell you." Kenzie glared at us, her arms clasped at her chest—ever the charmer. But it shut us up all right. "Listen up, because this affects some of you personally." Her eyes landed on me and flitted away again. "There was another murder. Tracer Judge is dead. They found the killer. Master McCloud has been taken into custody. He'll be staked. I don't know when."

There was another burst of questions as she strode to the front of the room. "You know everything I do," she shouted over the din. "Get to class. I'll keep you posted. I'm sure they'll want us at the staking."

That was it. She left.

I reeled.

All eyes landed on me. I didn't care, though. They could stare all they wanted. Screw them. Screw this island. I was over it. Done.

Judge was dead. Nice, decent, smart Judge. And now Carden was going to be right behind him, accused of crimes he didn't commit. Carden, whose eyes crinkled at the corners when he smiled. Who called me ridiculous names. Who might have been an all-powerful vampire, but he talked to me, confided in me. Softened for *me*.

He'd be staked unless I did something about it.

Talk about a no-brainer—I *would* do something about it.

Carden hadn't killed anybody, least of all Tracer Judge. How could he have? He'd been with *me* all night. Only there was no way to come forward as his alibi without outing our relationship.

That bastard Alcántara had something to do with it—I just knew he did. And now he wanted Carden dead.

Screw that. Screw the Directorate. Screw them.

Mei leaned over to whisper in my ear, "Are you okay?"

I startled and made myself nod. It was all I could manage at the moment. I turned and left, blind and deaf to her and everyone else.

Guilt swamped me. If it weren't for me, Carden wouldn't even be here now. It had to be up to me to fix it.

Someone was on a killing spree, and it wasn't Carden.

I'd deal with this. I'd help him. I needed to think. First things first. I couldn't call attention to myself. I needed to act normal. I'd go about my usual business and come up with a plan. What day was it? I'd go to class.

Wednesday. Combat Medicine day.

But Judge was the teacher and he was dead. Knowing the vamps, though, they'd have another teacher installed in there immediately, as though Judge had never existed.

Combat Medicine, then. I headed that way, knowing I'd need every ounce of discipline to sit in the classroom and act like I was paying attention as every girl stared at me. As Carden festered in a cell somewhere. As I pretended not to care.

Masha was leaning against the door to the sciences building as I entered. "Wonderful news," she said, smiling brightly.

"*Fabulous* news," I replied, grinning a little wildly. Was I having a psychotic break? I felt sort of giddy and unhinged. Kind of nuts. I'd worked myself into a lather as I'd walked across the quad. Whoever did this was going down. *I'd* take them down.

By the strange expression on Masha's face, my manic reply had confused and freaked her out a little. Good. I'd take *her* down, too.

And the thing was, in my heart of hearts, this intense, self-effacing focus felt saner than I'd ever been.

Ronan was at the front of the class—of course. He was the

likeliest temporary replacement for Judge. Seeing him standing there, though, alone and holding himself so stiffly, I felt a pang.

"Sorry," I whispered as I passed him on the way to my seat. And I was. Ronan and Judge had been close. He'd lost so many people—more than I had. I couldn't fathom it. Couldn't fathom why he stuck around. But like all of us, he had his reasons.

But then I messed up and heard myself add, "Carden didn't do it." It'd sounded more vehement than I'd intended.

Ronan only looked at me with flat, dead eyes.

I took my seat.

I couldn't think about Ronan just then. I felt bad, but if I were to do any good, I needed to numb myself.

I needed a plan. Investigating Trinity's death had been a dead end. All I'd discovered was that there were two men on the island, probably vampires, who may or may not have been German and who might or might not be involved. Their words ran in a loop in my head. *Is he in control? They grow reckless.*

I didn't know what to do with that. As I sat, waiting for class to start, I made a mental list of what I did know.

1. Alcántara was behind Carden's arrest, which meant he wanted Carden dead. That probably also meant the whole Directorate wanted Carden dead. But why?
2. Acari Kate had seen something on that cliff top the day she fell, and something about that whole episode nagged at me.
3. Carden was imprisoned somewhere. My guess was the castle on the hill. Which led me to . . .
4. The Trainees. They knew stuff we didn't.

My eyes went to Josh, settling in the seat next to me. *He* knew stuff that I didn't.

I watched him, waiting for him to look over. I didn't feel like talking, though, and he must've sensed that. When he finally did look at me, instead of his usual *giddaying*, he simply said, "Judge."

Judge had been a good guy. We'd miss him. We were scared, and something about teachers getting killed made things feel out of control, but we couldn't safely say any of that. For a moment, though, our eyes stayed connected, and we shared all that.

I held his gaze for an extra, pregnant moment before agreeing, "Judge."

"There are many ways to die," Ronan said, calling the class to order.

"Oh great," I muttered, sinking low in my seat. A lecture on death and the many possible flavors of my inevitable demise was just what I needed. Not.

First Amanda, now Judge. But there Ronan stood, essaying on blood loss. It was just like him to power through grief by slamming into it head-on. Discussing exsanguination. Pinching veins, compressing arteries. The jugular. The carotid.

I thought of Carden, and my fear for him was a physical pain. I grazed my fingertips over my neck, feeling for those veins, remembering how I'd longed for Carden to kiss me just there. To taste me.

How was he? How long could he last without feeding?

I shoved my fist against my mouth, keeping my emotions in check. Carden could've claimed me as an alibi. He couldn't have killed Tracer Judge if he'd been kissing me in a cave at the time of the murder. But here I was, still skipping around, going about my business, which meant he didn't tell. He was protecting me.

I'd protect him, too. I might've been reckless, but I wasn't stupid—I knew I couldn't do it alone.

But who could I trust? I considered the options.

1. Mei-Ling. She'd seemed eager enough to play Nancy Drew when we'd talked in our room. The girl had hidden depths—not to mention some not-so-hidden resentments at being kidnapped and forcibly brought here.
2. Emma. I trusted Emma with my life. But . . .
3. Yasuo? I trusted him, too. But lately there was something missing. I sensed he'd give his life to help Em, but friendship wasn't sophomore geometry. There was no *Yas trusts Emma, Emma trusts me, therefore I trust Yas.* Trust wasn't transitive.
4. Josh. Odd that he was in the running, because I sure hadn't trusted him at first. I glanced over at him. He'd helped me before, sticking his neck out to save me from hazing. Might he help me again?

He felt me looking and caught my eye. And yet again, rather than shoot me one of his signature doofy boy nods, there was something somber and supportive waiting for me in his gaze.

Josh, then.

Making like I was taking notes, I scribbled on a page of my notebook, tore it out, and passed it to him.

His eyes practically bugged out of his head as he snatched it up before anyone could see. Not a lot of in-class notes were passed on the Isle of Night.

"What the fuck?" he mouthed to me, then stole a quick look at the scrap.

I'd written: "We need to talk."

He gave me an incredulous *duh* look and mouthed back, "Later."

I tore another bit of paper, writing, "I want to know about the castle on the hill."

He crammed it in his pocket. "Not now," he mouthed impatiently.

I carefully ripped another tiny scrap, coughing to cover up the sound. Passing notes was a pretty stupid risk to take, but I was obsessed. And what was the worst that could happen—they'd lock me up with Carden? Though I knew instantly that wasn't the worst punishment. Maybe, deep down, I felt okay taking the chance because it was Ronan up there at the front of the class—and wouldn't he just blow a gasket to know I thought that way?

Either way, I needed to find out where Carden was being held, and the mystery began at the vampires' keep. "Promise you'll tell me about it," I wrote.

Josh kept the paper and shoved it in his pocket. "Stop," he whispered, not even looking at me.

I needed to get him to promise. I wrote on a new slip of paper, "No."

He scribbled, "STOP IT," flashed it at me, and shoved the paper into his pocket.

Ronan's back was turned, listing on the board the body's myriad pressure points. The topic was super-cool, and I regretted not paying attention. But Ronan might've been divulging the secret to the Vulcan nerve pinch for all I cared, and I wouldn't lose my focus.

I tried again, flashing Josh the corner of my notebook. "I lost something. Is it in the castle?"

He looked at me then, and this time his anger was gone. Instead he wore a tired, feeling sort of expression. He'd known what—or rather, whom—I'd meant. With a sigh, he wrote back, "You're going to get us in trouble."

I gave him a hint of a smile, knowing I had him. "Pretty handwriting for a boy. Now . . . CASTLE?"

Josh watched, making sure Ronan wasn't about to turn around, and he scrawled in his notebook, "We'll talk later. Not like you to not pay attention, nerdbot. So *stop*."

Ronan turned to face us, and I felt my cheeks go bright red. I had been just about to flash Josh my notebook. I stared blindly at the board, trying my best to appear completely engrossed. When Ronan turned around again, I quickly flashed what I'd written to Josh. "Don't split your infinitives. I won't stop till you promise."

Josh scribbled something, flashed it quickly, then flipped to another page. "Fine. I promise. Now STOP."

I practically jumped on him the moment class ended. I glanced around to ensure nobody was in earshot, making it a point not to catch Ronan's eye. We were among the last out the door, but still, I knew to be discreet and slowly said, "So . . . I need you to help me find something . . ."

Find Carden.

He gave me a quiet nod. So he *would* help. "Let's get out of here."

I was relieved, but I also felt a little thrown, too. I'd expected jokes and evasions. "Aren't you going to make a joke? No *that's what she said*?"

"We have all day," he said with a reluctant grin. "There. *That's* what she said."

His humor didn't annoy me. If anything, it broke the tension. I patted his shoulder. "There's the Josh I know."

We made our way down the path to the dining hall, and out in the open, we were able to speak a little more freely. "I just have a few questions for you."

He laughed. "So I gathered." When I didn't speak, he said, "So? Shoot."

I was still getting used to the concept of friends, and his openness and willingness to help made me wary. "What's the catch?"

"No catch. I assume this is about Master McCloud. You've got a thing for him, right?"

I stopped short. "How did you know?"

He shrugged.

"Seriously," I pressed. Had other people guessed, too? "What gave it away?"

"I've seen you. Don't worry," he added quickly. "I don't think other people would've noticed. Me, though . . . I see *all*, D."

Had he been watching me? Why? All of a sudden I was skeptical, and it made me nervous. "Why would you help me?"

"Let's just say I'd like to shake things up a bit." He paused just long enough for me to wonder what he'd meant by that. "Frankly, having the most badass Acari on the island owe me?" He tapped his head. "That's just smart. Come on," he said, urging me forward again. "I've got an idea where they're keeping him."

CHAPTER TWENTY-THREE

⟢ ⟶⟢⟵ ⟢

"But we're headed away from the castle." I stopped. Josh had taken a path that forked away from the top-secret vampire quarters. "I thought you were going to get me into the keep."

"Shhh." He looked around, looking half-amused, half-scared. "Are you nuts? I can't get you in there. They'd have both of us for breakfast."

"But I need to find Card—Master McCloud."

He narrowed his eyes on me. "Carden, eh?"

Of everyone, would it be *Josh* who ended up guessing at our bond? I couldn't worry about it now. But just in case, I quickly added, "Look, I was close with Amanda and Judge. I have some questions for *Master* McCloud. If it turns out he killed them, I'll stake him myself."

He gave me a sly smile. "Whatever you say, D. If McCloud is still alive—and seeing as the vamps are practically drooling for a public spectacle, I'm sure he must be—then I'm pretty sure he's in the caverns."

"The *caverns*?"

"Yeah, you know them."

I followed his line of sight to the standing stones. He was right. I did know the caverns. I'd seen them—or rather, fallen into them—while fighting Lilac. It was a vast underground network of tunnels and sea caves beneath the standing stones. The perfect spot for a dungeon.

"We don't need to drop into the water, do we?" I shuddered at the memory of our fight, of falling into the subterranean springs. They were hot, sulfurous, and very, very dark.

"*We're* not doing anything," he said. "*You're* going it alone. I'll show you a way around, though." He pointed to a faint trail, winding down to the sea. "Follow that down, and you'll see what looks like a rabbit's burrow. You're small—you can climb in that way."

"Gee, thanks." I eyed the trail—I never would've spotted it without him pointing it out to me. "It means leaving the path."

He shrugged, agreeing. "You asked where. I'm showing you."

I thought of Carden imprisoned. Again.

Except this time, would he be so willing to accept his death? I hoped not. I knew I had to see for myself. I had to help him, again.

But saving him meant breaking yet another rule. I faced Josh. "Should I take it personally that you just assumed I'd be game for leaving the path?"

"You should take it as a sign of my respect for you. You're one tough sheila. I hope you're on my side if I ever find myself locked up."

"I'll take that under advisement." I eyed the trail. We'd skipped lunch to come, and I needed to hustle if I wanted to do this today. Nobody was around now, but the chances of being seen would increase once kids finished in the dining hall and started heading to their afternoon classes.

I took my first step off the path, then paused, part of me still the tiniest bit skeptical. "I can't believe the vampires told you all this. About the caverns, I mean."

"Vampires didn't tell me anything. I spotted it the day of your fight, then went back later to check it out. I've been exploring when I can. I found a spot with a bunch of shackles. I think they must be holding McCloud there."

Shackles. Just the thought gave me a chill. "There are probably shackles all over this creepy island. Why would these be any different?"

"Because, Blondie." He paused, looking uncomfortable. "On the day of your fight, when I passed this particular tunnel, I could smell the blood. It was fresh."

I shuddered. Who else ended up in these dungeons? "Is *that* where they take all the bodies?"

"Please don't ask me too many questions," he said. "I'm walking a line here as it is."

It brought Acari Kate to mind. Ever since the day of her climbing accident, I hadn't been able to get her out of my mind. Had a bond with a vampire been what'd made her so unhinged? Had her mania been a glimpse into my future? What had she seen that'd sent her falling to her death? "Just one more question?"

He hesitated.

"Please," I pleaded.

Josh checked his watch, looking nervous. "Only for you, D. But make it fast."

"A girl died the other day."

"What else is new?"

I shook my head. "No, this was different. Acari Kate—did you know her?" He didn't, so I went on. "Well, she was acting all weird. We were far down that beach where Priti holds her combat classes."

"I know the spot."

"She was climbing up the rock face there. She saw something when she got to the top."

He only nodded, but I could see by his expression that he had some thoughts on the matter.

"She saw something," I said. "Didn't she?"

"Could be."

"You know something else, don't you?" But he just looked at me blankly, so I pressed. "Come on, Josh. This is important."

He sighed. "I guess it's not that big a deal. There's a man who lives out that way, near the southern part of the island."

"A man? Like, a human man?" I gaped at him. That was not the answer I'd been expecting. "What would he be doing out there? And why would some *man* scare her, anyway?" At this point, I imagined if I spotted an ordinary human male, I'd run to him with open arms.

"It's not who he is," Josh said. "It's who he would've been with. He's the keeper of the Draug."

I laughed, it was so ridiculous. But then the look he gave me was one part horrified disbelief and one part afraid. It was the fear that stole the smile from my face. "You're being serious."

He gave me a grim nod. "As a heart attack."

With that cheering thought, I thanked him and was on my

way, jogging down the trail before my small window of time ran out. I had Expeditionary Skills Training with Priti at three o'clock. She held class not far from here, but I'd need to double back and put on my gym clothes first. If I'd been thinking, I'd have put a change of clothes in my bag. But this morning I'd been too busy reeling from the news about Carden. I'd just have to go quickly.

Once I was out of sight, I could slow my pace a little, as I wasn't in as great a danger of being spotted. At least, not by a fellow student. If a vampire saw me out this way, I'd be screwed, no matter what. Something told me that not even Alcántara's weird fascination with me would save me this time.

I contemplated Josh's bizarre report. A Draug keeper? Was there a Draug pen? What did they eat? I shuddered to consider it.

More important, did the keeper have anything to do with the vampires I'd overheard? *Is he in control? They grow reckless.* Those words could apply to Keeper and Draug. Though I supposed they could be applied to most anything on this island and still make sense.

But then something else hit me: The keeper was a human man, living in solitude, on a high plateau. He'd have seen much. He might have seen the true killer. And like that, this mysterious keeper became my hope. I sure didn't have anything else to go with.

I almost jogged right by the entry tunnel Josh described. If his instructions hadn't been so clear, I'd have mistaken the small passage for the burrow of some animal.

With a quick glance in either direction, I dropped to my knees and crawled in. The darkness was immediate, swallowing me whole. The smell of brine and sulfur hit me, and I had to pause a moment to gather myself. The scent memory threw me back to the day of my fight with Lilac.

The old fear erupted from deep inside, setting my heart hammering against my chest. I forced myself to calm, to breathe, to be centered. And that was when I felt him.

Carden.

CHAPTER TWENTY-FOUR

───⟨⟨⟨⟩⟩⟩───

H e was near. He was reaching out to me. It wasn't clear, though, not like hearing his voice in my head or how I imagined ESP might be. But I felt him nonetheless. He was a tug in my belly. A buzzing in my head. A nudge in the back of my mind, a sensation telling me he was nearby.

Carden needed me to come. Maybe even wanted me to.

I upped my pace, crawling quickly through the darkness until my hands met damp, close air. It was the caverns.

I waited for my eyes to adjust, but there wasn't the slightest bit of ambient light. On the day of the Directorate Challenge, there'd been torches. There'd also been a terrible rent in the rocks overhead that'd let in fingers of watery sunlight. But the vampires must've patched it up, because it was pitch-black now.

I'd have to feel my way.

Without sight, my other senses overcompensated. I became hyperaware of the sound of my breath in my head. Of the *plip-plip* of distant condensation dripping onto rocks. Of the feel and taste of the humid air. And of Carden opening his mind to me.

"I'm coming," I whispered, teetering to standing. I made myself keep a steady pace, wary I might accidentally fall into the hot springs—or worse. I wouldn't have been surprised if this place held a crevasse leading straight down to hell.

I didn't know how much time passed before I heard the clinking of chains. Carden's voice was close, a harsh rasp saying, "You must leave me."

I forgot my fears of pits and pools and ran straight toward that voice. "Carden." I slammed into his chest, and he made an *oof* sound that made me feel such a swell of affection.

He chuckled. "We must stop meeting in dungeons, petal."

"Are you okay?" Though my body responded instantly to him, overcome with thirst and longing, those feelings weren't as powerful as this relief I felt, touching him again. Knowing he was alive. "We have to get you out of here." I ran my hands up his arms. The fabric of his sleeves was damp with condensation. I felt for his shackles. "Who did this? Was it Alcántara?" I frantically rattled the chains, trying to find some give. "I'll kill him."

"Be easy, love. But I speak truly. You must go. This isn't safe for you."

"What happened?" I didn't stop messing with those shackles—surely there was some way to pick them. "And who killed Judge?"

"I don't know who the killer is. They came for me—"

"Alcántara? The headmaster? Who?"

"Directorate soldiers. Young vampires. It doesn't matter."

There'd been an amused disdain in his voice that I didn't find funny at all. "It totally matters," I said. "Could they have been the ones who killed Judge?" Another thought occurred to me, and I struggled to wrap my mind around all the pieces. "Or maybe that has nothing to do with anything. Maybe Judge was killed because he'd planned to escape with Amanda."

"Annelise," he said sternly, and his use of my first name jarred me. "Stop thinking of others. You must leave now, before they return. How did you even find me?"

I hesitated, but I knew there would be no lying to Carden. "Josh told me how to find you."

"Josh?" His voice crackled ice-cold. "The Trainee boy? What are you doing meeting with him?"

"He's not just a random boy. He's my friend and he helped me find you." Saying the words, I realized they were true—somehow, in the past weeks, Josh had become my friend.

"He is just a boy, and you mustn't trust him or any of them."

I heard jealousy in his voice, but instead of it making me nervous, the sound exhilarated me. A guy jealous of another guy over *me*. I took a step back, unnerved that I couldn't see his eyes in the darkness. Was he really as vehement as he sounded? "He's okay," I assured him. "He's not like the others."

"The others," he repeated in a snarl. "None of them are *okay*. You must swear you'll no longer confide in any of them."

I had few friends, and I wasn't going to shut everyone out just because Carden said so. Who was he to demand that? "I'm not swearing anything."

He sighed, sounding so weary, and I wanted to take back my words. I considered making him any promise he wanted to hear, if it might mean hearing a smile in his voice once more. But I didn't. We were running out of time.

"There must be some way to get out of these." I pushed him aside, feeling for the origin of the shackles.

He grunted, and I realized he was holding himself at an angle.

I patted my hands along his body. "Did they hurt you?" His shirt was damp and warm. "Have you been bleeding? Do you need to feed?"

His tone changed, sounding as though he spoke through gritted teeth. "I need you," he said with a growl in his voice. "But we dare not risk it. They'll smell you on me. You must leave. Now."

I ran my hands along one of the chains to the base. I could feel the rust flaking under my nails. "Not without you."

"They'd only find me again."

Anger churned me. "Are you giving up?"

"Never," he said gently. "But the most important thing now is that you remain safe. Alcántara demands a scapegoat, and it appears I am he."

"Not if I find the real killer," I said angrily.

"You'll do no such thing," he said instantly, his tone hardening. "Think not of me."

"So," I said, speaking over him, "that's why you need to tell me about the Draug keeper."

"The Draug keeper?" he said, astounded. "What do you know of such things?"

"I know he's way up on that cliff top, south of the cove. I'm hoping he might've seen something."

"No," he said, so forcefully that I knew I was onto something. He repeated the word more calmly. "No."

"I will investigate this whether you help me or not."

"You're saying I cannot stop you?"

"Look, McCloud. I like you. As in, I really like you. I want to help you, and considering these shackles, it looks like you can't really stop me."

A moment passed. Finally he said, "I am honored." Emotion infused the words, and it was a foreign sound, striking me as sounding both moved and gallant. "I recognize that you are your own woman, Annelise, and that I cannot stop you. But you must also recognize that I will try. Just as you want to protect me, my compulsion is to keep you safe. At all costs. Even if the cost is my own life."

Sudden emotion swamped me so intensely that my throat ached with it. I tried to tamp it down, to shore up those emotions, because this was just the bond speaking, right? This was chemical.

Mostly.

His voice came to me in the darkness, hoarse and fraught. "I feel your sadness, but you mustn't mourn on account of me. You are strong. You have it in you to endure the fever. You will survive my passing."

"You're not dead yet," I said, so fiercely his body leaned toward mine in the blackness.

"There is a myth where I come from. The story of Josa MacIntyre, a sorrowful man, a fisherman who roams the world, gathering souls of the living. Sometimes I feel like this Josa, and the world is my sea, its despairing souls my only sustenance. But now I've met you, and it's been enough. So do not mourn me, love. My life has been long, and if my battle must end here, so be it. I'd rather die now than see you perish to save me."

"Forget your Josa." My spine stiffened. More than ever, I knew I needed to find the killer. I pulled from him. "Nobody is doing any dying anytime soon. Tell me what you know, Carden. Think of it as keeping me safe. Because if you don't tell me, I'll leave here and I swear I will search all over this island for clues."

"You would, wouldn't you?"

"I would."

"You brave, wee spitfire." He sighed again, but this time it didn't sound tired so much as resolved. "Touch me, Annelise. Quickly, now; we've not much time. I'd feel your hands on me as I tell you."

The words stole my breath. I stepped closer, sinking into him, cradling my cheek against that hard chest.

"That's better," he said. "I'll tell you what I know, which isn't much. I am an outsider here."

"But I thought you were from here."

"Aye, so I am. But I am not of these men. I've never pledged fealty to the Directorate, and they mistrust me for it. There are many things to which I'm not privy."

I fisted my hands in his shirt, wishing we were someplace else. Wishing I were brave enough to slide my hand under his shirt. That the day might come where I'd even have the chance. Such wishes galvanized me, focusing me back on my goal. "You must know something. You've been alive for hundreds of years."

"I do know things, it's true. I know there is a man, a human man, the one you call the Draug keeper." Carden was thoughtful for a time, then added, "Your instincts are good. The keeper sees much and speaks little, and he is perhaps a good place to start. More than one body was discovered at the base of that cliff."

"How do I find him?"

"He stays on an abandoned croft on the southern tip."

"Have you ever met him?"

Carden gave a startled bark of a laugh at that. "He won't speak to vampires unless forced."

I pushed away, looking up to where his face would be. I felt a pang of loss that I couldn't see his expression. "I can't believe the vampires would put up with that sort of disrespect."

"The keeper distrusts vampires, but they need him. His is a putrid, dangerous job—not many men would do it, and certainly no vampire."

I nodded in the darkness, feeling resolved. Giving our alibi wasn't an option, and giving up on Carden wasn't, either. But this—missions and secrecy—this I could do.

The last time I'd felt this optimistic, I'd been packing up my Honda, getting ready for what I thought would be my illustrious college career. "He may not trust vampires," I said, "but maybe he'll trust a girl from Florida."

"You seem to have that effect," Carden said quietly.

Had I misheard him? Was this vampire actually telling me he had faith in me? "Really?"

"Aye," he said with a low, rumbling chuckle. "Really. Trust is a foreign sentiment for me, and I thank you for allowing me to experience it once more."

I reached through the blackness, right to where I knew I'd find him, and cradled his face gently in my hands. His chains clinked as he strained his arms, leaning down to meet my kiss.

Sealing my resolve.

CHAPTER TWENTY-FIVE

A fter Priti's class, I lingered at the back as everyone headed from the beach to the dining hall. My plan was to slip away gradually until I could split away from the group unnoticed.

That is, until I was noticed.

"Well, look who it is," a menacing voice said from behind.

I stopped, blinked my eyes shut tight, gathering strength. Inhaling, I turned. "Rob the Trainee. What a surprise." I glanced down at his pants. "Glad to see you fixed your uniform."

For once, I was glad to be surrounded by the other girls. I'd humiliated him. It was only a matter of time before he demanded retribution. But surely he wouldn't do anything in a crowd.

Sure enough, he gave me his worst scowl, warning, "I'm coming for you."

"Yeah, yeah." Twerps like him no longer scared me. The repercussions of a feud between us—now *that* scared me. "You sound like a bad Vin Diesel movie."

"Oh, it'll be dramatic, all right. Someday when you don't expect it, I'll be there, waiting."

"Then get comfortable," I told him. "You'll be waiting a long time."

"It'll be worth it." His mouth peeled into a speculative grin. "So worth it. I think my friends might even join in."

I started walking again. I wasn't in the mood. "Perfect. I'll be happy to have an audience for when I take you down."

"Watch your back," he called to me.

"Maybe you should watch yours," I said over my shoulder. "Make sure there are no rips."

"Hey, D," Yasuo called.

I spotted my friends on the path and waved at them. Rob blended into the crowd of milling students, then was gone. I was sure he'd turn up again one of these days, like a bad penny.

Yas jogged over in that easy lope of his, and Emma was right behind him, weaving her way toward us.

I pasted a smile on my face. "Hey, guys."

"Hey, stranger," Emma said, giving me a hug. She glanced to where Rob had been just a moment before. "What'd he want?"

"Rob?" I rolled my eyes. I had more urgent issues to deal with than stupid adolescent Trainees. "Oh, we go way back. Forget him."

Yasuo looked impatient, his eyes aimed in the direction of the dining hall. "You going to dinner?"

I hedged. No. I was going to skip dinner and go in search of a mysterious Draug keeper who may or may not be willing to help me.

But I couldn't tell them that. Instead, I said, "No. I was just about to turn around. I left my towel down on the beach. I need to go back for it."

I hated lying; the words felt thick and awkward coming out of my mouth. Once I would have spilled my guts to them, but now I had no other choice.

I told myself this was Emma and Yasuo. They were different. But in my heart I knew there was an undeniable gulf between us now, one that I'd felt even before Carden's pronouncement echoed in my head. *You mustn't trust.*

Something else nagged in the back of my mind. An unsettling voice telling me, *Especially Yasuo.*

Yas was my buddy, it was true. But seeing as he spent most of our limited coed free time with Emma, our own bonding time had been cut way back. It'd allowed me to see from a distance the changes he was undergoing—his longer fangs, the more remote eyes, and most disturbing of all, an essential stillness and coldness that was gradually enshrouding his natural charisma like a fog.

His eyes were on me, and unlike the first time we'd met, they were unreadable. His arm snaked around Emma's shoulders, claiming her.

Was he claiming her *from me*?

But then Emma smiled, and it was as sincere as it'd ever been. "Want us to wait for you?"

Was that Yasuo's hand tightening on her shoulder? Was he giving her a silent message? "Yeah, D," he said. "We're happy to wait."

I didn't believe he meant it. "Don't sweat it," I told them.

If I'd been concerned before about the implications of their affair, now I was really worried. It wasn't healthy—or safe—for them to be so isolationist like this.

Amanda's death had made it clear that we girls were allowed to fraternize with only one set of guys, and they were of the undead variety. That meant no Tracer boyfriends and probably no Trainees, either.

I refused to contemplate my own singular relationship obsession, and if that made me a hypocrite, so be it.

"Can we save you a seat?" Emma asked.

"I don't know if I'll make it back." I'd have to last without this evening's shooter of blood. But since kissing Carden, I felt like I could go for days without the refrigerated stuff. "Grab me a couple dinner rolls, though, would you?"

The sun made its final dip behind the rocky horizon, casting us in cool gray twilight. Emma peered at me through the dusk. "You sure you're okay?"

How long had I zoned out, thinking of Carden?

"I'm fine," I replied, seeing how Emma didn't totally believe me.

But Yasuo believed what he wanted to believe. "Then we're outta here," he said. "Let's go, prairie girl. Gotta grab the good stuff before it's all gone."

Guilt gnawed at me as I watched them walk down the path, away from me. They were my friends, but my bond with Carden set me apart from them whether I liked it or not.

It'd set me apart from everyone. There was no one I could tell about it all. And I probably shouldn't tell anyone I was investigating on his behalf, either. Not even Ronan. If I told *him*, I knew I'd see only condemnation in his eyes, and I wouldn't be able to stand that.

I turned my back and pretended to return to the beach. When it was safe, with a quick glance all around, I jogged off, headed south. In search of the keeper of the Draug.

I smelled it before I saw it. It was something I'd smelled once before—the stench of sickness and rot. The scent of Draug. And by the distant echoing snarls, there were several of them.

I couldn't wrap my mind around it. Could they be tamed? Why were they kept? Was this what prevented them from roaming free, decimating the human population or coming to get young, tender girl flesh in the night? I shuddered, my skin crawling with revulsion.

I knew a spurt of fear, too. It was impossible not to be afraid—anyone who'd ever spied a Draug would be. They were neither vampire nor human, creatures for whom something had gone very, very wrong in their transformation. Which meant some of them had been Trainees. Maybe all of them were—I didn't know. I'd encountered only two in my life. One whose flesh was so decayed, all I'd been able to discern were rotted black strips of skin, a couple of shining fangs, and the creature's complete and all-consuming urge to eat me.

By the time I'd encountered the second Draug, I'd known what it was I faced and so had been able to keep my senses about me. Which only meant I was very aware of my tearing flesh, cracking bones, and imminent death. I'd thought I was dead meat until Ronan showed up to stake it. Where blood had once flowed, black tar oozed, seeping from its wound, bringing with it this stench I smelled now. It was the stench of evil.

Josh had said *keeper* of the Draug. Which meant they were *kept*. Which meant I was okay. Somewhat. Maybe. Because obviously they escaped sometimes.

Curiosity, reason, and need overcame raw fear. Carden would be staked if I didn't act.

My eyes swept the foreign landscape. I'd never been to this

part of the island before. It was craggier, hillier, with thin paths winding between towering rock formations.

But Carden had taught me about hills and climbing. Had he somehow intuited that I would need those very skills?

Sending up a silent thank-you to my vampire, I chose one of the higher rock faces that also seemed to have a manageable enough incline that I wouldn't need to do more than scramble up on my hands and knees. It would get me high enough to have a vantage over more land, but it wasn't so steep that I'd have to actually rock climb up the thing.

Night was coming fast now, and I needed to hurry. What I was doing was dangerous, and it'd become exponentially more so once it was curfew time.

With the darkness came cold. The moon was full and bright, though, and I felt its oddly charged light on my skin. I was still in my gym uniform, and I had that weird feeling of being cold and sweaty at the same time. It was just as well—I'd probably have torn up the knees of my leggings anyway.

A half hour in, and my knees were scraped and my nails blackened from the grit that jammed beneath them as I inched my way up. I was certain that technically the rock formation would've only been classified as a hill, but the thing sure felt like a mountain to me.

Finally I reached the top and eased onto the plateau on my belly. I felt a tug at my hips and adjusted my clothing. I'd tied a thin strip of fabric into a makeshift holster for my throwing stars and kept it hidden under my shorts. It was thin enough and tied tightly enough that nobody could see. Clinging as it did to the side of my hip bones, the shuriken didn't hurt me when I took a hit to my abdomen, and only cut a little when I fell on my side. Unfortunately, both were common occurrences.

It was a small price to pay. These days, it just felt stupid to go out unarmed. I thought of the homemade stakes Ronan kept hidden in his sleeves. I was sure I wasn't the only Acari who kept hidden weaponry.

Scooting along on my stomach, I inched out as far as I dared to the opposite edge, scanning below for the keeper's cottage. I opened my senses all around me. I'd been surprised from behind by a Draug before. It wouldn't happen again.

"Come on." I spoke under my breath, and it came out as smoke, disappearing at once into the blackness. "Where are you?"

The moon was bright way up here, but this rock that gave me such a great vantage point also managed to cast the valley in shadow. I blinked hard, peering into the darkness.

Nothing. I opened my ears to the distant snarls and groans. Caught their scent on the wind. I spun slowly on my belly to look down from the far ledge. And there I spotted him.

A figure in the darkness, moving amidst large structures. Were they cages? I squinted hard. The wind gusted, sending goose bumps shivering up my legs and arms, but it blew the clouds overhead, sending a finger of moonlight down, illuminating hands, reaching from between bars.

Draug hands, clawing in the darkness, moaning, pleading. They wanted blood.

I saw the figure more clearly now, too. It was a man, and something in his gait told me it was an older man. He had something long and thin in one hand—a stick maybe?—and a walking staff in the other. It was long and curved at the top, like a reaping hook. It gave me the creeps.

A hand swiped at him, and I heard his curse from my perch, an unintelligible, thickly accented bark. He swung that stick at the cage and there was an electrical *zzzt* sound, followed by an explosion of shrieks and snarls. Not a stick, then—he held a cattle prod.

It chilled me. But then I realized I was chilled because it was freezing. It was full dark, and now that I wasn't moving, the air was bitter cold.

I needed to get the hell out of there. I could get away with skipping dinner, but I couldn't get away with missing curfew. As it was, I'd have a real job explaining myself if I ran into any vampires on the way home.

I'd come back, though.

I didn't think the Draug would be capable of the murders. They were like zombies down there, mindless undead stumbling around like pure id—thirsting for blood and herded like cattle.

But the old man was a different story. I had questions, and he looked like someone who knew answers.

I scrambled back down the other side as quickly as I could, scree and small rocks scraping me as I half galloped, half skidded, slid, and crab-walked my way down. Panic was trying to set in, like a demon scratching at the back door of my brain. I'd taken too long. It was full dark now.

"What are you doing?" The voice came out of the shadows, as bitter cold as the night air.

Caught.

CHAPTER TWENTY-SIX

A hand came at me from behind, snatching me. Fingers dug into my elbow, immobilizing my arm. But I swung into action with the other, struggling with the waistband of my shorts.

"Shit, shit, shit," I cursed, clawing for the stars at my hip. I hadn't thought this out well enough, not nearly at all, this stupid, stupid homemade shuriken belt that I'd thought had been so clever, and now I'd die because of it.

"Settle down," the voice snarled.

Instinct clicked in, assessing the situation, scanning my training for options. Close proximity, restrained, no weapons—no choice but to head butt. I wrenched my body to face my attacker.

"Ronan," I shrieked as recognition clicked. My heart had exploded, hammering in my chest, and I fought for breath. "God . . . God . . . God*damn*." I yanked my arm free. "What the hell? What the . . . what the hell?" I repeated, getting my nerves back to normal. "You scared the crap out of me."

"I scared you? *I* scared *you*?" He grabbed the arm back and pulled me into a jog. "We have to get out of here."

"You're hurting me," I said, even though he wasn't really. I yanked my arm back, but still did a quick shuffle to catch the rhythm of his pace. "What are you doing here?"

"I was looking for *you*. I don't know why, though. You seem determined to get yourself killed."

"You were looking for me?" We were jogging at a steady pace now, and I wished I could've seen his expression.

"When you didn't show up for dinner, I became concerned." He stopped, getting his bearings in the dark.

I pointed. "Campus is that way."

"As I am well aware," he said flatly. "But we can't go that way. Too risky. We need to head to the water. That way I can make up an excuse if we get caught."

He slowed to a walk, and I followed him, barely making out the winding path in the moonlight. His shoulders, his arms, every part of him seemed strung tight.

For a while, all I heard was the chuff of his breath and the scuffing of our footsteps along the gravel. When Ronan finally broke the silence, he sounded no less angry. "You haven't answered me."

"What do you mean?" I asked, knowing full well what he'd meant.

"Does this have to do with the vampire McCloud?"

"No," I replied quickly. Too quickly.

He stopped short and spun to look at me. I almost ran into his chest, and I took a step back. His eyes were focused hard on me, and even in the darkness I could see his anger shimmering there. "Don't trust anyone. Least of all a vampire."

"Does that mean I shouldn't trust you?"

"Annelise." His tone had flipped from angry to tired, and the sound of it made something inside me feel very, very sad. "Sometimes you can be so foolish." I opened my mouth to speak, but he put up a hand, stopping me. "I know you do these things because you are loyal. Your heart is true, and I admire it. But please. Don't let it get you killed."

I was truehearted? Suddenly my throat ached with emotion. I wanted to assure him that I wouldn't get myself killed, but I couldn't bear the lie. Instead, I told him, "You could help me, you know."

I sensed his hesitation as he began to walk again. "What are you up to?"

I answered his question with a question. "Why would the vampires want to kill one of their own?"

"Don't see my honesty as an opportunity to take advantage."

"I'm not taking advantage—everyone knows Carden is going to get staked."

"*Carden?*"

I panicked at my slip and quickly asked, "When will it happen? Tonight?"

He shot me an annoyed look. "No. They're planning a public trial."

I tried to keep my sigh of relief quiet from Ronan. "Any excuse for a little pomp and circumstance."

He gave me a lingering, sidelong look. "I caution you."

Had he heard my relief? Was that what he cautioned me against, or was it just my snarky comment that'd bugged him?

"And there'll be a public execution, I assume?"

"One would assume." Sensing my question before I had a

chance to voice it, he added, "Don't ask me why, Annelise. The Directorate has motivations that are beyond my understanding."

"The Directorate," I repeated. Only recently had I heard the term. It made me think of some sort of star chamber and a bunch of cloaked vampires sitting at a round table, passing judgment. Not unlike what I'd seen on the other island, actually.

Ronan probably heard my question forming, because he upped his pace as the backside of the Acari dorm came into view.

I didn't have much time left, so I spoke quickly to get out one or two of the million questions that were pinging around my brain. "Does that mean not every vampire is in the Directorate? Are they the ones in charge of the island? What are they up to?" By the time he edged around the side of the building, I was jogging to keep up.

We arrived at the front stairs, and Ronan turned, his expression unreadable. He didn't answer me, though. He only told me in a tired voice, "Go to sleep, Ann."

I'd been going on guts and stupidity, and as the heavy dorm door shut behind me, the reality of what I'd done and how I was back safely hit me. As the adrenaline left my body, a weird jiggly feeling creeped up my legs, weakening them beneath me. I held on to the banister as though I were scaling Everest instead of the stairway back to my dorm.

I found that I was eager to see Mei-Ling, to talk to someone and actually have a normal conversation. I wondered if Emma snagged me a dinner roll like I'd asked her to. I was starving.

Between the hunger, the adrenaline, and all my many, many questions, my hands were trembling by the time I managed to unlock my door and get back into my room. My vision had tunneled into two tiny black points.

Mei would be there, waiting for me—I could almost feel her presence in the room. She'd be a friendly face. A voice of reason. I'd confide in her, and we'd figure out how to proceed. Maybe she'd play her flute, and it'd relax my mind, opening it to calm plans and bright ideas.

I shut the door, leaning my head against the doorjamb, feeling so very, very relieved. "You would not believe the day I had."

"Tell me, *querida*."

I shrieked. I actually shrieked, and let me tell you, I wasn't proud of it. But hearing Alcántara's voice was like hearing the chiming of my own personal death knell.

A vampire. *The* vampire.

In our room. *My* room.

Not good.

Distantly, I wondered what he'd done with Mei.

I made myself look calm. Made myself look like what Alcántara might've been expecting, which was a scared, startled girl instead of what I realized just then I really was in my heart of hearts: fearless and focused.

I had new knowledge. I had choices to make. I would no longer be suppressed and controlled. I'd be Annelise Drew, in-control, empowered girl.

And in-control girl had to get her act together. I put a hand to my chest, faking a girlish swoon. "You surprised me."

I summoned strength from deep within. I felt how some of that courage sprang from the wellspring that was Carden's life force flowing through my veins. Was it merely a chemical thing, the vampire's blood giving me a false sense of bravado? Or did this strength spring from the sense that I was no longer in this alone?

BLOOD FEVER

I didn't have time to consider or decide.

Instead, I thought of what the suppressed, fearful girl might say and told him, "I'm not allowed to have boys in my room."

I hoped the naive words made me appear less guilty. Hoped that they would make it seem like I just saw him as a guy, not a vampire. That maybe it would erode the teensiest bit of his power.

"You know very well that I may come and go as I please. You, however. It is perilously close to curfew, and you have been out. Where have you been? You missed dinner."

"I . . . I was working out. I thought I'd go for a run."

"You look pale." He stepped closer. "Strained. Perhaps you need to drink."

Oh God, was he going to try to feed me? From his own body? Instead of fear, it was revulsion that swamped me. My stomach clenched and turned, and it took everything I had not to gag at the thought.

I lied. "I drank earlier. At the dining hall."

"But you were not at the dining hall." He had a half smile on his face, challenging me with the false innocence of his statement.

I lied again. "I swung by super quickly. I wasn't hungry for food, so I didn't stay."

He stood close. My legs were trembling more than ever, my body reeling from the earlier adrenaline dump that'd been followed by relief, followed by this new adrenaline dump. I leaned back against the doorjamb to prevent myself from accidentally swaying into him.

I thought of Carden, shackled in an underground chamber. I thought of the stake that would pierce his body if I lost my cool now.

Alcántara ran a fingertip down my cheek. "You didn't use to lie to me, *cariño*."

"I'm not lying." *Lie, lie, lie.*

He paced a semicircle around me, scanning his eyes up and down my body. He inhaled deeply, and my guess was, he was sniffing for Carden.

I decided an innocent girl would ask, "Is there something wrong?"

He made a throaty, considering sound—"Mmm"—then came to stand before me once more. He wore a peculiar expression. Carden had been very careful with me in the dungeons. If Alcántara thought he'd smell another vampire on me, he'd be mistaken.

And if I'd thought that meant I was in the clear, then I was mistaken.

Because that was when he touched me.

CHAPTER TWENTY-SEVEN

———— ∞∞∞ ————

I n an instant, Alcántara was standing close, and he stepped closer still, tracing his hand along my neck, down my arm.

I repeated my question, my voice gone weak. "Is everything okay?"

"That is just it," he told me in a husky, intimate sort of voice. "I fear it is not all okay. And like a remiss guardian, I wonder where it is I've gone wrong."

He might not have smelled Carden on me, but I could tell he still suspected something—big-time. I thought fast. "On the contrary." I made myself give him a big, brave, beaming grin. "You're an excellent guardian. I've learned so much."

He barked out a laugh, and I had a moment of thinking I'd saved the day, until he said, "Perhaps I've trained you too well?" He pinched my chin between his fingertips, tilting my face up to his.

That smile stayed pasted on my face even as I felt the blood drain from my head. "What do you mean?"

He wasn't giving me an inch of space. "You have been busy, little *Acarita*. What is it you've learned?"

He was in my face, and I could barely think because of it. "I've learned lots of things on the island," I replied in a falsely bright, pretend-innocent tone.

"Don't play with me, girl." His coal black eyes were cold and sharp on me.

The air grew thin around me, and my head became hollow, like I needed oxygen.

Those eyes. He was pulling me in with those eyes. His hand went back to my arm, stroking down; then it swept to my waist. I swallowed hard. He'd touched me before, but never like this. His thumb moved in small circles along my stomach. I couldn't look away.

His voice went hard. "I asked, what do you know?"

Keep it together; keep it together, I chanted in my head, forcing myself not to fall into that gaze. And then another chant came to me, and it was what braced me.

I am roots in the earth. I am water that flows. I am grounded. I am Watcher.

I inhaled again, only this time it was long and slow. A deep breath that brushed the cobwebs from my mind.

"You evade the answer." He raised his other hand and pinched my ear hard between his fingertips.

I fought the urge to flinch away. "I—"

"Do not try me." His thumbnail slid down and sliced the tender flesh of my earlobe.

Pain as sharp and thin as a razor seared me, followed by the hot ooze of my own blood down my neck. I barely felt it, though. I'd had a revelation. I'd learned a thing or two on this island, and

BLOOD FEVER

I could turn it against the vampire who'd brought me here. Oh, the irony.

I could fight his mind, which meant I could fight him.

Could I use these skills to help myself and the people I cared about? Could I use them for what was right instead of unquestioningly helping every vampire who came across my path?

Roots in the earth. Grounded. He wanted Carden dead. I was Carden's alibi, but I could never confess to it without getting us both killed. Because vampire or no, Carden and Alcántara clearly played on different teams.

"My apologies, Master Alcántara," I said in my sincerest tone. He stared at me a moment. I felt that cold hollowness pressing at my mind again, but this time I knew how to hold it at bay. I recalled my climb, focusing on the smallest part of it, a snapshot image of my hand in front of my face, gripping the rocks. "I've been out practicing my new climbing skills, and if I've learned anything, it's that I need to increase my arm strength."

Apparently, my answer had enough of a whiff of truth that he lowered his hand.

I peeked around him, desperate for him to step away and give me an inch of space. It all called for a topic change. I forced my voice to be cheery. "Hey, where's Mei?"

My feigned innocence seemed to mollify him. "The Guidons are keeping her occupied."

The words sent a shiver of foreboding up my spine. He'd wanted me to protect her, but now he'd sent her off with the older girls. Was he done with her?

I didn't want to think of the implications. I could protect her if the Directorate wanted her protected, but once they changed their minds? I couldn't watch her 24-7—I needed to sleep sometime—and I didn't think she had the chops to make it on her own, kooky flute skills or not. "I've been watching out for her, like you said."

I mentally assessed. Mei was so much younger than the Guidons. Some of them wouldn't be able to stop themselves. Amanda had warned me on my first day here—once these girls scented weakness, they became wolves.

"And how is Acari Mei-Ling?" His question might've been on topic, but his voice was distracted. He shifted his weight, stepping closer, brushing his thigh against mine.

I inhaled sharply and covered it up with a tiny cough. He'd flirted with me before, but never like this. I'd have taken slashing fingernails over his *thigh* any day.

"She's great." I tried to lean back, but the doorjamb was hard at my back. It was so weird to have this conversation as he was touching me in totally inappropriate ways. "I think if she can survive this first year, she'll be great." I was rambling, but anything to keep this exchange on the spectrum of normalcy.

"Have you heard her play?"

"I have. She *seeeems*"—the volume of my voice spiked as he leaned in to nuzzle my neck—"really talented. She said she can play a lot of instruments."

He pulled back. "So, you did not find anything extraordinary about her performance?"

How to answer? The urge to protect her overwhelmed me. Being Mei's guardian had gone from an assignment to something personal. I liked her and wanted her safe.

The vampires knew she had a gift, but did they understand just how hypnotic her playing was? If they were to experience the true potency of her power, she'd never be safe from them.

And then a selfish thought flashed into my head: Once the vampires realized what they had in Mei-Ling, she'd be under scrutiny forever—that meant, as her roommate and guardian, I'd be under even more scrutiny.

I decided to play it cool and downplay her talents. "Sure, yeah. Flute's not my thing, though."

Alcántara tilted his head, considering. "Not your . . . *thing*?"

I shrugged it off. "It's kind of shrill, you know?"

His gaze swept along my face, studying me. Finally, he said, "Perhaps she doesn't need your help after all."

Oh God. What had I done? Had I given the wrong answer? The only thing worse than vampires having too much of an interest in her would be them not caring whether she lived or died. "I could tell she was good," I added with quick enthusiasm.

My mind raced ahead. The moment Alcántara left me, I'd need to find her. If she was with a bunch of Guidons, she was probably being eaten alive as we spoke. I didn't know if Vampire/Watcher bonds were common, or how they even worked, but if Alcántara was somehow connected to someone like Masha and he gave the green light, Mei-Ling was toast.

"Let us forget her." His intensity flared, like fresh wood catching in a fire that'd waned. He stepped so close, I had to look up to meet his eyes. "Now it is just you." He brushed the hair from my brow. "And me."

I strained to listen, hoping I'd hear voices of other girls in the hallway. But it was silent. It didn't stop me from saying, "She could come back any minute."

He chuckled. "I've ensured we won't be interrupted. We have been interrupted too many times recently. Too often, another has come between us."

Heat flooded my face—I couldn't help it. He was talking about Carden. "What do you mean?"

"You know who I mean." He pressed the backs of his fingers to my cheek. "Such a pretty blush. It confirms the truth of my words."

I forced myself not to flinch. "I . . . I'm just hot, I think."

His lips peeled into a seductive smile. I saw the glimmer of his fangs and looked away. Looked down. Maybe he'd think I was just being demure.

But then I felt cool pressure under my chin. His fingertip, tilting my face up to his. "Hot indeed, *querida*." The naughty way he said it implied so much more than just my temperature.

These attentions, this intensity, it was like he'd suspected my interests lay elsewhere, and his response was to force the issue with these creepy lingering touches and suggestive words.

Alcántara had flirted with me before. I once thought he might kiss me, in the library, what felt like so long ago now. But his bizarre wooing was different now. There was something in his eyes that hadn't been there before our mission. Or rather, something was *missing* from the look he was giving me, like he was a snake viewing me through glassy, bottomless eyes. Teasing me. Trifling with me.

He cupped my cheek. His other hand remained gripped on my waist. The feel of his fingers curling into the soft flesh of my torso was the only thing reminding me to keep breathing. "There have been certain . . . elements thrown between us."

He began to lean down.

Oh God, oh God, oh God. The words keened in my brain. There was no calm mantra now. *Oh God.*

This was it. There was no escaping. I was pinned between the door and Alcántara's cold, hard body.

"I have met obstacles," he whispered, his mouth so close I felt his lips brush mine. "But no longer."

And then he *kissed* me, and it wasn't like kissing Carden, not at all.

Alcántara's kiss was studied, methodical. Conscientiously thorough. I waited to experience some emotion—desire, longing, any sort of tingling whatsoever—but I didn't feel a thing.

And it wasn't just because we weren't bonded. Alcántara's kiss was different from Carden's because Carden could *kiss*. He'd been my first, so I hadn't realized it before. But now, kissing Alcántara, I knew. Carden . . . just . . . wow.

But I knew better than to spurn the affections of a vampire, particularly one whose fangs were *right there*, and so tried to sense what Alcántara wanted me to do. Technically, his kiss was fine, but something about it was coldly precise. Passionless compared to Carden's all-consuming touch. His lips were cool, and as much as I tried to follow his lead, I felt how my movements were just as stiff and studied in return.

He pulled away. Compared to my kiss with Carden, the contact had been brief. With Carden, I'd fallen into the kiss, into him, from the instant my lips had touched his.

"I thank you for the small intimacy, *mijita*. It was most illuminating." Alcántara gave me a tiny half bow. "I will bid you good night," he said, his voice chilly and polite.

The keening in my mind hitched up a notch, but this time my panic was for an entirely different reason. Had I been too reluctant? Or worse, had he sensed Carden? Detected our bond?

I wouldn't know, because the Spanish vampire swept me aside and was out the door before I could shut my mouth.

CHAPTER TWENTY-EIGHT

ast night, I'd been lucky. Lucky the Guidons hadn't eaten Mei-Ling for a midnight snack. Lucky that Alcántara hadn't torn me limb from limb when he sensed whatever it was he'd sensed in my kiss.

He'd left, and Mei-Ling had been sitting on the floor outside the door, curled into herself.

"Mei." I was still shaky and weirded out from Alcántara's kiss, and it took me a moment to register that she was there and relatively unscathed.

She looked up at me. "Are you okay?"

"Me? How about you?" A welt was rising on her cheekbone, and it made my blood boil. I recognized Masha's whip in that mark. Anger focused me, wiping away the remnants of Alcántara's surreal and creepy touches. "What did they do to you?"

"It's no big deal." She stood and brushed herself off.

I could see that it was, in fact, a big deal. But I knew Mei, which meant I knew not to press the issue. Instead, I asked, "What are you doing out here?"

"They told me not to go in." She glanced at the door as though a dozen vampires might spring out. "You know, while he was in there with you."

I glanced down the hall, the lights dimmed for curfew. "You could at least have waited in the lounge."

She shrugged. "I wanted to be close . . . just in case."

"In case . . ." I'd thought I knew Mei-Ling, but apparently I still had much to learn. "In case I needed help?" My shoulders slumped, I was so completely touched by the sentiment. Though if Alcántara decided he wanted me dead, how anyone could help was beyond me.

"Yeah." She gave me a flicker of a smile.

I scanned her, standing there in her gray Acari uniform tunic and leggings. "Do you even have your flute?"

She shook her head.

I considered the situation. Mei-Ling had been kidnapped here against her will. I was bonded to a vampire who was going to be staked because another vampire decided he stood in the way of a goal. Oh, and apparently, I was the icing-on-the-cake part of that goal.

I was embroiled in a game that was far more complicated than the girl gladiator torture they'd subjected us to in the first semester.

I shooed her into our room, shutting the door behind us. There was work to do, and I didn't waste any time. "Okay, lesson one. Always have that flute. We'll make a special holster or some-thing. You need a way to tuck it in your pants without anyone seeing. It won't break, will it?"

"No," she said, sitting on the edge of her bed, not taking her eyes from me. Her attention was avid, but not in a slavering, I'll-do-whatever-you-tell-me sort of way.

I appreciated the trust. It made me want to help her all the more. "That's good," I told her. "You'll have enough to occupy you with lesson two."

"What's lesson two?"

"I'm making you a better weapon than just a damned flute."

She raised a brow, giving me a sassy look. "I think it's more than just a damned flute."

She'd sounded amused, but when I replied, I was more serious than ever. "Yeah, but can it pierce a heart?"

She looked appalled. "I can't pierce someone's heart."

I had no patience for her revulsion. "First of all, it wouldn't be some*one*'s heart. It'd be some*thing*'s. And, if it were your life or theirs, you bet you could do it. But first, you need a stake."

I'd been thinking about this since the day Ronan had revealed his handmade stakes, slim but lethal, hidden beneath the sleeves of his sweater. One of those stakes had saved my life, killing the Draug that would've killed me. And now I was going to make some for myself. For *us*.

"Where will you get a stake?"

I stood at my bureau, sad but resolved. Because the trouble was, you needed wood to carve a stake. And the only wood I had was my shuriken box. "*Stakes*—plural. I'm gonna make them."

"You're making us *stakes*?"

I opened the drawer. Pulled it out. I hated to do it. I'd not received many gifts in my life, and this had been one of them. Even though it came from a bunch of vampires, it was impossible not to appreciate the gorgeous antique, stained a deep red. The wood had been notched and pieced together by hand. Someone had spent much time carving a crane, etched in black on the lid. "Yup. Hopefully I can get a few out of this."

"Oh, you can't," she exclaimed, seeing the box. "That's too beautiful."

"Then they'll be some mighty pretty stakes." I set aside the throwing stars, wrapped in a swatch of dark velvet. I'd tucked my pencil rubbing of the runes in there, too, and pulled it out, sliding it under my clothes instead. It was a weird compulsion, keeping this memento, but somehow the snippet of ancient Viking graffiti served as a reminder of how banal humanity actually was. How banal it was supposed to be.

I held up the empty box, studied it. And then in a violent motion, I began to wriggle the lid free of the base.

Mei leapt to her feet. "You'll ruin it."

I swung my back to her, holding it out of her reach. "Better the box than us." The hinges slowly gave way, and then my arms jerked as the lid ripped free.

I got to work, popping off the edges of the top and the sides. I'd use it all. "Hopefully, we'll each get two good stakes out of this. Maybe three. They'll be crude, but sharp enough."

I began to sharpen the chunks of wood, using the edge of one of my throwing stars. It reminded me of peeling potatoes.

She sat next to me, enthralled. "What are we going to do with them?"

"You're not going to do anything. You're going to learn how to protect yourself, so you can keep yourself safe if anything happens to me."

"What's going to happen to you?"

Deep in thought, I swept the edge of my shuriken along the

stake, working methodically. Lethal points were gradually emerging from the blunted, splintered ends. "The vampires in charge want Car—Master McCloud dead, even though I'm certain he's innocent. There's more going on with this island than Watcher training."

"And you think if you throw Master Alcántara off stride, you'll get one step closer to uncovering the truth?"

I stopped carving, amazed. "Wow, you really are going all Nancy Drew on me."

"I prefer Buffy references." She gave me a sly grin. "And I want to help."

Ironically, it was the grin that turned my stomach, stopping me. My hands froze in midair. She should've been grinning with friends at the mall, not smiling with me over this macabre endeavor. "I can't let you help me. I mean, you could die, Mei."

She grew serious. "I know."

"Why help? And why me? I mean, we just met. Seriously, I'm just a messed-up seventeen-year-old who's trying to go down swinging. I am so not worthy of your help."

She looked away, thinking, and I expected an adolescent response. But what I got was something far wiser.

"My grandmother used to tell me not to be afraid," she said. "She said the only thing in this world that we should fear is standing still." She met my eyes once more, her expression hard and focused. "The vampires ordered the Tracer to kill my boyfriend. They would've killed my family if I hadn't come. I must not remain still. Evil has been done to me. I can lie down and take it. Or I can stand up and take revenge."

I looked at the crude stakes in my lap. "But this could get you killed."

"I can take action, help you figure out what's going on in this crazy place, and *maybe* get killed instantly. Or I can sit here, doing what I'm told, waiting to get killed *eventually*." She gave me a wry look. "I prefer just ripping off the Band-Aid, thanks."

My mind went back to my creepy run-in with Alcántara. Something had shifted in his lizardy eyes, telling me he might've been done with Mei-Ling. It gave me a chill, but I thought her assessment was probably right. From now on, she would simply be waiting for her eventual death. And it wouldn't be a long wait.

I gave her a quiet smile, then looked down to continue my carving. "Okay, here's what we're going to do."

CHAPTER TWENTY-NINE

———∞∞∞———

I began to explain the situation, but my roommate interrupted
me almost immediately, and I guess I understood why. The
phrase "There's a Draug keeper I need to spy on" wasn't something you heard every day.

I gave her one of my stars to help with the carving, and as we
worked, I told her about Draugs and about the keeper and about
the dire warnings I'd heard about the other side of the island.

I hoped she was right and that she wasn't helping me in vain.
That this actually would be one step toward unraveling the mystery of the island. Because I really liked my peculiar, unpredictable young roomie, and it would devastate me to lose her as I'd
lost Amanda and Judge.

When Mei spoke again, her question was the last one I'd expected. "Is this about that vampire you like?"

I froze. "What do you mean?"

"Oh, come on," she said at once. Then she laughed, and I
realized I'd never heard her laugh before. It was a high, tittering

sound that made me smile despite myself. "You may be able to use your brashness to manipulate and confuse other people, but it doesn't fool me."

"Wait." My hands dropped to my lap. "Full stop. My brashness?"

"Yes," she said, trying not to smile. "*Arrogance* seemed too harsh a word."

"Wow." I gave a little breathy laugh, amazed at this study of my character. "Well, thanks, I guess. So, you're saying I'm— what?—*brash*? And that I use it to *confuse* people?"

She shrugged. Her eyes didn't budge from me, and they were unflinchingly honest and steady. "Maybe *cocky* is the better word."

I laughed nervously. "I like your style, Mei-Ling. Very *Mei-the-Merciless.*"

"See," she said, not to be interrupted. "Just like that. You're dismissive and pretend to be careless, and it confounds people. Nobody ends up seeing the real you. Then they either fear you or hate you, or they just help you, hoping you'll help them someday."

I had been smiling at this bizarre evaluation, but that last statement gutted me. I was reminded how Josh had offered his help, claiming an alliance with me was only smart. "You think people help me because they *fear* me? That just kind of completely bums me out."

She put a tentative hand on my arm. "Not all of us. Not those of us who really know you. We really like you."

I shook my head, unsure what to make of it all. "You're way too much, Mei-Ling."

"So what's the answer?"

VERONICA WOLFF

I laughed again, getting back to my stake, picking up the carving stroke where I'd stopped. My hands were a little shaky after all those true confessions. "You're relentless. I don't even remember the question after all that."

Her smile was prim, and it made her look all of fourteen years old. "Is this all about the vampire you like?"

Discussing Carden seemed like child's play after my very own character assassination, and I caved. Anything to change the subject. "Okay. You win. It's about Carden, the vampire I like." I caught her eye. "Is that what you were after?"

I could only hope she'd noticed my thing with Carden because we were roommates and roommates noticed things and not because my attachment to him was so obvious.

"What's the deal with you two?" Mei-Ling's question was probing, but her gaze was glued to the star and stake in my hands.

Her averted eyes somehow made it easier to reply. "The deal . . ." I wouldn't tell her about the bond, but if she was going to risk her life to help me, I owed her a partial truth. "The deal is, I really like him."

She made a face. "But why? He's a vampire."

"*Why?* He's just different," I said, without thinking.

Her brows scrunched even more. "How?"

"How . . ." I wondered just that. There was the bond. Obviously. But I couldn't tell her that. I trusted her, but that seemed like information that could get her killed, and I was exposing her to enough risk already.

So what else was there? Why did I feel strongly enough about Carden that I'd risk my life—risk my friend's life—to save him?

"He treats me like a real person," I began, trying to put exact words to my feelings. I swept the blade down the wood, sharpening it, putting all my emotion behind it. I opened my mind, opened my *heart*, probing just what it was that I felt. "Like I'm my own unique individual. Not some kid, or someone who's been slapped around, or someone who's good at school. Maybe it was because we met on the other island, away from here, without a context. But when I met Carden, he met me as *me*."

I considered my feelings in light of what Mei had just said about me. Carden didn't fear me—the thought was laughable. And he definitely didn't need my help. He needed me, because of the bond—but I imagined he could bond with any pretty young thing.

No, he liked me. And I liked him. He made me laugh. He was light where I was dark, seeing the humor in things that'd felt so grimly serious to me. Carden gave me hope.

I couldn't lose that hope.

"I think I need him." It went beyond the physical need of our bond. To lose Carden now would make me feel lost. It would steal my purpose, my hope. "I can't lose him," I told her, and it felt like a confession, dredged from the darkest depths of my soul.

"Then count me in." She'd completed a stake, and she put it on the bed with confidence. It was crude, marbled red and brown and black where she'd scraped the paint from the wood, but it looked sharp. It looked like something that could pierce a heart. "So, you think the Draug keeper knows something."

"I didn't see him up close, but the guy looks like he's seen some serious stuff. For all I know, he could be the killer."

"Check," she said with a nod. "We're going to find the Draug keeper. And then what?"

What *would* we do next? Good question. "Sit down for a nice chitchat?"

"Yeah, right." Mei selected a new strip of wood and began to carve. "We could capture him. Interrogate him. Like a citizen's arrest."

"You've been watching too much *Law & Order*." I considered it. I knew I—*we*—needed to take action.

Seeing my star wielded so carefully in her hands somehow cemented our friendship. It made me feel like we could figure this out. As I watched her painstaking strokes, a plan formed in my head. "I could act as bait. Have a Draug attack me. If the keeper is good, he'll help me. If he's bad . . ."

"He'll sic the whole herd on you?" Mei looked aghast. "That doesn't sound like a great plan."

"No, listen, you'll be there with your flute." The more I thought about it, the more perfect it seemed. "When you play, everyone will get all calm and tractable. If he's the killer, we'll tie him up and Carden goes free. If not, we'll ask him questions, maybe get proof enough to show that Carden's not the murderer."

"*Carden*, huh?" She raised a brow.

I sat tall, placing my last stake on our small but respectable pile. "Yes. Carden." It felt good to be honest, if only partly so.

But then Mei frowned. "What if you're hurt?"

"I'll be fine," I assured her, trying to believe my own words. The truth was, I expected to get an injury or two. It didn't thrill me, but one or two more scratches taken for the cause wouldn't kill me.

She put her last stake down and we admired our handiwork. Six wooden stakes. They weren't nearly as pretty as my antique box had been, but they promised extra protection, and that was all the pretty I needed.

"Nice work," I said.

Our eyes met. Mei-Ling asked gravely, "Will we leave to-night?"

"God, no," I exclaimed with a laugh. "Do you know what's crawling around out there at night? *Eeesh*." I shuddered. "No. We'll go tomorrow, when the sun is at its highest." Alcántara had once told me himself—vampires can roam about in the sunlight, they just don't relish it. "Daylight won't protect us from every-thing, but it might offer a little cover."

I'd gathered from Ronan that we had a little time before the trial—though I wasn't ready to confess Ronan's sympathies just yet. There'd been enough revelations for one evening. Instead, I added simply, "No need to go off stupidly half-cocked."

"Right," she said with a smile. "We'll go off stupidly *all-the-way*-cocked."

We smiled grim smiles, and though I was nervous, it felt good to share this resolve. To be taking action.

I crawled into bed, praying we woke to an unusually bright morning. Honesty had cleared my conscience, and sleep came fast and hard.

Fantasies of Carden were waiting for me there.

CHAPTER THIRTY

I awoke feeling heat. Vague images of Carden shimmered on the edges of my mind, but as hard as I tried, I couldn't grasp them. I couldn't remember my dream.

It angered me. Focused me. Intensified my urgency.

I wouldn't lose him. I would have that heat. I would make it real, experience it live and in person, and not just as a stolen moment in a pitch-black dungeon, either.

The thought shot my eyes open. "Rise and shine," I croaked to Mei, still asleep in her bed.

I hopped up to peek out the blinds. Warmth still pulsed through my body, enough that part of me could almost believe we'd woken to a warm day.

Mei rolled to her side, watching as I pulled aside the blinds. "Well?"

I scowled. "It's as gray and bleak as ever."

"Of course it is," she said, throwing off her blankets.

I fumbled into my uniform as quickly as I could, the brisk morning air a shock. "You ready to play that flute later?"

"Always," she said, sounding slightly shivery as she pulled on her own clothes. "But are *you* ready to be attacked by the weird Draug guy? Wait"—she stopped and held up a hand—"don't tell me. You were born ready, right?"

It elicited a much-needed smile from me. "Right."

The day took forever. We had only three hours between the time her Phenomena class ended and my Medieval Musicianship class began. It'd have to be enough for us to sneak away and find the Draug keeper.

"We need to go as fast as we can," I told her, breaking into a jog. "You up for it?"

She nodded, falling into my rhythm. "What should we do if we're spotted?"

"If anyone sees us, we'll tell them we're just out for a run."

"All the way out here?" She shot me a look. "This is way off the path."

"The vamps don't tend to roam around this time of day," I said, hoping I was right. "Nobody will see us." But I upped my pace all the same.

I knew to keep to the hilltops, and as we neared the spot, I got onto my belly to scoot to the edge, gesturing for Mei-Ling to do the same. We studied the valley below. When I'd last spied the keeper, it had been nighttime, but the sun was up now, and the place didn't exactly sparkle in the light of day.

"Creepy," Mei whispered.

"Totally creepy," I agreed in what was the understatement of the year.

"It's like a horror movie down there," Mei said.

I'd seen the cages glimmering in the dark, and I saw them clearly now, a row of steel pens, holding Draug in various states of decay and derangement. Some rattled cage bars, some snapped and snarled at each other, and every one of them looked feral and very rabidly hungry.

"Is that where he lives, you think?" Mei pointed to a small, one-story building set off from the pens. Thick, sloppy coats of graying whitewash couldn't conceal its crumbling stone walls. At my shrug, she said, "Maybe he is the killer."

"Sure seems like a decent candidate." Creaking caught my attention. The body of a goat hung from a nearby tree, spinning and swaying slightly in the breeze, blood dripping from its slashed throat into a bucket underneath. "Looks like he's familiar with the concept of exsanguination."

Mei put a hand to her mouth, looking ill. "I'll bet he drains his victims to feed to the Draug."

"We'll see soon enough," I said, trying to keep a level head. "You stay here."

Mei put a hand on my arm. "Are you sure about this?" She looked pale, and I imagined I probably did, too.

"I'm sure. You stay on higher ground. Just keep that flute handy."

"The stakes, too?"

"All of it." I scanned until I found him—the Draug keeper. He was in a corral on the far side of the valley, bustling his way through a mob of goats who were bumping and nipping at him. "Looks like it's feeding time." Other goats ignored him, instead skittering and hopping around, looking wild-eyed. I wondered if they'd caught the Draugs' scent and recognized a predator.

"It's go time," I said. "I'm going to sneak down while Farmer John is dealing with his herd. I'll wait till most of the Draug are back in their pens; then I'll show up and see what attacks."

Mei held up her flute. "I'll be waiting."

Our eyes met and held, and we shared a grave nod. Mei-Ling was just a kid from Long Island, and here she was, ready to play her weird little instrument, risking her life to save mine. And I'd thought I didn't have friends.

Giving her a small smile, I said, "I know you will be."

I eased over the back side of the hill, cursing the pitter of displaced gravel as I skidded down. I just had to hope the groans of hungry Draug would drown out the sound.

I edged around the base of the hill and sprinted to a rocky outcropping. It'd provide cover enough for me to spy on the scene before acting—I needed to make sure every last one of those Draug were penned before I opened myself to attack. I figured Mei and I could easily handle one sociopathic Draug keeper—he was probably only human, right?—but I wasn't so sure what would happen if we added some undead to the mix.

Panting, I leaned against the rock to catch my breath. Time for a weapons check. I wriggled my arms, feeling the reassuring poke of my stakes where I'd hidden them at my forearms. My stars, though, those I needed to see for myself. I pulled all four from my boots and held them at the ready.

I heard the goats now, *mehhing* and *baahhing*, their voices comically low and unconcerned. The smell came to me clearly now, too, the stench of rotting Draug masking any livestock stink there might've been in the air.

Inch by inch, I edged around to peek from behind the rock. I'd heard the goats, and now I saw them, jostling each other, eating.

And the Draug keeper was . . .

Gone.

My heart kicked up a notch. I pressed my body against the rock, trying to see as much as I could without actually revealing myself. Did Mei-Ling still see him from her perch? Because I'd lost sight of the guy completely.

"Who they sending now?" a man's voice asked.

"Oh crap," I exclaimed, stumbling backward, startling like a child.

It was the Draug keeper, up close. I braced for him to eviscerate me for my language, but he only laughed. His face was weathered, but he wasn't ancient, not by a long shot. Rather, he looked like someone's very vital, somewhat eccentric, and fairly soiled grandpa.

He studied me, taking in my uniform and the stars in my hand. "You work for the vampires. Well, you tell them things you're not the best spy, eh?"

"I'm not a spy." Was this his way of toying with me? Because he sure wasn't acting like he was going to kill me.

His eyes narrowed to slits. "Who sent you?"

I pulled my shoulders back. I stood tall, but I felt cornered. The rock was a cold wall cutting into my back. "Nobody sent me."

"Mm-hm," he grunted, continuing to give me a critical eye.

I gave him a critical eye right back. He carried a shepherd's crook and a thin, yellow stick that I assumed was some sort of cattle prod. I wouldn't let him get close enough for me to find out.

He twitched his head. "Well, girl? You don't get up off that cold rock, you'll catch your death."

Catch my death. His ominous words galvanized me. I readied

for his attack, and let the star I held in my right hand slide between my fingertips.

He curled his lip. "You come to kill me?"

"What?" I inched sideways and felt the tug of my uniform as
it snagged on rock. "No."

He pointed at the stars I gripped in my left hand. "Then why
you got those? You gonna kill me, just get it over with. Or don't.
It's time for tea."

It was the weirdest, most normal thing I could imagine hearing. But then his eyes widened, and suddenly he looked like a
crazy man.

Here it came. His attack. I braced.

"Stop there," I warned.

But he didn't listen. He leapt.

CHAPTER THIRTY-ONE

M y arm shot up. Pebbles rained down on me. Mei-Ling,
getting into position on the hillside above. She wouldn't
let me down.

"Back!" he shouted, bounding forward again.

"*You* get back, old man." I took aim, my eyes zeroing in on
his throat.

But then I realized he wasn't looking at me. He wasn't attack-
ing *me*. Instead, he lurched past, shoving me aside. He waved that
yellow stick, shouting again. "Get back."

I spun. "Oh God," I yelped. A Draug. *Close.* "What the . . . ?
Crap!" I skittered back, scraping my arm along the rock. "Where'd
that—"

"Fool thing." He clouted the Draug on its head, then jabbed
it with his prod. "Get back." There was an electrical *zzt* sound
followed by the stink of burnt flesh.

The Draug hunched and held its head, and the keeper prodded
it all the way back into its pen.

I could only gape at the man as he returned. "Aren't you afraid?"

He gave me a funny look. "Of that thing?"

"Yes, of that thing." I'd almost been killed by such a thing twice now. Had known several girls who *had* been killed.

He shoved his cattle prod between his belt and waistband. "It don't scare me."

My eyes shot to the pen. "But they could kill you." They writhed madly now, riled up, sensing aberrations—a new human, unusual activity, singed flesh.

"So could you."

I looked at him, dumbfounded. I guessed I *could* kill him. Probably pretty easily, especially if I could get that cattle prod out of the equation.

He sucked at his teeth and spat. "It's just a dumb beast," he told me, and it sounded like he meant his matter-of-fact tone to be reassuring. "Think of 'em like livestock. My father did this job, and his father before him. Probably *easier* than working livestock."

He headed toward his stone hovel, and I hopped into step, catching up and following close. "How come they don't kill you?"

"You got a lot of questions for a girl who's nobody's spy."

I tried my best innocent smile. "It's because . . . I've got a curious mind?"

He stopped at the front door and gave me a frank look. "Maybe that's it."

I repeated my question, rephrasing it. "So how come you're safe with them, but they'd kill me?"

"How come this, how come that." He went inside and pulled

a chain, lighting the room's single hanging bulb. There was a small fireplace along the back wall, a cot in one corner, and a sink, ancient stove, and old-fashioned fridge in the other. Long cords dangled from a lone wall socket in what looked like a major electrical hazard. The place was dim and smelled musty and damp.

I did a quick scan, looking for a cleaver, or machete, or ax that he might bust out and use to slaughter me, but didn't see any.

"Well? You gonna sit?" He filled a banged-up kettle with water and put it on the stove. "Or did those things in the castle whoop your bottom too hard?" He cackled at his own joke.

I ventured all the way in, pulling a three-legged stool from what I guessed was his dining table. "No, I can sit."

"You're not scared, are you?"

"Should I be?" It took no time for my eyes to adjust to the gloomy lighting, and I stared openly now.

He cackled again. "It's why you're alive. The Draug, they feed on fear."

"And blood." I made a little chuff of a laugh, as if to say *duh*.

But the old man didn't like that much. His face hardened. "You're not listening, girl."

I hadn't realized he was telling. "Oh. Sorry. I didn't realize. So . . . you'll tell me why they don't kill you?"

"They don't kill me because I'm not afraid."

"I don't get it."

He stopped what he was doing at the stove to turn and face me. "Draug drink blood, sure. They need it to live, like you need water. But what they *crave* is fear. Crave, like you crave meat or sugar or love. They're creatures of fear. Fear makes them feel alive. They'll cut you for your blood, but they kill you for your fear."

His speech silenced me.

He put a chipped teacup in front of me, and it was surreal, seeing this formerly fine piece of china, decorated with tiny pink rosebuds, its rim tarnished a faint tinny color where it'd once been painted gold. "Drink," he said. "Hope you like the goat blood."

I stared in horror at the cup, and he cackled again, long and loud, ending in a racking cough. He cleared his throat and spat into the sink. "You'll face down demons, holding naught but those wee Christmas stars, but you can't take a joke." He nodded toward the teacup. "That's good tea, girl. Scottish breakfast. Drink up."

I kept wary eyes on him as I picked up the cup. I was still trying to decide if the old man was simply eccentric or full-on insane.

But the warm cup stilled my trembling fingers and the tea did smell divine. I blew on it and took a sip. It was good, and it warmed something inside me that I hadn't realized had been chilled. It gave me courage. "What are they, anyway? The Draug, I mean."

He plopped down on a stool across from me. "They tried to be vampires. Didn't make it."

I pictured the creatures in my mind's eye. They were in the shape of men, though I knew that many had been no more than boys. "No, I mean, how do they come to be? Did the vampires mess up? Did something go wrong in the change?"

He shrugged. "There's a test. These are them what didn't pass."

I tried to make sense of his weird accent. "You mean like a written exam or a physical or something?"

"A test. *The* test. Boys go into the cave and they either come out Vampire or they come out the Draug."

He'd said *the* cave, not *a* cave. It struck me who could tell me about this test and this cave. Carden. The need to save him was more urgent than ever, and it felt like this was somehow connected. "What happens in the cave?"

"Can't say for sure." He sipped his tea as casually as though we were discussing the weather.

I studied the old man, studied his features and his movements, wondering—as I did whenever I spotted a human—if this might've been some relative of Ronan's. "What's your name?"

He peered hard at me, looking bemused. "That's something I don't generally tell strangers."

"I'm Drew. Well, Annelise Drew, but people call me Drew. So there. No longer a stranger." I sipped my tea, trying hard to look as nonchalant as I'd made my voice sound.

He did that cackly laugh of his, only lower this time. "I'm Tom. And folk just call me Tom."

Was this guy actually okay? Granted, he was a strange old dude and, wow, he smelled, but he didn't strike me as a sociopathic killer. Which brought me back to square one: Who *was* the sociopathic killer?

What the hell . . . I figured I had nothing to lose and said, "So, Tom. I don't suppose you've seen anything strange, have you?"

He looked at me like I was the nutter, not him.

"Okay," I quickly amended. "I know there's lots of strange stuff. But girls have been dying." Something in his cheek twitched, and I sped up. "I know—that tends to happen a lot around here. But there have been mysterious killings, too, stuff like bodies being drained, and nobody knows who's doing it."

He bristled. "Why would I know?"

"Because you seem like the type of gentleman who notices things," I said, turning on the charm. I was rewarded with another cackle.

He nodded, looking decided about something. "Aye, and so I do see things. Like that new vampire who's roaming about."

A horrific thought sideswiped me. *Carden.* Carden was a new vampire.

I'd been with him during one of the killings, though. I knew he was innocent. Wasn't he?

Still, I had to ask. "What does this new vampire look like?" I held my breath, waiting for the answer.

"Pale. Shifty. Like all the vampires look."

"Please." I'd aimed for exasperated, but my voice came out sounding helpless and lost. "Dark hair? Light hair?" After a moment's hesitation, I added, "Kilt?"

He gave me a cockeyed look. "Kilt? Nah, not the kilted one. This one is smaller, with white hair."

"White hair?" I hadn't seen any white-haired vamps.

"Dead white."

I sat forward on my stool, feeling electrified. "You mean he's old? Or, rather, was older when he changed?"

Tom's expression shuttered. "Teatime's done. Talk's done, too. You be off now. Feeding time. Gonna get messy around here real soon."

I carried my cup to the sink. Before he could disappear out the door, I asked, "One more question?"

"Can I stop you?"

With a smile, I shook my head.

"Well, girl." He rapped his staff impatiently in the dirt. "Spit it out."

"What you just told me . . . If there really is a rogue vampire wandering around . . ." This man had seen the real killer—it could be the ultimate proof, clearing Carden for good. "Would you tell the vampires for me?"

"Already did."

CHAPTER THIRTY-TWO

———— ∞∞∞ ————

"He already did?" Mei–Ling looked at me in disbelief. We were half jogging, half running back to campus. Not only was it getting perilously close to class time, but we were also beginning to freak out about being so far off the path.

A small trail led down the hillside, to a narrow stretch of beach. I felt exposed on the foreign terrain and hoped to do a big chunk of our backtracking along the coastline. The stretch of navigable beach wouldn't last forever, but a wall of rocks might shelter us from view.

"What do you mean the Draug keeper told the vampires Carden was innocent?"

I shot her a look. "Exactly what I said. He told the Directorate he'd seen the killer and it wasn't Carden." The beach flattened out, and I upped my pace. "We need to hustle. Can't have you late for Dagursson."

But being late wasn't the biggest thing on my mind. I feared there'd be no stopping the Directorate. They didn't care about catching any killer—they just wanted Carden dead. Part of me was terrified they might've even killed him already. Though some other part believed I'd know instantly if he were gone.

Either way, I wanted, longed, to be closer to him. Being so far apart made me feel . . . off. Wrong.

And, realistically speaking, if I were to be caught now, it'd raise all kinds of alarms. It was no secret Carden and I had often been seen together. Me off-roading so blatantly would get both of us killed.

"Slow down a sec." Mei-Ling held up her hand and stopped, bending and grasping her knees to catch her breath. "If they know he's innocent"—she looked up at me, panting—"why haven't they freed him?"

They didn't free Carden because this was all a ploy—*Alcántara's* ploy—to frame him. To see him killed. But why? An old grudge? Jealousy? And what did *I* have to do with it? But I was too afraid to say all that. Finally, I spoke all the truth that needed to be said. "All I know is that I have to get him out of there."

Mei stood, and we set off again. "What now?"

We were still moving briskly, but not as fast as before, and it frustrated me. I wanted to race home. But seeing her hand clutching the stitch in her side, I forced myself to let up. I used the easier pace as an opportunity to think. "I guess we stick to the original plan, only instead of using me as bait to catch the Draug keeper, we're going to lure a rogue vampire instead."

"No way," she said. "You'll get kill—"

The sound of heavy footfalls startled us, silenced us—bodies jumping from the rocks, landing behind us. "Hello, Acari. You're very far from home." It was Masha. *Of course.*

I grabbed Mei-Ling's arm as I turned, shoving her behind me. "I could say the same about you."

I needed to protect my roommate, and not because Alcántara had ordered it. I'd guard her because it was what I wanted to do.

"I've been looking for you." She prowled toward us. "Hunting for you."

How to play it? With bluster? Humor? Aggression? I opted for some mix of the three. I plucked the stars from my boot. "Did you miss me?"

"Nobody will miss you. This time, you're not going back."

"Wow, so you're really going to kill me? Because, you know, you've tried before." My expression was calm, but my mind raced, assessing. Masha was with two girls, both Guidons. I spotted a butterfly knife and one throwing knife. I didn't see her whip, but I knew it was there, waiting for me.

"I won't fail again." She strolled closer, eyeing us with a wicked smile on her face. "I think it's time to dispense with *all* the *hos* on this island."

I had to laugh. "So dire, Masha. And yet so predictable."

Mei tried to push out from behind me. "Can't you come up with some new material?"

I dug my fingers into her arm, holding her in place, hissing, "Easy." I adored her spunk, but was painfully aware that all she had were a few homemade stakes plus a flute in her pocket—and a fat lot of help *that* would be. The vampires saw it as a weapon, but it was one of magnificent subtlety, an instrument to dull and control the masses. Unless she used it to jab at an eye or two, it wouldn't do us any good in a brawl. And if my roommate got close enough to be jabbing at these girls with a flute, it'd be the last thing she ever did.

I took a step back. A rock wall on one side and the sea on the other—*not* a great place for a fight. "Yeah, Masha, how about some new slurs to add to the mix?"

"I believe I am done talking," she said, and unfurled that whip.

"*There* it is," I said. "I was beginning to think maybe Alcántara had confiscated your weapon again."

"Oh no. And I have better news. Hugo said I might kill you now." She laughed at what must've been my goggle-eyed expression. "Do I surprise you?"

I gathered my wits, and quick. "Not at all," I told her with what I thought was admirable calm. But I *was* surprised. Alcántara had sanctioned my death, which meant he hadn't been fooled by my act. He knew there was something between me and Carden—I was sure of it now. "He *told* you to kill me?"

"Not precisely." She waved her hand as though annoyed with such minor details. "He told me he wouldn't stop me. Same thing."

I hoped it wasn't the same thing. If I survived, I didn't want to return to campus only to be butchered by Alcántara himself.

But I couldn't think about that now. I had more pressing issues, namely Masha and her pals. She looked eager to knock me off for good. If she was playing for keeps, it meant only one of us would be getting out of this alive.

I had more than just weaponry at my disposal—she might've had a whip, but my tongue could get in some pretty savage lashes—and if I wanted to survive this, I'd need to bring every last skill. I gave a dramatic shrug. "I guess he didn't like our kiss any more than I did," I said, aiming straight for her jealous little heart.

Masha's face turned ugly with fury. *Bull's-eye.*

I gave her an innocent smile. "Oh, you didn't know we kissed?"

"Hugo kisses many girls. But he keeps few. You, he is done with." Her arm flew out before I had a chance to react. Her whip snapped, and leather kissed my jaw, the pain instant and hot. She smiled. "I've been waiting for this day."

"Oh—me, too." Ignoring the trickle of blood tickling down my neck, I opened my senses to the periphery, trying to guess everyone's next moves.

Mei-Ling was doing something at my back. Pulling out her stakes, I guessed. But I couldn't let her get in the fray. She didn't have enough experience—not against trained killers like these Guidons. Chances were, if she pulled a weapon on them, it would only get turned and used on *her.*

"I only wish we had an audience," I said as I backed into the rock wall. It'd stop Mei from doing something brave and stupid, plus it'd protect both our backs. "Everyone could watch as we take you and your gal pals down."

"We?" One of the Guidons laughed. "*We?* Seems like your *ho* friend here is useless."

The other girl stepped forward, closing in. "Good luck with that."

Masha cut in front of them, pacing a half circle before me, poised like a boxer. "We don't need an audience. When I kill you, everyone will hear about it. Everyone will finally know what trash you are."

The other Guidons pulled out their weapons. I heard that butterfly knife flicking open and shut, *click-click. Click-click.*

Three against one, not counting my roommate, whom I

needed to get out of there. I'd concealed Mei-Ling's gift from Alcántara, and now it was my fault that her life was forfeit. I'd do everything in my power to continue protecting her *and* her secret.

This wasn't going to be a normal stand-in-place-and-duke-it-out sort of fight. Outnumbered like this, I'd need to keep moving, getting in whatever hits I could. I couldn't guard Mei and keep myself alive at the same time.

I must've had a death grip on her arm, because she snarled in my ear, "Let go." I'd backed us against one of the rocks and was edging along the side. "I can help."

I ignored her, keeping my sole focus on Masha. "You don't have to do this, you know." I'd keep her talking as I inched farther sideways, waiting for a plan to present itself. If I stood still and three girls jumped me—jumped us—that would be it. They'd be clearing bits of us off the rocks for a vampire snack.

"I don't have to do this," Masha agreed magnanimously. "But I want to. I want to see you dead, Acari Drew. Your friend, too. Hugo says she also no longer matters." She craned her neck, trying to catch Mei's eye. "Hear that, little girl? You no longer matter. Step out from your hiding place. I'll make it quick. I promise."

I stepped aside, shoving Mei. "Run."

My roommate flinched away, pushing out from behind me, looking pissed. "I won't leave you."

"Go, run, little girl," Masha purred. "We like to chase."

"Leave her out of this." I shoved Mei again, but she didn't budge. "*Go.* Get out of here."

Masha shook out her whip, a cascading strip of black leather, so elegant and fluid in her hands. "Hugo thought he wanted her. He said she's fair game now."

"I won't let you touch her." I honed in on Masha's neck. Only one of us would survive.

Masha giggled. "Said *you're* fair game."

"All's fair, isn't that what they say?" I pinched a star between my fingertips, eyes on her jugular. I threw.

But Masha darted aside, and my shuriken flew past her, arcing and dropping into the sand. "Too slow," she said. "You're not fast enough to beat me. Not strong enough." Large rocks littered the base of the hillside, and she sprang onto one of them, cracking her whip at me as she spun into place.

But I was faster this time. I ducked and threw, and my star hit her arm, still extended in midair. I laughed, feeling momentarily giddy with the tiny success. "I am smart enough," I said. "Smarter than you, Masha. And you hate that. It's why Alcántara—why *Hugo*—wanted me."

"He doesn't want you anymore." She shook her whip out, twirling it from where she stood on her perch. "You're not good enough. You're nothing anymore."

I slid another star into position. Only two left—I'd run out soon, and if I had any hope of surviving, this fight would have to get sloppy. Fists, sand, seawater . . . whatever it took to win.

Which meant I really had to get Mei-Ling out of there. I slammed my hip into her, hard. *"Go."*

Finally she listened. She took off, and hearing her scuffling, frantic footfalls, something in my chest released. I needed her safe—I wouldn't have her die on account of me.

But then one of the Guidons took off, chasing her. She was a strong, broad one, and she sped after Mei, flicking open her butterfly blade as she ran.

I didn't think. My right hand wasn't in a good position, so I punched my left arm out, sliding the stake from my sleeve into my hand, and impaled the Guidon in the chest as she flew by.

Her body bucked in midair, and she dropped, spasming in the sand. Dead.

Masha's face hardened, her eyes narrowing, glittering with hatred. "Lucky hit."

I spared a quick glance for the remaining Guidon. "Two on one, Masha. I think you should leave Mei-Ling out of this. You might need all the help you can get."

"We'll find her," Masha said. "Don't worry. We'll just get rid of you first."

I'd pinned my focus on Masha and realized too late the other Guidon was on the move, rustling with something. Masha cracked her whip, aimed at my face, and I ducked, but as I did, I heard the sickening meaty *thunk* of the other girl's throwing knife skewering my shoulder.

I stumbled back a step. "God*dammit*."

I tore the blade out, which was stupid. Combat medicine rule number one: When stabbed, do not remove object from wound. Blood flowed from my body in a hot gush, soaking the front of my shirt almost instantly.

I slung the blade back at her, but it was my left hand, wet with my own blood, and my throw went wide.

I clutched my shoulder, backing away. So much blood. It would summon something to us, for sure. I imagined I heard the distant snarling and moaning of the Draug already, rattling in their cages.

The Guidon plucked her knife from the sand and closed in. "I think it's *you* who needs help, Acari Drew."

I needed to keep moving. Blood loss would weaken me. I

backed up, but slammed straight into the wall of rocks. I darted a look up and from side to side. It was boulders to either side of me and the steep hillside above.

"Cornered," the Guidon taunted. "Like a little rat."

Masha was on the move. I heard the click of scattering rocks as she began to climb. I couldn't let her get above my head. I had to separate my two opponents.

"Crap." I knew what I had to do, and I hated it. Masha had disappeared onto the rocks, but I knew better than to worry about her when I had a deadly Guidon right in front of me. *"Crap,"* I repeated, taking off toward the water.

I heard the girl follow, and I spun, jogging backward, and threw my star. Hit.

"Bitch," she shrieked. Stumbled. Fell. But she rolled back to a squat at once, glaring at me. She didn't pull her eyes from me as she plucked my star from where it'd embedded in her foot. She did a little limp-hop and began running after me again, almost as fast as before.

I turned and hauled ass for the water, not sure what my plan was. I took up my last star and spun around again, facing her. I threw, but she bobbed out of the way at the last second and laughed as it went wide.

Slowing to a jog, she held her throwing blade between her fingers, showing it off. "Need a weapon?"

"Nah, I'm good." I slid the last two homemade stakes from my sleeves.

"Clever." She prowled toward me, her blade poised for action.

I lunged, taking her by surprise, slamming my stakes at her from either side. Water, sand, and blood made my grip slick, and one grazed her arm in a nearly useless hit and flew from my hand, but the other managed to penetrate the thick muscle at her shoulder.

She yowled and pulled the wood free, hurling it into the water.

I gave her a gratified smile. "Clever. That's me."

Furious, she ran at me with her knife, slashing wildly, and her blade sliced my arm.

I sidestepped toward the water, managing to avoid another of her wild thrashes. "Easy, cowgirl."

"Oh, it is easy." She bobbed toward me, stabbing at the air like a fencer, and I hopped back. But then she leapt, slicing too quickly for me, slashing my belly. The wound was shallow, but the stinging seawater brought tears to my eyes. "Time's up, Drew."

I flew into her, grabbing her head. "Not quite." Her hair was done in a long braid, and I snatched it, wound it around my hand, and yanked her head down.

She grunted and sprang away, still holding on to that blade, and stabbed at my belly. I flinched aside and felt the hot sizzle of steel along the side of my waist.

We were in the breakers now, and a big wave slapped us, sending us both stumbling. As she twisted back into position, she threw her knife. I saw the move coming and swatted it away before it could pierce me, but still it slashed the side of my hand, a hot sting to join all the others.

I looked down to see if I could find and retrieve her weapon, but it was gone. Blood had turned the seawater pink at my feet.

Neither of us had any weapons now. I dove for her, and we fell into each other, and the calf-high waves swirled and sucked at our feet as we grappled. I had to be faster, meaner. I grasped at the air for whatever I could grab, pulling a fistful of hair, scratching at her cheek, flailing my legs to get in whatever kicks I could.

She did the same, pulling my ear, biting my shoulder. I slammed my hand against the side of her head, cupped over her ear. She stumbled, momentarily dazed, and I hit again, curling my body hard, tangling my fingers in her braid, bringing her head down and my knee up into her throat. I heard a bone crunch. Heard her exhale a strange, squeaking breath.

She dropped, facedown in the surf. Her body bobbed up and down, looking like a peaceful bit of seaweed floating in the breakers. Dead.

I swiped a hot tear from my face, shaking from adrenaline. I hated this.

But I wasn't done. Would I ever be done?

Because now there was Masha.

CHAPTER THIRTY-THREE

I was tired. All I wanted was to find Carden. He'd make this all better. It'd been so long since I'd tasted him. I needed him, only now I didn't know where my physical need for the blood ended and the simple needs of my heart began.

I could run. But Masha would be there waiting for me at the top. I couldn't stay on this beach forever. No, I needed to face her. To fight.

And then it hit me. *Mei-Ling.*

She was out there. Maybe even now, facing down Masha.

I raced up the beach. I needed to get to higher ground. My legs pumped while I scanned the hillside for the best route up.

It was steeper here, barely a hill, almost a cliff face. I'd have to clamber on all fours. Then climb.

I sprang onto a low rock, hopped onto another, hoisted myself atop a boulder, and set to climbing. Carden's words came to me. *Trust your legs,* he'd said. My legs were strong. *I* was strong. I could do this.

As I wriggled over the top, I sent a brief thanks to Priti for putting us through so many arduous climbing drills over the past weeks. I'd never complain about one of her classes again.

I rolled onto my feet, and there Masha sat, waiting for me, looking like Buddha on the mountaintop. "You have no weapons, Acari."

"Hasn't seemed to hinder me before, *Guidon*." I was relieved she'd waited for me—it had to mean Mei was safe.

But something about that last fight had deflated me—maybe it was that I still didn't even know the girl's name. Whatever the reason, I had an idea and it didn't involve weaponry.

I walked toward her. "Why are you doing this? Why are you always fighting me? Think how strong we'd be if we sided together. If the girls were in this together. It doesn't have to be like this."

She looked at me like I'd gone insane. "Who's to say I don't like it like this? You're so stupid. You brag how smart, how clever you are. But you are just stupid. You had a chance with Hugo, and you threw it away."

"This is about Alcántara? Are you kidding? We're out here in the middle of nowhere, fighting for our lives, and you're making this about a *guy*?"

"Not just *a guy*." She gave me a suggestive smile.

"Ew. Whatever." I put up my hands—the last thing I wanted was to hear Masha's naughty details. "Why are you even siding with him? He'd have you as his slave if you let him." I stepped closer, feeling brave that her whip had yet to make an appearance. "They're killing us, Masha. Where do they take the bodies? Don't think for a second they wouldn't take *you* there. Don't you want to go home?"

"This is my home now. Hugo, my family."

It zeroed in on a suspicion I'd had. "You're bonded with him, aren't you?"

She flew to her feet, whip in hand. "What do you know?"

I put my hands up. "Easy. I don't know jack about you and *Hugo*." Though I did have a million questions, like, why had Alcántara been interested in me? Had he wanted to bond with me, too? Could vampires bond with more than one person at a time, or would his interest in me have eventually meant Masha's decline?

I sensed I was onto the reason for her irrational hatred of me, only now was totally not the time to address it with her. Instead, I said, "I'm just saying, Master Al seems like a pretty crap family. And I should know." I'd left a man who'd kept me under his thumb.

I'd never be under another thumb again without giving a fight.

I took a wary step closer. "It doesn't have to be like this."

"You're right. I don't have to listen to your boring chatter." She unfurled her whip. "I'm going to kill you. Then I'll find your little friend and kill her, too."

"Good luck with that." I knew what was coming and got into a fighting stance, only this time I slid my sleeves over my hands. "Isn't that what your friend told me earlier?"

"My friend wasn't as strong as I am." She gave her whip a twirl. "My friend didn't have Hugo's blood running through her veins."

"Ah, so you are bonded." But I smiled anyway, because I knew something Masha didn't: I had *Carden's* blood running through *my* veins. It'd make me just as strong.

Masha hauled back her arm and cracked her whip, but I'd seen it coming. I covered my face, and as the leather hit my palms, I grabbed and pulled. It cut into me, but my sleeves gave my hands some protection. I pulled again, and Masha held on, an absurd tug-of-war.

But years of jump ropes and schoolyard bullies had taught me a good trick. I let go suddenly, and she stumbled backward, catching herself before she toppled.

She teetered along the cliff's edge now, and I couldn't waste a moment. I snatched a rock from the dirt and lobbed it at her as hard as I could. "Think fast."

She automatically flinched and swatted it away, losing her balance as she did. Her foot slipped along the ledge, and she dropped. It was surreal, like she'd suddenly shrunk two feet. She'd landed on her knees and was sliding, grappling in the dirt for a handhold, sinking, scrambling, skidding down to her belly, finally dangling from the cliff side by her elbow, holding on to the rocks by her hands.

For a moment, everything stopped. I'd hated her for so long, dreamed of this day for so long, it seemed unreal that it'd finally arrived. More unreal was my next impulse. In that moment, I knew a flash of insight: The enemy of my enemy was my friend.

I couldn't help it. I was tired. So tired. I dropped and grabbed her arm. "We don't have to fight."

"Fuck you, Acari trash." She scrambled to get footing, but only slid further. Rocks dislodged and tumbled down, striking the cliff side with a *bounce-bounce*, then they bounced right off a sharp ledge and down, away from view.

"They're not all bad," I said, putting words to my revelation as I had it. "Vampires don't have to be bad. It's these guys who are bad."

"Your *vampire*," she spat. She didn't look at me as she spoke, but rather her attention was fractured, eyes skittering all around as though she'd missed some obvious solution to her problem. "He doesn't deserve the name. He won't survive. Hugo won't allow it. He'll kill your McCloud." She looked at me then, her lips peeling into a lizard smile. "Hugo said he'd let me stake him. Staking a real vampire is so much more spectacular than the Draug we've—"

I lost it. I forgot how weary I'd become. I forgot about making peace. I let go of her arm. Shoved her away.

Bounce, bounce.

A horrific thud echoed along the rocks, her body hitting the ground forty feet below.

I rolled onto my back, looking up at the white-gray sky. "I tried, Masha."

I WANTED TO JUST LIE there. To sleep. To pretend I was anywhere else. I needed to save Carden, but could I? I seemed capable only of killing and screwing things up.

I'd killed Masha, and it took a minute for the reality to set in. She'd bonded with Alcántara. Would he be furious his Russian pet was killed? Would he be feeling her death even now? Would he find out I was the culprit?

I was on the verge of freaking out, but freaking out was a luxury I didn't have. I made a mental list to calm myself.

I would:

Gather my stars.

Find Mei.

Go to class.

Pretend nothing had happened. Pretend I wasn't hysterical.

Frantically try to find the killer before Carden was staked before my eyes.

Could I blame the Guidons' deaths on the mysterious rogue vampire? But they weren't drained, and exsanguination was one thing I was incapable of doing. I had to hope that removing my weapons from the scene of the crime would be enough to erase any evidence pointed my way.

As I climbed back down, I called quietly for Mei. No answer. Hopefully she was back on campus by now, headed to her music class.

With that thought came strains of her flute, high and keening, echoing along the rocks, as though I'd summoned her. I stopped to listen. I was imagining things, surely.

But the sound came louder. And I detected another sound, too. Guttural moans.

I shivered. I'd found my stars and stakes, and hastily wiped them clean of sand and blood and holstered them. "Like nothing ever happened," I muttered, then took off at a jog, headed for the sound of the flute, which, unfortunately, was coming back from the direction we'd come.

Alone, I moved quickly, mesmerized by the rhythm of my steps, a soothing drumbeat in my head. But then I saw them.

I skidded to a stop, my heart exploding double-time.

In an instant, my stars were in my hands. I'd thought I had nothing left, but there I was, squatted, poised, ready for another fight.

Draug. A whole slew of them.

Coming right for me.

CHAPTER THIRTY-FOUR

———

O ptions flew through my mind, scattershot, like a pinball in a machine. I could run. But if that were Mei-Ling's flute, it meant she was out there, probably in danger. Was she playing to give me a message? Was it a call for help?

There'd be no running. I'd have to fight this one out, at least until I found her.

But how to fight a dozen Draug with only four throwing stars? They were moving slowly, like zombies. Maybe they'd just eaten. Maybe their bloodlust was temporarily dulled. Or maybe, like Tom had said, if I didn't show fear, they'd not hunger for me.

Either way, fear was something I couldn't afford. I put two stars in each hand and took off running, headed straight for them. "Best defense . . . good offense."

I heard Mei-Ling scream and ran harder, but then I made sense of her words and skidded to a stop, close enough to the Draug to see the whites of their eyes.

"Stop, Drew," she cried again. *"Stop."*

She meant me. She wanted *me* to stop.

Her voice came from above, and I looked along the hilltop. She was walking, her flute in hand. Tom walked beside her, looking grumpy to be there.

"What the—?"

She half slid, half ran down the hill to me, a proud smile on her face. "I thought I'd bring backup."

I had the oddest flicker of temper. I was slashed all over my body, and despite the rapid healing of my wounds, my shoulder still ached like crazy. I'd been freaking out with worry for her, fighting to protect her, and here she was, scampering toward me with a smile on her face. "What the hell are you doing?" I snapped.

She looked stung. Hurt. It made me feel like an ass. "I thought I'd help you," she said quietly.

"Sorry. You're right." I sighed and looked toward the Draug, and it hit me what I was witnessing. They weren't acting like zombies because they'd been fed. This was Mei-Ling's doing. I looked back at her for confirmation.

She waved her flute. "Cool, huh?"

I stepped closer, fascinated to see the creatures up close. Their eyes were glazed, and they held themselves utterly still, like they were waiting for something. The stench was overpowering, but I couldn't look away. Each face was so distinct, all in various states of decay.

My eyes went to a patch of brown curly hair, and I recognized one of the Trainees who'd been in my Phenomena class last term. I whirled and ran to the hillside, leaning on the rocks for support as I retched up every last bit of food in my system.

Tom's voice sounded at my shoulder. "Get a hold, girl. Be calm, like your friend here."

Astounded, I looked up, wiping my mouth, gathering myself. Sure enough, Mei-Ling *did* look calm. Composed. I remembered how she'd been through a crisis before, watching as her boyfriend was killed, but it hadn't destroyed her. This time, when crisis struck, she'd had the wherewithal to use music to pacify the Draug. She'd needed me to protect her, but it appeared in this situation *I'd* needed *her*.

"Yeah, Drew," she said with a teasing smile. "Be calm like me."

I used my sleeve to wipe my mouth again. "Jeez, Mei. Your flute did this?"

She shrugged, looking pleased.

Tom, though, had that grumpy look again. "Her whistle shut them right up."

I bumped up against her, giving her a half hug. "You're like the pied piper."

He scowled at my arm around Mei's shoulders. "You girls done? We gotta get a move on. My Draug ain't the only ones called by blood."

That focused us quickly enough. There was a rogue vampire out there somewhere, who'd be called by the scent of blood in the air. It also reminded me how there were bodies—bodies that might easily be linked back to me. "There are three of them," I said gravely. "They were Guidons."

Tom sniffed and nodded up the beach. "I smell 'em, all right. This way?"

I nodded, nervous. How would we dispose of them? Even if I didn't get in trouble for killing three Guidons, I knew I'd get it for going so far off campus. "What should I do?"

"We'll see," he said mysteriously.

We reached Masha's body, and the full impact of what I'd done hit me. Masha was dead.

I knelt to study the body. I'd killed a girl before, only to see her pop up on another island. I didn't want another Lilac. I felt for her pulse, for her breath.

Really dead.

My eyes went to the injury on her arm, and ice filled my veins. I'd retrieved my shuriken, but that cut was short and razor-thin . . . like something a throwing star would leave. "My fingerprints are all over this."

Tom spat in the sand, looking thoughtful. "Not for long."

"What?" I didn't understand what he was saying to me.

"You"—he waved at Mei-Ling's instrument—"play that thing again."

She pulled it out, and just holding it seemed to give her comfort. She began to play, and it wasn't just the Draug who were affected.

My mind lulled, as though my brain got heavy, and those snapshot memories flickered on the edges of my consciousness again. She made me feel nostalgia.

Could she make me feel *happy*, too? Might her music have the power to make me no longer Acari? To make me, for just once, simply a teenager?

He shooed at me, startling me from my thoughts, and waved me away. "My boys got this. You don't want to watch."

He was right—I really, really didn't.

For once, the sea called me, and I headed to the water, walking in the breakers, away from the body of the girl I'd killed. She'd washed onto shore, and the waves rolled over her, pushing her a little higher on the sand with each ebb and flow of the tide.

I walked away, walked deeper, longing to feel the waves pound my legs. Maybe they would cleanse me.

I walked until the crash of the surf filled my head more loudly than the hideous gurgle and snarl of the Draug as they consumed the bodies.

When I returned, Tom was spattered with gore, looking like some sort of macabre butcher. Draug still crouched, sniffing around where Masha's body had been. Through their huddled bodies, I spotted bones, tufts of black hair. I looked away, sickened to my soul.

"Nobody can pin this on you now," Tom said.

I nodded, tried to say the words "Thank you."

Mei looked as shaken as I felt, and I went to her, linking my arm in hers.

Tom began to walk up the beach, farther away from campus, beckoning us to follow. Even though it meant missing class, going way too much farther from the path and surely sealing some grim punishment for ourselves, we followed.

I dared not refuse him. I owed him.

I turned and looked back at the Draug. "What about them?"

He waved it off. "They're more scared of this island than you are. They'll go back to their pens now. They like it familiar."

Apparently, at its heart, a Draug was no more than a frightened, feral child. The concept astounded me.

We walked for some time, and I guessed I was committed now. Far away and in deep—too far from the dungeons to help Carden. And now I wasn't even sure if I'd be able to help my own self, either.

To take my mind off my nerves, I asked, "Why'd you help us?"

"Help comes to them who help themselves."

I frowned at him. The way he spoke in riddles confused me, and my patience was flagging as quickly as my courage. "What does that mean?"

"Maybe it's that you've got a heart. Maybe I'm bored. Maybe you're different." He cackled and shook his head. "Or maybe I just helped because I like the look of you two."

We grew quiet as the beach grew rockier and harder to traverse. Eventually we came to a small cove I'd never seen before.

Tom hiked away from the water toward the cliff wall and disappeared into a sea cave. "Come on then," he shouted from inside. "Don't got all day."

We followed him in, and the stench was overpowering. I hid my nose in the crook of my elbow to dull the acrid tang of urine stinging my nostrils. I smelled dung, too, and over it all was the cloying sweet smell of hay. "What, is this like your barn annex or something?"

My eyes adjusted to the dimness, and I saw there was a boat pulled up onto the rocks. Bits of hay were strewn all along the cave floor. "Wait," I said. "It smells like a barn because it *is* like a barn."

"I got a boat, you see." Tom gave a weighty nod toward it. Nodded back to us. "How do you think I get the goats here? We go through the things pretty quick."

It was a flat-bottomed craft, maybe twice the size of Ronan's rowboat, only this one had an ancient engine to propel it. Old boards walled off one end into a makeshift corral, piled with old hay.

Just right for a girl to escape.

I glanced back at Tom, and the smile in his eyes told me he'd thought the same thing.

This was my chance. It was my moment.

But in that moment, I knew. It was Mei-Ling who would escape, not me.

I went to Tom, putting all my heart and soul in my next question. "Will you take her?"

He scoffed at my intensity. "Why do you think I brought you here? I can fit both you girls."

"Not me," I said. "Not yet." I turned to Mei-Ling. "But you need to go. Run. I'll tell them you're dead. Your family won't be safe if the vampires think you're still alive."

She reached out and took my hand. She looked scared and so young. "Come with me."

I stared longingly at that boat. I couldn't go now. I'd faced escape once before only to realize I'd found a place and it was by Carden's side. Now I knew I'd also found a fight.

I couldn't leave *Eyja næturinnar*. I didn't know who I'd be if I ran away now, but I knew who I'd be if I stayed.

I wouldn't go down easy. I'd see this through. Help the girls who wanted it. Stick by my friends.

"I need to stay," I said. "I'm in too deep. I need to figure out who these vampires are. What they are. But first, I need to save Carden."

I looked at Mei-Ling, feeling my heart crack. Friends were too rare to be saying good-bye to one so quickly. But I had to put her on that boat. She wouldn't survive otherwise.

"Be safe." I felt emotion threatening, and to stifle it, I went into robot mode, reciting all I knew. "There are shipping lanes throughout the North Sea. Wherever Tom takes you, you can catch a larger boat to Norway, or Iceland, or Scotland. Get food first, though. Jerky, stuff like that. More important is water. You can live for weeks without food, but without water, you're dead in a few days. Find a boat; then stow away if you have to. But I imagine ships all need kitchen or cleaning staff. Don't trust anyone." I realized she was looking at me funny, and I gave a humorless laugh. "I've thought about this a lot."

"Apparently." She smiled at me until I couldn't help but smile back.

"One more thing." I removed a throwing star from my boot. I couldn't let her go without some sort of weapon. I handed it to her. "Don't try to throw it. I mean, you can practice—you *should* practice—but you never know when you'll need something sharp."

She pushed my hand away. "I can't take your shuriken. I've got those stakes."

I pressed the star into her hand. "Stakes won't cut meat. No, you need a sharp edge. Take it."

I'd consider later what the implications were of parting with one of my treasured throwing stars. For now, Mei-Ling needed it more than I did.

Her eyes went to the boat, then back to me. "You sure you won't come with me?"

"I'm sure. You just find your way home."

A peculiar expression washed over her face, and as it did, I watched Mei transform from a child to a young woman. "I won't be going home," she said. "I'm going to get revenge."

My reaction was instant and vehement. "No way. It's not safe out there."

She shook her head. "I *can't* go home. You said it yourself. The vampires will kill my family."

Tom had been readying the boat, but apparently he'd been

listening because he interjected. "You think I'm a fool? I'm tak-ing her to friends."

Friends? I filed that away for later. If I ever saw Tom again, I'd ask who these friends were.

I looked at Mei-Ling, studying her, wondering if this would be the last time I ever saw her. I hoped it wouldn't. "Maybe this isn't good-bye."

She smiled broadly. "Maybe it's more like *see you later.*"

I laughed, but my eyes were serious. "Seriously, Mei. There's some scary stuff out there. Be careful."

She held up her instrument. "I've got my flute."

"But I'm worried you'll need me."

She gave my arm a shake. "The world doesn't revolve around you, Drew."

"Well, *my* world does."

Tom had dragged the boat into the water, and it bobbed furi-ously in the breakers. He called to us, "Now or never."

"I guess this is it." I walked her to the water's edge, frantically trying to think of whatever more words of wisdom I needed to impart. "If you see some tall rich bitch mean girl with hair the color of maple syrup, look out."

She laughed. "Lilac?"

I could only shrug. "Who knows anymore what's out there."

She clambered into the boat, and Tom held it so we could finish our farewell. He wore thick rubber wellies on his feet, but still, the poor man was getting soaked.

"You be safe," she told me. "And mind yourself."

I stared hard, trying to read her meaning in the shadows of the sea cave. "Mind myself?"

"My grandmother had a saying. It's a Chinese proverb. The loudest duck gets shot. So yeah, Drew, mind yourself."

"You're a pain, you know? And I'm going to miss you." I leaned over the edge to give her a quick, hard hug, putting all my heart into it. I whispered good-bye in her ear.

But then I shoved her away.

And Tom pushed off, hopping in as the boat rose on the water. He revved the engine to life, and the overwhelming stink of petrol obliterated the goat smell. Mei-Ling nestled in the bed of hay, disappearing from view.

I stood there for some time, watching them fade into the distance. Watching my roommate as she made the escape I'd dreamed of.

CHAPTER THIRTY-FIVE

I wanted to mope. I wanted to hide. I wanted to avoid what hell might be awaiting me back on campus.

What would I say? What would my excuse be? Not only was I missing class, but I'd have to fabricate a pretend Draug attack and Mei's death. Oh, and I'd also need to act surprised when people realized Masha and her pals had disappeared.

I bore the injuries to support the Draug story, but could I lie convincingly enough?

I couldn't mope. I couldn't hide or avoid. That thing deep inside me that'd survived my father, that was surviving Watcher training—that thing kicked in. It was my instinct to survive.

It was my will to live that got me shaking out my shoulders and kicking into a strong, steady run back up the beach. I was practicing my looks of surprise and dismay when I heard a weird noise.

I slowed to a jog, spinning a circle to see where it came from. The Draug had all gone, and even if they hadn't, I was no longer so afraid of them. There were other, much deadlier things out there, and those were the things that I searched for now, scouring the horizon.

There it was again. A hissing, just barely audible over the crash of the waves.

I spun and spun, searching. What'd I been thinking, running along the water? I was too out in the open, with my back exposed.

Again it hissed. Then there was laughter, male laughter, deep and rolling. He hissed louder.

I spun once more, and there he was. Suddenly. Right there before me.

It was the vampire. The rogue vampire.

I knew the moment I laid eyes on him that this was the creature responsible for the murders. This was the thing that'd killed mercilessly and without reason, draining bodies dry and leaving them to rot like trash.

It wasn't just the white hair that told me he was the rogue. This vampire was different. It was something in his manner—the way he studied me as though I were an alien creature. It was in the feel of him, too. He radiated power—I felt it like a tug in my gut. Like electricity penetrating me, rippling deep beneath my skin.

He was ancient. I felt it. He was beyond pale, his skin pallid, lacking any color whatsoever.

He was simply dressed and a lot less soiled than I'd have expected a rogue vampire to be. No, somebody was housing this creature. Cleaning his clothes. Weirdest of all, he wore sunglasses. I realized I'd never before seen a vampire in sunglasses.

I looked away, desperately scanning, searching for an escape route, even though I knew there wasn't one.

He laughed, and compared to his hissing, it was a bizarrely human sound. "Such a pretty pretty."

Cold dread washed over me, and I backed up. Slowly, I edged away from the water. This thing would probably kill me, but I refused to be drowned.

He followed slowly, his head tilting as he studied me. "Normally I wait until dark to feed. But I can't avoid the pretty pretty."

So creepy creepy. I backed away faster now. I inventoried my weapons: three stakes and three stars. Maybe if I could get to higher ground, I could figure something out.

He laughed again, chanting, "Here, pretty pretty."

Cold sweat prickled my skin. I broke into a backward jog. He was so foreign to me, so terrifying, so powerful, and yet I couldn't take my eyes from him. I went faster, even though I knew he could overtake me. He was toying with me. And it was working. My heart hammered in my chest, and I fought to breathe normally. My skin had gone clammy. I shot a quick glance at the hillside. It wasn't so steep here. I'd spied the trail. If I could climb up, maybe I'd be able to make a run for it. Maybe someone would see me.

Maybe maybe maybe . . .

I spun and broke into a flat-out run, my arms pumping, sprinting as fast as I could. But the damned sand made it so hard. My feet chuffed and thumped along, and I grew winded quickly. But I made it to the bottom of the hill and instantly began to clamber up, using hands and feet to pull and hoist myself up and over.

I made it.

But then he appeared—he'd just jumped, and there he was, standing before me, blocking my path, whispering, "Pretty pretty."

I tried to dart around him, but each time he'd appear in front of me. Laughing and muttering.

I thought maybe I could distract him, and I tried, asking ridiculous things, like, "Who are you?" and "Did you kill those people?" All the while, I wriggled my arm, working the stake out from my sleeve. My stars would do no good against this thing. My only chance would be if I surprised him. Finally, a stake slipped loose, slid into my hand, its tip concealed in my palm.

I scrambled around him—I had to get away from the ledge— and this time he let me. But he was always just there, at my shoulder, chanting, "Here, pretty pretty."

His voice was changing. Intensifying. He was growing bored, or thirsty.

I had to do something. He'd act soon, and I'd need to beat him to it. I stopped short, whirled, and lunged for him, slamming my arm up, until my stake met flesh. The impact reverberated up my arm.

He screamed and flew backward. I'd pierced him, but it was lower than his heart. His eyes locked with mine as he pulled the stake from his body and tossed it over the cliff. He smiled at me, and it was chilling.

"Pretty pretty likes to fight," he said, and his voice was unexpectedly sultry.

It was the most disturbing thing I'd ever heard. I gritted my teeth, mustering bravado. "Don't think you can creep me out."

He frowned at that. "A creep, am I?"

Disgust shriveled his features, and he lunged at me. It was too fast. I didn't have a chance to pull my other stake all the way out. He held me, held my skull crushed between his hands. I fumbled, squirming and fighting against it, but he wrenched it back, exposing my neck.

He held my head, but he didn't have my hands. I clawed at his face. Tore off his glasses.

He hissed again, shoving me away, flinching from the daylight. His eyes were pale and red. He squinted at me, staring, raging. No longer did he resemble a predator toying with his meal—he was all fury and retribution and malice.

I stumbled backward, screaming.

He opened his mouth to hiss, and kept his mouth hanging open. Other vampires hid their fangs, or at least tried to create the illusion of humanity. Not this one. This one kept his mouth open, hissing and hissing like a rabid animal.

I'd scratched a deep welt on his cheek, and reddish black blood oozed down. He stretched out his tongue, slowly licking his own blood, and it was obscene, almost sexual. I shuddered, watching as his skin healed, slowly knitting together before my eyes.

I pulled out my other stake, but he flew at me, swatting my hand, sending the bit of wood flying over the ledge. I fell from the impact and scuttled backward.

My stakes were gone, but I still had my stars. I had to hope they'd be good enough. He watched, avid curiosity on his face, as I plucked them from my boot. Seeing the steel stars in my hand, he laughed.

He wore the strangest cockeyed grin as he began to prowl toward me.

I threw a star. And another. And the third. Two hit; none did any damage.

His grin turned dark. He looked hungry, stalking toward me like an eager lover. "What other treasures do you hide, sweet pretty?"

I backed up, screamed. He backed me against the ledge. I hated how I screamed. But this was it. I had nowhere else to go. The end. My screams filled my head.

The vampire bent down to me. Cold, bony fingers threaded through my hair, so gently. But then he pulled, yanking me to standing. I yelped with the shocking pain of it.

"They all scream," he said angrily. He wrenched my neck back, locking his eyes with mine, and I was instantly lost. "Silence," he whispered, and the words came to me as though through a tunnel. Those pale red irises became my gravity, sucking me toward him, in and down. "Yes," he cooed, sounding so pleased. "Yessss."

I shut my eyes, waiting for it. Waiting to die.

CHAPTER THIRTY-SIX

———— ✦ ————

Ashout cleared my head. A "No" growled so fiercely, it pierced my consciousness. "No," bellowed in a voice deep enough to reverberate through me. Shaking me.

Carden.

I exploded to life, wriggling and scratching and fighting. This thing wouldn't kill me. Not today.

"No," Carden shouted again.

I watched as fingers appeared around the rogue vampire's neck. I watched Carden, and his fury had altered his face to some other thing, some powerful, savage force I hadn't seen before. He grabbed harder, and harder still, until his fingertips disappeared into the vampire's flesh. He grasped the rogue's neck and lifted him off the ground. Flung him away.

The vampire landed hard and bounced, but then he was up again, swooshing right back to Carden, swinging at him.

But Carden had seen it coming, and as he ducked, he reached

back and swung. His arm arced wide, his fist slamming into the vampire. The creature flew backward, off the cliff.

I clung to the ledge not to fall. "How did—" I began breathlessly, but Carden jumped after the rogue, disappearing before I could sputter a thought.

I skittered down the hill after him, gathering up a stake and a star as I went. I didn't have time to find the other weapons.

I slid down, and something punched me from the side as I landed. The world went black for a moment. I came to and found myself restrained. The rogue held me. I flailed, struggled, and kicked, but those hands only clawed more tightly into me.

"This one is mine," the thing said to Carden.

I heard Carden's approach, footfalls in the sand. But this time the creature was ready, and he hauled his arm back and punched Carden, sending him flying.

The vampire curled over me, hugging me. "Time to die, pretty. Are you ready?" His whole body enveloped mine.

I was unable to move. I felt his breath on my neck. I forced my eyes to look away.

Where was Carden? I was frantic to find him. I'd see Carden as I died—I'd have *Carden* be the last sight I saw.

And I found him—he was running back toward us. Running back for more.

Carden, who'd somehow gotten free of his dungeon. Carden, who could've left me—he could've fled the island—but we were in this together, and he was running toward *me*.

Time slowed. He ran at us, his focus only on the vampire.

But then I had an idea, and the moment the thought came to me, his eyes flashed to mine.

The stake.

I still held a stake in my hand. I reached my arm back to toss it in the same instant Carden opened his hands to catch. It was as though we were one being, having the same thought at the same time.

I threw. Carden caught. And he staked the vampire.

The creature released me, shrieking a cry so piercing, I had to clap my hands over my ears. I stumbled backward as he turned black, shriveling and sizzling before my eyes, howling and screaming.

And then he was dust.

My knees gave way, but Carden was there, and suddenly I was in his arms. He carried me to the water's edge and gently put me down. I saw I was covered in gore and leaned over to splash my hands, my face. But I was shaking too badly.

Carden stilled me. "Hush," he said, cupping water and sloughing the blood from my arms. He worked down to my hands, tenderly rubbing circles over them until I was clean.

When I stood, his eyes were on me, bleak and relieved both.

"I heard you," he said. "I heard your screams as though they were in my own head."

I fell into him, crumpling into his arms. "Did they let you out? I don't understand."

I looked up at him, and finally I registered his injuries, huge bands scored into his wrists, deep scrapes along his hands. I gently took one of those hands in mine. The wounds were healing quickly, but I saw how deep they'd been. How bloody. I gently rubbed away the flaking blood to reveal fresh skin, looking so angry and red beneath. "What did you do?"

"A man can do much when driven." He took my face in his hands. "There is no chain that can keep me from you."

He'd known I was in trouble. He'd come for me.

Carden had told me of his Druid ancestry, but it was then I saw firsthand how my Scottish vampire had abilities and powers that made him a threat to Alcántara.

"Come, sweet. We must go back."

"Will this"—I nodded to the pile of ash—"will he be enough to clear your name?"

"Aye, more than enough."

I gave him a weak smile. "Ding-dong, the witch is dead?"

He wrapped an easy arm around my shoulders. "As you say, you peculiar, wee thing."

I looked at the pile of blackened dust and grew serious. "How will we prove there even was a rogue vampire? How will they know we're not lying?"

He bent and picked up the vampire's sunglasses. "These."

"This is our proof?" I took them from him, studying them.

"This vampire was too old to go out in daylight. The Directorate will see these and know the meaning. Perhaps they'll even recognize them. Either way, they'll guess he was here, if they didn't know already."

"They must've known," I said. "Somebody did. That guy was way too clean to be completely *rogue*."

"My thoughts exactly." He took the glasses back and pocketed them.

As we walked back to campus, I mused, "Why don't more vampires wear sunglasses? Seems like a clever way to get around light sensitivity."

"Simple. One cannot hypnotize one's prey when one's eyes are concealed."

"Oh." I gazed up at him, staring at his profile, trying to make sense of it all. My thoughts drifted to Ronan, who'd used his own hypnotic powers to get me onto this island. "Did you ever want to hypnotize me? Did you ever try?"

He stopped short, looking amused by the notion. "Now, where's the pleasure in that?" He cupped my cheek, and his next words were spoken low and husky, bringing all sorts of sexy implications to mind. "Seems I've been able to convince you to do things without resorting to trickery."

I cleared my throat, feeling a blush rise to my face. "Seems so."

We returned to campus and blamed the deaths on the vampire. All the deaths, even Masha's, and it was just as well. I was a lousy liar, and a half-truth would be easier to maintain than pretending I hadn't seen her.

Nobody questioned how Carden had known so many girls were under attack, how he'd sensed he was needed enough to break free and act as rescuer. The vampires weren't surprised, and it wasn't because they'd detected our bond. There was something about Carden that made him more powerful than the others, and powerful was dangerous.

Dangerous enough to have caused the bad blood between him and Alcántara. I wondered if my mission off-island really had been to save Carden, or if it'd just been to ensure his silence.

But all that mattered was that he was free, and it was back to normal on the island. Except for Mei-Ling. Her absence left a hole that I felt already.

"What came of Mei-Ling?" Ronan had asked me gently.

I'd had to look away. I couldn't let him see the lie in my eyes.

Carden spoke for me then. "There was nothing left of her."

They believed us, or at least I thought they did.

All except for Alcántara.

I was out of it at dinner that night. Shaky and empty, still trying to wrap my head around what'd just happened. Namely, Mei-Ling was gone.

It was possible to escape from here.

Worse, I hadn't had a moment to be alone with Carden. All the refrigerated shooters of blood in the world weren't enough to stand in for this need I felt for him. I wanted to see his easy smile and to feel that heavy arm around my shoulders. It would've been enough.

I was numb as I scooped a pile of gelatinous spaghetti on my plate. Grabbed a small, tart-looking apple. Walked to my usual spot with Emma and the gang.

My tray clattered as I put it down. The chair scraped hard against the floor. I sat.

Only then did I realize everybody was staring at me. "What?" I met everyone's eyes in turn. "What's going on?"

Yasuo's eyes didn't budge, pinned hard on me. "Alcántara posted a new fight bracket."

I dropped my forehead into my hand. "What now?"

"You're fighting me," Emma said quietly.

The blood drained from my head. I'd dreaded this day. "We have to fight each other?"

At her nod, I looked to Yasuo. "Rules?" I asked, though I was terrified of the answer.

"Two girls in. One girl out." His eyes were razors, slicing into me. "To the death."

CHAPTER THIRTY-SEVEN

"Two go in, only one comes out." I stared at the notice, posted outside the gymnasium. "Sounds like a nineteenth-century circus playbill." I felt a slender hand on my shoulder. Emma's. I turned to her. "This is my fault."

"Don't be ridiculous."

"No. It is." It was never a good idea to cross a vampire. First I was a less-than-enthusiastic recipient of Alcántara's kiss. Then Masha had gone off after me and never come back. "It *is* my fault. This is Alcántara's way of punishing me. I'll make it right."

"You bet you will," Yasuo said.

I glanced over Em's shoulder to find his eyes glittering cold on me. Everyone knew she and I were besties, just as they knew I'd beat her in a fight. But never in a thousand years could I hurt her. Though, just in case I did, there was Yasuo, ready to thrash me quicker than you could say *catfight* if anything happened to her.

Disturbed, I tore my eyes from him to look back at my friend. "We'll find a way so you don't get hurt. I'll throw the fight."

"Or else," Yasuo said.

"Please," Emma told him in that quiet way of hers. "Trust Drew. I do. We'll figure this out. We have before."

"Yeah, Yasuo." I tried my best playful scowl. "We have before."

It didn't bring a smile to his face. "You have to let her beat you."

"I will."

"How?"

"I don't know, Yas. I'll figure it out."

"Well, you better figure it out now," he snarled, "because the fight is tomorrow."

"It's okay," Emma said soothingly, taking his arm in hers.

He glared down at her. "It is *not* okay. You read the freaking poster. Two in, one out. Are you really going to kill her? Is she going to kill you?" He turned his glare on me. "I know how this'll play out. Miss Selfish here will win the day, like she always does."

The comment felt like a Mack truck rear-ending me. "What's that supposed to mean?"

Emma looked distraught now. "Please stop, Yasuo. You're not helping."

"Well, somebody needs to do something."

I put my hands on my hips. "I will so totally do something." My mind raced, and a plan began to form. "Emma *will* take me down. We've been studying the vascular system in Combat Med. She can get me in a hold, pin me down, and make like she's choking me." I spoke faster, the idea taking hold. "Listen, this could work. If she cuts off the blood flow to my carotid artery, I'll pass out. I'll look dead, but the moment she lets go, it'll be all good.

I'll look pretty blacked out for a while, and by the time I come to, she'll be out of that ring. Okay?"

"Wow, that is good," Emma said. "So simple."

I hoped it was simple in an elegant way, and not simple in a stupid way. She'd need to time it just right—if she waited too long to let go, I'd be dead, and if she let go too soon, then we'd both be dead.

"What happens when Alcántara realizes you're not dead?"

"I'll take the heat for that," I assured him, though I left the rest of my thoughts unspoken. Namely, if I got in trouble, Carden could always swoop in before my punishment and we could make a break for it, maybe find those mysterious *friends* of Tom's. "Don't worry."

Emma smiled up at Yas. "See? All good."

"It's me Alcántara wants to punish," I assured him. "Not Em."

He didn't speak, though. His eyes were narrowed on me, and for an instant I saw something flicker there. Red. Like the rogue.

Goose bumps crept along my skin, and I fisted my hands to get the blood flowing again. This was Yasuo. My pal. He was just playing the part of protective boyfriend. Still, it took a mental effort not to take a step back from him.

I was still chilled from that exchange and headed back to my dorm when I ran into Alcántara.

"Greetings, Acari Drew." He bowed his head, looking the part of chivalric fourteenth-century courtier. "I see you are recovered from your ordeal."

"Recovered, yes," I said, mustering a weak smile, then added with a little chuff of a laugh, "Though I'd feel a lot more recovered if I didn't have to fight my friend." It was a stupid thing to say, but I felt like I was at the end of my rope. I was done lying down and taking it from these guys.

I'd watched Mei escape—I'd learned there were options. I'd learned hope.

"You do not wish to fight your friend?"

Was he being serious? Would he give me an option? "Not particularly, no."

"You have no friends." He gave me a chilling smile. "This is merely my way to prove it to you, once and for all."

He'd liked me once. With that in mind, I tried a different angle. "And what if I die instead?"

His lip curled. "You're a trying girl. There was a time I enjoyed the challenge you pose. Now I tire of it." He began to walk off. "What will be shall be."

Carden. I needed Carden. He'd be my comfort.

Somehow he knew. "You're sad," he whispered to me later that night. Lights-out had come and gone hours ago, and it was dark, with just a blade of moonlight cutting in to light my room. His being able to sneak in after hours was the one consolation for losing Mei-Ling.

"We have to enjoy this while we can," I said, avoiding the topic. "I'll graduate to Initiate at the end of this term." Soon I would get a new room. A new roommate. New fights and new enemies.

"Initiate." He sighed. "Such tomfoolery. The Directorate would have you think this is boot camp. While most of those creatures have never seen a day of battle. But, Annelise?"

"Yes?" I asked, staring at the ceiling. I felt full of emotion and, even in the dark, I couldn't bear facing him for fear of letting it show.

"Annelise." He cupped my shoulder. "Face me."

I couldn't resist that husky voice in the darkness. I rolled to face him, and it took a moment to get adjusted. He was ever the gentleman, and refused to lie under the covers with me. The old-fashioned gesture touched me.

"You're avoiding what's really troubling you," he said.

"What's the real trouble?"

He raised his brows, waiting for me to come around.

I sighed. "Okay, yeah, I am sad. And more than sad." The rogue vampire was dead, and the Directorate ruled a return to normal. They'd proclaimed Carden innocent. This was an aberrant event, they'd said. Carden and I were left only with our suspicions and no proof that Alcántara had anything to do with the killings. Now all I needed to do was fight Emma; then it'd be back to our regularly scheduled program. If we both survived. "I'm worried about who planted the rogue. I'm worried Al has you in his sights. I'm worried I'll accidentally kill my best friend."

"First," he said, "you shouldn't worry for me. You're a braw spitfire of a woman, but I've survived for hundreds of years without you. I imagine I'll get through the coming weeks as well."

I felt a tiny smile begin to play at the corner of my mouth. "I'm a woman?"

He chucked my chin. "You know you are. And you're strong. Do you know there was once a time when we Scotsmen went to battle, leaving our women to protect the home? It was *women* who ran the homesteads, raised our children, fought for our land. And from what I've seen, you are stronger even than that. Braver than that."

I bit my lip, feeling that emotion trying to bust through. "I just . . . I worry, is all. I worry I won't be able to find a way to survive this. For Emma to survive it. I'm sick of losing people—even the girls who'd see me dead. I'm sick of all of it."

"You will do what you always have done, which is what is necessary to survive. I cannot predict what will happen in your fight. There is no plan Hugo has not yet conceived himself, and I fear he will stand in your way." He cupped my cheek, holding my gaze to his. "But whatever happens, hear this: I will not watch you die."

I turned and pressed my lips to his palm. I thought of stoic prairie-girl Emma. I had a centuries-old vampire secretly in my corner—whatever my best intentions were, it wouldn't be a fair fight. I couldn't bear the thought anymore. "Take my mind off this," I pleaded. "Show me your powers."

"My powers?"

"You know. Your Druid powers. Predict the future or something." I blinked my eyes shut. "Tell me what I'm thinking."

His hand ever so gently cradled my neck. "I'm thinking perhaps you'd like me to kiss you."

I opened my eyes and what I saw blew me away. His features had gone soft, as though he were glimpsing heaven. And heaven was *me*. There'd been a time when I thought I didn't want to kiss a vampire. Now it was all I wanted.

I slid my hand over his. "I would like it, yes."

He kissed me, and there wasn't the hunger of our previous kisses. This was a tender kiss. A bolstering kiss. A kiss to give me strength and tell me I wasn't alone.

When we parted, I stared at him, memorizing him. How strange to find myself with this creature, whispering intimacies in the darkness. "How is it you're so different? I mean, all the other vampires come from another time and they're all sexist pigs."

He smiled at that. "They're naught but frightened boys. They don't know what I do."

"Which is?"

"That in the body of a wee blond spitfire lies the heart of a warrior."

Just then, hearing his conviction, I felt that warrior's heart. In Carden's words, I heard how he'd once had a mother, a sister. Aunts and grandmothers whom he'd honored.

Someday I'd ask him for his history, but I didn't think he was ready to tell me, not yet. And I wasn't ready, either. Because somewhere in his stories, I imagined how a girl might find love for a vampire. And that was something I definitely wasn't prepared for.

CHAPTER THIRTY-EIGHT

———❦———

"Don't worry." I gave my friend an uneasy smile. It was surely the strangest prefight march this island had ever seen—two competitors, about to fight to the death, clinging together like they were each other's life raft. "It'll be just like in *Star Trek*."

"What do you mean?" Emma asked nervously. "I don't understand."

She sounded nervous, and I chattered in an attempt to calm her. "You know, like Spock. You hit the right pressure point, and *boom*—I'm out cold." She still looked blank, so I said, "You didn't watch *Star Trek*, did you?"

She shook her head.

"Of course you didn't."

"But I know what to do. I grip your neck."

"No, you'll *pinch* my neck. There are two carotid arteries, one on each side. Doubles your chances, right? Pinch, and I'll black out."

"What if you don't wake up?"

"Just don't hold on too long. If you let go in time, I'll be fine."
I gave a brittle laugh. "Several thousand brain cells short, but
alive." What I didn't mention was that it could also stop my heart,
send me into shock, and kill me. But I pictured Carden, remembered his words. *I will not watch you die.* I gave her an encouraging
smile. "Seriously. Don't worry about me. I'll be fine. Just make
it look convincing."

"Convincing." She nodded solemnly. "I can do that."

We'd reached the gymnasium, and I could hear a commotion
inside. A crowd had gathered already.

We stopped and locked eyes. We'd been distant lately, but it
hadn't been because we were mad at each other. It was purely
due to circumstances—class schedules for one, though Yasuo
was the biggest reason. Him, and Carden, too. She'd been enjoying having a secret boyfriend, while I'd been in my own weird
world. But I *knew* Emma. Emma was my friend. We'd get
through this.

She held out her pinky. "Friends forever?"

"Forever," I agreed, twining my little finger with hers. "Pinky
swear."

I opened the door for us, and the shouts and taunts of the
crowd swelled—mostly girl voices. Neither of us had many
friends in the audience. It girded me. I needed to do this, to fake
my own death, to save Emma.

"Ladies," Alcántara greeted us from his perch outside the ring.

The crowd hushed as we climbed in between the ropes. I
caught Emma's eye. We were together. We could do this.

"Two girls in," he announced like a boxing emcee. "One
out."

We went to opposite corners of the ring and stood there unmoving, staring silently at each other. *Friends forever.*

He tipped his head toward us in a dramatically somber gesture. "Commence."

Emma slid her Buck knife from a holster at the back of her belt. It was thick and serrated, and just seeing it gave me a shudder. She gave me an apologetic shrug.

I flexed my foot, feeling the stars in my boots. I bent to pull one out. My aim would need to be better than ever—not in an effort to kill my friend, but rather to make sure I *didn't* kill her.

I stepped forward and gave her a small, reassuring smile. We'd agreed we had to make it look convincing before she pinned and pretend-killed me. Which meant we'd have to draw some blood. I just hoped that, when the time came, she remembered not to twist that knife.

She advanced a few steps, looking reluctant to leave her corner. As she moved, the gym's overhead lights gleamed white on her wide blade. She might've been unwilling, but there was nothing uncertain about the sharpness of that steel.

Once more, I was grateful for this term's Combat Medicine. I knew the least painful, the safest places to be stabbed. The spots where we'd be least likely to bleed out, those parts of the body that wouldn't sustain permanent, crippling injury.

Major arteries = bad. Extremities = good.

Feet, hands, fingers, toes were all prime spots, as long as we avoided critical tendons in the hands and stayed far from the arms and legs, which housed some major veins.

The butt, believe it or not, was also a great target, as long as we were careful to avoid nearby arteries. Nick the wrong spot in the butt and you're toast.

The forehead was definitely something to consider, if we had the opportunity. It'd bleed a lot—head injuries always did—and that would provide some necessary high drama, with the skull protecting all the valuable bits.

The crowd began to hoot and catcall. They wanted carnage, but Emma was hesitating. She was having trouble doing this. I'd have to wake her up, jostle some life into her. See if I couldn't bring out a spark. It'd be up to me to draw first blood.

I approached and prowled around her, trying to look eager to go in for the kill. I drew a second star, holding one in each hand. I widened my eyes, hoping she'd understand the message. *Stand very, very still.*

She froze—she got it. I had only a tiny window to act before we looked too obvious. I threw the stars in quick succession. The first I threw at her head and breathed a sigh of relief as it skimmed her hair. The second hit her foot and stuck there.

She made the tiniest shocked whimper, and I had to purse my lips against the emotion. I had to be strong. We could do this.

It was her turn to act, but she wasn't, so I stalked toward her, hoping to make it easier for her. I shoved her, then shoved again. *Come on, Emma, fight.*

I grabbed her hair and pulled her down hard, making like I was kneeing her in the gut. I tugged back up, and she didn't need to fake the sound of pain. I hissed in her ear, "A real friend would fight me." I hated to do it, but I had to goad her to action or she really would be killed.

Emma flinched back, and finally I saw fire in her eyes. She lunged toward me and slashed at my thigh, managing to tear only the fabric and scrape the skin in the most superficial of wounds that also happened to draw a dramatic amount of blood. She'd been using a Buck knife since she was little and she was *good*. Thank God.

I realized the crowd was chanting, *"Knife, knife, knife."*

The sound turned my blood cold. I guessed I had some real fans in the audience. Not.

Emma's eyes had narrowed—she was finally feeling the battle lust, and for a surreal moment, I believed it. I believed she'd turned on me. That she wanted to kill me.

It made me feel so alone.

I had to glance at the crowd. I had to. I had to see Carden and feel some sort of support. I looked to the audience, but my eyes lit on Ronan instead. He stood close by, looking like he might spring into the ring and intervene. I had to look away.

Then I spotted him. *Carden*. He looked calm. I'd be calm, too.

Staring back at Emma, I squatted to pull out my other star, flexing my thigh as I did, encouraging the blood to flow where she'd slashed me. I stood and sprang toward her, pretending a slight limp. I threw as I ran, as lightly as I could, hitting her in the belly. I hoped it was shallow enough not to do any damage. I'd had to do something—it'd look too suspicious if I hit her in the foot again.

Weaponless now, I grabbed her and we began to grapple. I spun, trying to flip her in a move we'd practiced a thousand times in our sparring. She slashed, and her knife sliced my butt.

I shouted, shocked at the pain. It was technically one of the "safe" places to be injured, but man it stung. I stumbled backward.

My uniform leggings were soaked with blood. Emma left red footprints on the floor of the ring as blood oozed from her abdomen and foot. We couldn't take much more of this.

I needed to end it.

I didn't give myself a chance to think twice. I just ran for her and swatted her hand. Her knife went flying. With its scalloped grip, I knew she'd never have let that thing go so easily, but I had to pretend to disarm her to make my strangulation more convincing.

We grappled, and I put a foot behind hers to trip her. We fell, and I let her roll on top of me. Here it came. We made like we were wrestling, but we had to make it quick. Anything more and it'd look too staged, too fake.

She slammed my shoulders down, and for a moment my head swam for real with the impact. I felt her hands wrap around my neck. Her eyes locked with mine, and I detected the slightest twitch in her eyelids. I twitched mine back. *Do it, Emma.* We were in this together. Friends forever.

Time to let my bestie kill me.

She squeezed, and panic swelled. I tried to suppress it. This was pretend. I'd be all right. We'd both come out alive. I had to trust her. I did trust her.

But still, cold panic and solitude began to swallow me. I was alone. I was being choked to death.

Not alone, I told myself. I tilted my head to catch another glimpse of Carden, standing at the edge of the gym. His strawberry-blond head rose above the rest as he waited for the moment I might need him.

I wouldn't be afraid. I trusted Emma. Trusted Carden.

I pretended to writhe, but she pinched harder. Even though I'd pushed away the panic, as my vision dimmed, I began to writhe for real. My deep-seated animal instincts flared to life—I couldn't suppress those. I didn't need to act out the hammering of my heels against the ring, the gasping of my mouth, automatic, like a fish out of water.

I let go. Forcefully, I crushed every one of my instincts. I suppressed my all-consuming urge to survive. I let it all go.

I blacked out.

The first thing I felt was cool air in my nostrils, filling my lungs. It felt so good, tasted so good.

My eyes fluttered open. I felt Carden, but I saw Ronan. Fury distorted his features. I didn't understand. Was he angry I was dead? I willed him to look at me so he could see I was alive.

But he didn't look, and then I caught sight of Yasuo, too, fuming, raging, his fangs bared. It hit me that everyone in the crowd was looking where they were.

I turned to see, and the pain in my neck was severe. I coughed, and my throat convulsively gagged and gulped, and I had to spit out the saliva that was too painful to swallow. I focused, and it took a moment to make sense of what I was looking at.

Emma's feet dangled above the ground, kicking at the air. A hand held her up by the neck. Alcántara. He held her, dangling and flailing, but he stared at me. He waited for reality to register in my eyes and then gave me a slow smile.

I tried to mouth words, but couldn't speak. I coughed again. *What are you doing?* I wanted to scream.

Her hands clawed at his, but he only tugged her closer. He wrapped a hand at her belly and used Emma's own knife to slash her down the middle.

He dropped her to the ground, a lifeless, bloody heap, and finally I was able to make a sound. A keening, nonsense wail that tore my throat as it came out.

"There is no cheating." He looked out at the audience and proclaimed, "Only one shall emerge alive."

I scrambled to my hands and knees, scuttling to Emma. She was dead. I shrieked, pleading, "But it wasn't her fault. Blame me. It was my idea. Punish me."

Alcántara slowly turned his head, looking at me with those eyes, cold like black stones. "I just did."

CHAPTER THIRTY-NINE

W ith the end of the semester came my ascension to Initiate. There weren't many girls left from my original group, and the vampires held a torchlight ceremony for us in front of the standing stones. In the darkness, I couldn't see the castle on the hill, but I felt it out there, looming. Full of secrets. The secrets of men.

Once it'd scared me. Now I saw it as a challenge.

The rest of the year was a numbed blur, and how bizarre it all was. Vampires and an oddly sentimental acknowledgment of Christmas, or Yule, as some of them chose to call it. There was a night of lights and incense and familiar melodies sung in eerily somber Latin.

It was so weird to think that somewhere in the world, people were out there, shopping at Target, and doing Black Friday and Cyber Monday and all that. While it felt so timeless here, just me and my new, dark blue catsuit.

Carden gave me a small gift—a replacement for the throwing

star I'd given to Mei-Ling, only this one bore a delicate feather pattern etched along its blades. "A lethal wing, for my wee dove to fly," he'd told me. There was nothing in the world that could've been more perfect.

Well, maybe there was one thing. I don't know how or from where, but Ronan had managed to steal back the photograph of my mother that'd been confiscated. He gave it to me as a gift . . . but also as a warning, he'd said, and it was his accompanying advice that was the only thing to sully what was such an extraordinary surprise. The photo was a reminder, he'd said, of who I was. Of being human. In those words, I heard his recognition and admonishment of my relationship with Carden.

I tried to shrug it off and just enjoy the picture. Because I was also determined to enjoy my vampire. McCloud was a greater comfort to me than I'd ever known.

I tried to contact Yasuo, had even asked Josh to intervene, planning "accidental" run-ins, all to no avail. Once, in the dining hall, I'd caught his eyes on me, gleaming with fury and blame.

He hadn't spoken to me since Emma's death. He was so angry. So sad. But it was okay. So was I.

Yasuo wasn't the only one who wanted revenge.

Read on for an excerpt from

VERONICA WOLFF's

next **Watchers** novel,

coming soon from

NEW AMERICAN LIBRARY

It was a new semester, and this term Martial Arts Intensive was my combat class. We were practicing some basic Brazilian jujitsu, doing sweeps. Half the girls were lying on their backs, swiping the feet out from under their partners, who stood above them.

Apparently *my* partner had different ideas. Before I'd regained my footing, she clipped my heel out from under me, sending me toppling.

"What the hell?" I hopped up, giving a shake to my ringing head.

"What?" she asked, playing dumb.

"You're supposed to let me get into position before you sweep me." I approached again, taking a tone that was more ridicule than reprimand. "This is practice, Audra."

"I'm *Frost*," she snarled, though I didn't need to be reminded of her ridiculous new name. I'd become acquainted with her when she was Emma's roommate, and I remembered the day she'd announced it, chosen in honor of her love of life on *Eyja nœturinnar.* Shudder.

I couldn't help it—I smirked. "Isn't that one of the X-Men?"

The girl was a nerd the caliber of which made *me* look cool. I mean, I might've been smart, but I wasn't a dork, *thankyouverymuch.* But under that white-blond bob she had a tiny heart and a brittle mean streak that, when combined with her slavish affection for everything the vamps represented, made her a natural fit for the island.

She swatted at my leg, glaring at me with almost comically narrowed eyes, but I skipped out of her reach.

"Are those your angry eyes?" I stifled a giggle, hearing the voice of *Toy Story 2*'s Mrs. Potato Head.

"I hate you."

"I'm sure there's a club." I began to step over her hips to straddle her where she lay on the floor, but before I got into position, she cuffed the back of my knee, hooked my ankle, and whipped my foot out from under me. I crashed to the floor, cracking my head against the thin mat.

I rolled upright more quickly than before, angry now. It was wrong of her to catch me unawares during a simple workout, but I hadn't tucked my chin, and falling incorrectly was definitely my bad. I hated when I messed up, especially in Priti's class.

"Stop it." I stepped over her and quickly found my balance, positioned over her. "You're not even doing the move right."

She cupped her hands behind my ankles, but I was doing all I could to make it difficult, imagining myself anchored to the floor, and this time it took her a few tries before she could topple me.

I felt Priti's eyes on me, so finally I let the girl sweep me. I then popped back to standing, asking sweetly, "Do you need me to give you some pointers?"

Frost and I had been butting heads since we'd found out we were to be placed together as roommates in the Initiate dorm. We both hated the situation—me because Frost was a brownnose with the vampires and the last thing I needed was a snitch roomie, while she just hated me . . . well . . . apparently there was a constellation of reasons I was still only beginning to understand.

"I'm doing something right," she said. "You fell, didn't you?"

"This is class, not a fight to the death."

"Kill or be killed," she said, trying to sound cool.

"So tough." I rolled my eyes. As if I hadn't learned *that* lesson already. "Look, I don't like the new room situation any more than you do."

Honestly, I blamed much of her attitude on jealousy. Enamored of anything with fangs, the girl fancied herself a bit of a scholar on island matters. But here I was, someone who was considered a genius, who'd also attracted the attention of two of the island's most notable vampires.

First and foremost, there was Carden McCloud, the swoon-worthy Scottish vampire I'd bonded with. Nobody knew just how intense our relationship really was, but there was no hiding the fact that we spent a lot of time together. Increasingly, his eyes gleamed with lust—and somehow even more unsettling, fondness—when he looked at me.

Then there was Hugo de Rosas Alcántara. I detested the ancient Spanish vampire, but I was undeniably obsessed with him, too. My best friend, Emma, was dead, and I blamed *him*. The dream of revenge had become the thing that spurred me to get out of bed in the morning. It was what drove my workouts. What kept me up at night. It might take me years to exact my vengeance, but I would have it.

"Time for holds," Priti called, and her bell-like voice momentarily elevated the place into something more transcendent than just a stinky, sweat-stained gym. Her lithe grace promised a female power that I, too, might carry inside, though I had yet to access it fully. "On the floor, little birds. Time to grapple."

Everyone dropped to their knees, awaiting her next instruction.

"Begin in the cross-side position. Five minutes. Go."

I moved quickly, pinning Frost on her back before she had a chance to get up. "How about I go first?" Draping my body across hers, I began to go through the rote moves we'd learned.

"This is such a joke," Frost said, snarling. She bucked her hips, and I lurched forward, releasing my grip to catch myself before my nose crunched into the mat. "I can't believe they put me with you."

I felt Priti standing close by but out of view. She chuckled. "Ladies, please don't kill each other."

"We won't," I said, but my eyes on Frost added a silent *yet*. I stole a glimpse of the girls next to us, going through their moves in a way that rehearsed mechanics, not gave bloody noses.

I resumed my original position, lying across her body, putting her in a hold. "You just can't stand that the vampires like me." I tilted my head, whispering for her ears alone, "More than you."

She let out a feline snarl and grabbed my arm. "No." Her nails dug into me as she wrenched my elbow to her chest, thrusting her hips and flipping me onto my back. "I can't stand you because you think you're better than everyone else." She straddled me, pinning my shoulders with her knees. "You think you know so much. But guess what, Drew?" Little bits of spittle flew from her mouth, and I squinted against the onslaught. "I know more."

The girl was making this a real fight and it was pissing me off. "You need to learn, *Audra*." I hooked a foot around hers, propelled my hips upward, and flipped her back under me. "All this posturing just smells desperate. Vampires hate desperate."

"Is that what you told Emma?" She wrapped her legs around my waist, hooking her feet at my back, but she was unable to get leverage.

"Screw you." We were grappling hard now, but our strength and size were well matched. She bucked and squirmed, but I held on, keeping her pinned. "Don't you dare mention Emma."

"You think you're the teacher's pet." She shifted her weight, and I just barely escaped a choke hold.

"There's always Master Dagursson," I said sweetly, referring to the remarkably unattractive ancient Viking vampire. "He *loves* you."

"You think you're better than everyone else."

"Maybe I am."

"You think you're the vampires' little darling." She wrenched her legs up and cinched them around my neck. "But I know better."

I smacked her repeatedly, the universal sparring language for *Stop killing me*, but there was no stopping her.

"You killed Emma," she said.

I rolled to my side, forcing her legs to unclench, and sucked in a breath. "A vampire killed Emma. I didn't kill Emma."

But deep down I worried I did. Deep down, I tormented myself with thoughts that I could've done more. How I might've sacrificed myself to somehow save her.

The memory of her body, limp in Alcántara's arms, brought

fresh rage and anguish. Power shot through me, and I broke Frost's hold, flinging her away as though she weighed nothing. "Get the hell off me, freak."

"Your roommates are cursed." She crouched on her hands and knees, and I could see her mind working furiously, looking for her chance to pounce. "I refuse to be run off to the castle like Emma was just because you're some vampire's pet."

I froze. "What did you just say?"

But she'd frozen, too. "Nothing."

"Was she still alive when they took her?" The words came out slowly, a chill creeping over my body.

"You saw her," she replied, giving me a nonanswer, but her eyes betrayed the secret she'd spilled.

I pressed. "They took Emma to the castle?"

"How should I know?"

I could tell she was lying. Frost didn't want to be *run off to the castle.*

Like Emma.

What happened to my friend after Alcántara slashed her down the middle? As they did with all the fallen girls, Tracers had come into the ring and taken her away.

I thought of the vampire's castle, a hulking granite keep looming silently beyond the standing stones. Was that where they took her body? If so, for what purpose?

Was it possible Emma still lived, enduring Alcántara's torture?

I needed to go, to find a way into the castle to see for myself. I wouldn't rest until I uncovered the truth. I would find out what happened to Emma, and then I would have my revenge. I'd expose Alcántara's hideous secrets.

And then I would take him down.

Like her heroine, **Veronica Wolff** braved an all-girls school, traveled to faraway places, and studied lots of languages. She was not, however, ever trained as an assassin (or so she claims). In real life, she's most often found on a beach or in the mountains of northern California, but you can always find her online at veronicawolff.com.